LAW OF

LAW OF THE GUN

Edited by Martin H. Greenberg
and Russell Davis

PINNACLE BOOKS
Kensington Publishing Corp.
www.kensingtonbooks.com

PINNACLE BOOKS are published by

Kensington Publishing Corp.
119 West 40th Street
New York, NY 10018

PUBLISHER'S NOTE
Following the death of William W. Johnstone, the Johnstone family is working with a carefully selected writer to organize and complete Mr. Johnstone's outlines and many unfinished manuscripts to create additional novels in all of his series like The Last Gunfighter, Mountain Man, and Eagles, among others. His story in this anthology was inspired by Mr. Johnstone's superb storytelling.

All Kensington titles, imprints, and distributed lines are available at special quantity discounts for bulk purchases for sales promotions, premiums, fund-raising, educational, or institutional use. Special book excerpts or customized printings can also be created to fit specific needs. For details, write or phone the office of the Kensington sales manager: Kensington Publishing Corp., 119 West 40th Street, New York, NY 10018, attn: Sales Department; phone: 1-800-221-2647.

ISBN-13: 978-0-7860-4233-3
ISBN-10: 0-7860-4233-8

First printing: November 2010

10 9 8 7 6 5 4 3

Printed in the United States of America

First electronic edition: November 2010

ISBN-13: 978-0-7860-2581-7
ISBN-10: 0-7860-2581-6

Contents

Introduction

Russell Davis

As a reader, author, and editor, there is little that fascinates me more than those archetypes of a particular genre that have grown in stature, somehow surpassing the trite and clichéd and reaching up and out to become mythical. The landscape of the American West, from novels and short stories to films and music, is filled to the brim with the mythic.

How is it possible that this landscape is both so known and yet unknown? How is it possible that it keeps changing and growing, continuing to offer surprises of place and character and story? Perhaps it is because we ourselves are responsible for the continued reinvention of our view of the frontier, of the places and people, the rivers and mountains. Perhaps because what is now myth was once common, and one day, we will in our own turn, take our place in some strange fashion as part of the mythic American West.

In the first anthology I edited for Kensington/

Pinnacle, *Lost Trails,* I encouraged the authors to take advantage of the many unknowns in history about famous or infamous people—to tell a story of a lost moment in their lives. They responded with stories about Mark Twain and Buffalo Bill, John Wesley Hardin and Billy the Kid, and so many others. They are stories of real people who have risen to mythic stature by way of their deeds, both good and bad.

The anthology that followed, *Ghost Towns,* went in another direction—and often in unexpected ways. I asked the authors to explore the notion of ghost towns, real or imagined, and to feel free to utilize elements of the supernatural, should they so desire. It should come as no surprise that they did, in fact, feel free, and the anthology showed places that were both haunting and haunted, taking the reader to places that once were, and might never be again. These were the stories of mythic places in the West. That there are elements of the unknown or the supernatural should come as no surprise. Mythic places are often haunted by the spirits of those who lived and died there.

In this volume, I asked the authors to explore the most famous mythic archetype of the West: the gunfighter. Now, I must admit that part of this request was purely selfish. From my earliest memories of books and movies, I've liked gunfighter stories. If one enjoys western tales, it is almost impossible to not be steeped in the lore of this mythic figure. From the earliest days of the dime novels and the first movies all the way to the present day, the gunfighter has a mythic stature much larger than virtually any other western archetype.

As in the first two anthologies, I found myself surprised by the direction taken by the authors. Most of these stories are not the gunfighters imagined in popular films or dime novels, but rather very human characters, often trapped by circumstances into using the best tools they have to survive, make a living, or protect those they care about. In many ways, there is an air of dignity to these characters, and a sense of inevitability, as though they know their time is slowly winding down. Rather than go into detail about the stories, I'll let you discover them much as I did, and hope that you find these mythic figures to be as engaging and interesting as you might have when you first read the term *gunfighter*.

One final note, then I'll exit stage left, and allow you to continue on your journey. If Tombstone, Arizona, is "The Town Too Tough to Die," it is entirely possible that the literature of the American West is much the same. It will continue on, albeit in changing forms, for as long as there are those who remember these mythic people, places, and archetypal characters. There will be books and stories, the occasional film or miniseries, and—it needs to be said—the oral traditions that continue in so many families today. Yet I dream of something more than this. I dream of the day when the American West once again captures the imagination of many, and there is a renaissance, bringing all of this to life for another generation.

The question of how this dream may be fulfilled is a difficult one, and the answer is ultimately up to those of us who write or edit in this genre, who make movies or television shows, and it is also up to you—our readers. On one side, we must continue to reach out, with new ideas and new stories, and let me assure you that the mine of the form is hardly even tapped yet. There is a great deal more to be told. On the other side, we must ask you to reach out, spreading the word that the literature of the American West is like a river. It is not gone, but changing and fluid, while still holding true to its essential course.

Working together, sharing these stories with your friends, family, and children, we can ensure that western stories in all their forms continue to live and breathe and bring excitement to future generations who need to know the West is not just a few museums, but alive and well *today*. There are still famous and infamous people, ghost towns and thriving communities, horses and cowboys and gunslingers still riding the ranges and living the mythic dream that inspires us all.

Thank you for your support of our shared genre, and remember to always keep one chamber unloaded for safety.

Stagecoach, Nevada, *Spring 2010*

Note: The editor is not responsible for the sequence of the stories in this volume. The order was set by the publisher.

The Trouble with Dudes

Johnny D. Boggs

The silver had tarnished, the etchings faded, the chain and fob long gone, and he couldn't read the sentiment engraved on the inside of the case, which he had to pry open with a fingernail since the release mechanism hadn't worked in years.

Snapping the cover shut, Lin Garrett wondered why he even kept the pocket watch. It didn't work. *Much like me,* he thought.

Oh, he worked. A man had to work to eat, but Garrett didn't put his heart into it anymore. He worked so he wouldn't starve or freeze, but a proud man would never find enjoyment in mucking out stalls, swamping saloons, sweeping out stores, or being polite to dudes.

Staring at the broken watch, he sat on an overturned bucket inside the barn, trying to figure out how he had gotten so old, so worthless, so forgotten. Nothing to his name but a silver Aurora watch that had stopped keeping time ages ago. Years earlier, people had called him sir, spoken to him with respect, sometimes admiration, other times fearfully. Now, they hardly spoke to him at all.

Those dudes had, though.

They had driven up in a pair of Ford Model Ns, mud-splattered two-seaters about as basic as a body could find in a big city, but mighty fancy for a ranch in southern Wyoming. When one of those horseless carriages backfired, the noise and the odd sight of the automobiles sent his horse pitching, and Garrett found himself tasting gravel. Which, years ago, wouldn't have embarrassed him. By grab, he had been dusted so many times he had lost count, had broken both arms, a leg, his collarbone and wrists at least once, and his nose was about as crooked as the road leading to the Aurora Cattle Company & Guest Ranch. Yet the dudes had braked their Fords hard, jumped to the ground, and raced to the corral. They pulled him to his feet, fetched his hat, dusted off his shirt, anxiously asking if he were all right. Even the Aurora foreman had ambled over from the bunkhouse and told Garrett he should call it a day.

The dudes hailed from New York, had come to Wyoming to live the West. They'd called him names like old-timer, hoss, and pard.

"The name's Garrett," he told them with irritation.

"I'm Seth Thomas," said the tallest of the four. "Like the watch company."

Garrett started to tell Seth-Thomas-Like-The-Watch-Company to go to hell, but he caught the foreman's hard frown, realized that these dudes were paying customers, and, more important, he needed this job. So he shook each dude's hand.

"That what brought you to this ranch?" he asked the tall one.

Seth-Thomas-Like-The-Watch-Company stared at him blankly.

"Aurora," Garrett said lamely. "Like the watch company."

The kid, maybe in his early twenties, shrugged. "Never heard of it."

"Before your time," Garrett said, and had headed for the barn.

The watch had been new when the mayor presented it to him in 1884, among the first solid silver watches produced by the Aurora Watch Company. Back then, Garrett had been a lawman, and the watch was a token of appreciation for valuable service to Flagstaff, Coconino County, and Arizona Territory. Or something like that. He had been written up in territorial newspapers, even in the *National Police Gazette.* Street & Smith had published a couple of dime novels that were supposedly based on his life. Or something like that. Garrett had never read the damned things. The Aurora Watch Company had failed in 1892, though, and around that time Garrett had pretty much become a failure himself. He couldn't understand what had happened to him, other than he had just gotten old.

The barn door's hinges squeaked, and Garrett

slid the watch into his vest pocket. He pushed himself off the bucket, joints popping, hip and shoulder stiffening, as lanky foreman Sam Cahill, about twenty years younger than Garrett, approached him.

The foreman spit out a mouthful of tobacco juice, then hooked his thumb toward the door.

"You made an impression on 'em dudes," he said.

"I been bucked off before. Ain't the first time. Won't be the last. Didn't hurt me none." He relaxed, forcing a smile. "Just my pride."

"Uh-huh. Leader of the group's Jason C. Hughes, nephew of Charles Evans Hughes. That's *the* Charles Evans Hughes."

Garrett said nothing. Charles Evans Hughes meant as much to him as the Aurora Watch Company meant to young Seth Thomas.

"Charles Hughes, the governor of New York, the gent William Taft offered the vice presidential nomination to, only Hughes turned him down. Those kids all just graduated from Brown University. Plan on enterin' Columbia Law School, but first, they want to see the elephant." He spit again. "They been readin' Wister's book."

"Seems like everybody has."

"Uh-huh. 'When you call me that, smile.' All that nonsense. One of those dudes asked me if I had knowed Trampas. Guess I'll never understand book-readers."

Garrett waited.

"Well, Wister spent some time on a ranch like this

one. So did Teddy Roosevelt, or so I hear tell. So Jason C. Hughes has come here to shoot an elk, work cattle, chase mustangs, play cowpuncher with his friends. They've come to see the West, least the West they read about thanks to Mr. Wister." Sam Cahill sighed. "Never thought I'd be nurse-maidin' dudes, but it's a new century, Garrett, and beef prices ain't what they used to be."

Garrett nodded just to do something. There wasn't anything to say.

"They want you to take 'em."

He had something to say to that. "What for? You got two hands to ride herd on your guests. You hired me—"

"I hired you so you'd have something to eat, Garrett. I put those boots on you 'cause what you had when I found you at the depot had more holes than leather. I put that jacket on you, and I hired you to take orders. Those dudes think you're a bona fide Western man, a by-God Owen Wister hero, and I allow you look the part, or once did. They want you to show 'em the West."

The foreman shifted his chaw to the other cheek, then shook his head. "Look, Garrett, I didn't mean to speak sharp to you, but you see the fix I'm in. The kid asked for you, and he's a top-payin' customer from a mighty important family back east. At least three of our board of directors live in New York, so these are important guests."

Board of directors! When Garrett had ridden for

various brands back in his prime, before he had become a lawman, ranches were run by ranchers, not boards.

"Way I figure it," the foreman kept saying, "you could take 'em down by Muddy Creek, show 'em some country, maybe find a bull elk or some muley, and check the herd down that way—my line rider quit two weeks back—let 'em push a few dogies, then bring 'em back here and we'll send 'em back to the U.P. depot with their ear-splittin', putrefyin' horseless carriages. Give you some time in the open country. Got to beat muckin' stalls. Do a good job, maybe I'll let you be my line rider down yonder."

With a final spit, the foreman held out his hand.

Sighing, Garrett clasped the extended hand, knowing he should have quit, knowing he was making a mistake.

He just didn't know how big.

Jason C. Hughes, Seth-Thomas-Like-The-Watch-Company, and the two other dudes—one named Todd and the other Abraham, although Garrett couldn't remember which was which—were advertising a leather shop in their chaps, brand-spanking-new boots, dressed like they had stepped off the cover of one of those dime novels. Sam and the wrangler had put the boys on the gentlest horses the Aurora had, and then sent Garrett, pulling a pack mule, toward Muddy Creek.

"Bring 'em back in a week," Sam Cahill had

instructed him, and with a wink added, "and try to bring 'em back alive."

He kept the pace easy, pointing out a golden eagle, some curious coyotes, and letting the dudes chase after a handful of mustangs. At dusk, he watered and grained the livestock, boiled the coffee and fried the bacon, and even scrubbed the dishes while Abraham, or maybe it was Todd, fetched a flask from his saddlebags, and the dudes started drinking.

"Ever seen anything like this?" Jason C. Hughes asked.

"I'd be obliged," Garrett said, "if you wouldn't point that rifle in my direction."

Hughes laughed. "It ain't loaded." He swung the barrel toward Seth Thomas and pulled the trigger. It clicked loudly. "You're dead, Seth," he said, and all the boys laughed.

He held the rifle up to show Garrett, worked the bolt, and laughed. "It's brand-spanking new, old man. A Mauser, and I got the scope sighted in, so I'll be able to drop an elk from more than a thousand yards. Dumb animal'll never know what killed it."

"That's mighty sporting of you," Garrett said.

"What's that on your hip, Garrett?"

"An old Colt."

"Old?" Todd or Abraham sniggered, pulling one of those newfangled hammerless automatic pistols from a holster. "That's an understatement. This is what a Colt looks like now."

"You learn that from *The Virginian*?" Garrett said.

"Thought you boys wanted to live the West. We don't carry toys like that in this country."

That seemed to shut them up, and he poured a cup of coffee for himself, wishing he had thought to have brought along a flask. *Six more days*, he thought.

By the third day, he had had enough.

When Jason C. Hughes aimed the Mauser at the pack mule, Garrett charged across the camp, jerked the rifle from the New Yorker's grasp, and heaved it into the arroyo. He wanted to scream at the kid, to tell him he had warned him about pointing it, that all weapons should be considered loaded, and that he wouldn't tolerate this foolishness anymore. Yet all he could do was put both hands on his knees and try to catch his breath. The effort pained him more than getting dusted by a horse.

"You crazy old man!" Jason C. Hughes leaped to his feet, scrambling into the arroyo, kicking up red dust. "Do you know how much money that Mauser cost my father?"

As he filled his lungs, a shadow crossed over him. "Better watch yourself, old-timer," a voice told him. "We don't want you to keel over from a heart attack."

Garrett instantly straightened, and smashed Todd's nose. Or maybe it was Abraham's.

A second later, the gunshot ripped through the camp, echoing across the countryside, and Garrett lay on his back, spread-eagled, thinking how this was a bitter end to sixty-five years. Killed by a bunch of greenhorns in the middle of nowhere for a miserable job that paid him thirty a month and found, the same wages he had drawn forty years earlier, only back then he had worked with and for men he had liked.

"Criminy, Abraham, put that thing away!"

"Hey, what's all that shooting?"

"Abraham has killed the old fart! Fool almost broke my nose!"

The mule screamed, and hoofs stomped. More voices, but Garrett couldn't understand the words.

Seth Thomas knelt over him, his face ashen, lips trembling.

Garrett flexed the fingers on his right hand, blinked, moved the hand and placed it on his chest. He felt blood leaking down his side, then slid a finger into the vest pocket, pulling out the shattered remains of the Aurora watch. Slowly, he sat up.

"He isn't dead!" one of the dudes screamed in a nasal voice.

Garrett looked across the camp. Abraham sat on his bedroll, mouth open in surprise, the Colt automatic on the ground beside his boots. Todd stood over his friend, holding a rag against his bloody nose. Well, now he could tell those two apart. Jason C. Hughes had climbed out of the arroyo and wiped the dust off the Mauser with a handkerchief, more concerned about his rifle than Garrett's health.

"You all right?" Seth Thomas asked.

He nodded. The .25-caliber slug had smashed the watch, then cut a nick across a rib before it spent off somewhere. The wound wasn't much, although he'd have a hell of a bruise come morning. He smelled whiskey, realized Seth Thomas had unscrewed a flask and was offering him a drink, which Garrett accepted.

After pulling himself to his feet, he forced himself to walk over to Todd and Abraham, and just stood there, right hand on the butt of his old Colt. He kicked the automatic pistol into a clump of cheap grass. "Last person who shot at me got killed," Garrett said.

Abraham swallowed. "It just went off. I didn't mean—"

"That's why I warned y'all about not pointing them things."

"Old man," Jason C. Hughes said, "you attacked Todd. Abraham was protecting our friend. Thought you had gone crazy."

What he wanted to do was draw his .44, but he kept thinking about Sam Cahill, and kept remembering how cold winter got in Wyoming, how the bunkhouse stayed pretty warm, and that he needed a job. Criminy, it was an accident. The dude didn't mean to shoot him, had just been scared. *Let it go. Give you something to laugh about during the long winter.* Then Seth Thomas's voice sounded.

"My lord . . . you're Lin Garrett, the famous Arizona lawman."

He fingered the circular piece of tarnished silver, now punctured by a .25-caliber bullet, and could barely make out his name. He could see far just fine, but close-up, well, that was another story.

To Marshal Lin Garrett
From the People of Flagstaff, A.T.

The bullet had obliterated the rest, and Garrett tossed the remains of his watch case into the fire.

"My grandfather told me stories about the famous Lin Garrett," Seth Thomas was saying. "Grandfather came from Boston bound for Arizona with . . . oh, I can't remember the name."

"The Arizona Colonization Company."

"That's it!"

"You never told me your grandfather was a Westerner," Jason C. Hughes commented.

"Oh, Grandfather didn't stick it out." Seth Thomas shrugged. "He returned to Boston after a couple of years."

"What was your grandpa's name?" Garrett asked.

The dude told him, but Garrett shook his head. He couldn't remember names anymore, especially names from thirty years back.

"I've heard of a Pat Garrett," Todd said, just to say something. His nose had stopped bleeding.

"He got killed a short while back," Jason C. Hughes said. "Read about it in the newspapers."

"No kin," Garrett said.

"Grandfather showed me a book that had been written about you," Seth Thomas said. "One of those penny dreadfuls. He read parts of it to me, but I can't remember much about it."

"Nothing to remember," Garrett said. "Just lies."

"So you used to be famous, eh?" Jason C. Hughes laughed. "Maybe Owen Wister should write a book about you. And to think, Abraham almost killed you. That would have been something."

"You aren't going to tell Mr. Cahill, are you?" Abraham asked.

"No harm done," Garrett answered, warmed now by Seth Thomas's bourbon.

"Well, I haven't killed my elk or deer yet, old-timer," Jason C. Hughes said, "and I want to round up some longhorns!"

Garrett returned the flask to Seth Thomas. "We can check cattle in the morning, but they'll be Herefords. Longhorns are a thing of the past in these parts. You can try out your cannon on the way back to the ranch. We'll hunt up some elk in the hills." He stared at Abraham. "Don't forget your pistol. And don't ever pull it on me again."

He swung off his horse without a word, trying not to flinch from the pain caused by Abraham's bullet, and fingered the closest track. The dudes slowly reined in, although Todd's sorrel came close to plowing over Garrett as he studied the sign.

"What is it?" one of the dudes said.

"Elk?" asked Jason C. Hughes.

Polled Herefords, branded with the Triangle A, grazed nearby. Garrett rose, holding the reins to his bay, and walked a few rods farther, not answering the guests, and studied more tracks.

"Those are horse prints," Seth Thomas said.

Still Garrett kept quiet, found a mound of horse apples, and broke one open, feeling it with the tips of his fingers.

"I hope you plan on washing your hands before you fix our supper, old-timer," Jason C. Hughes sang out, and his pals laughed.

After he wiped his fingers on his chaps, Garrett mounted the bay, turned in the saddle and spoke with a purpose. "Tracks head toward those hills." His chin jutted in that direction. "We're following them."

"There are plenty of cows here." Stretching his aching legs, Jason C. Hughes pointed at the Herefords. "Why don't we just work them?"

"I ain't interested in those cattle."

His boots scattered the ash from the fire in the small box canyon.

"When are we going to eat?" Todd asked.

"We ain't." Garrett muttered a curse as he looked

at the four boys riding with him. One was off in the bushes answering nature's call, two others looked just too tuckered out to even climb down from their horses, and the fourth, Jason C. Hughes, filled his stomach with whiskey.

"What is it?" Seth Thomas asked.

Garrett climbed into the saddle. "Four riders," he said, "came into the pasture down there and gathered what I reckon to be twenty head of Triangle A beef. Most likely, they used a running iron on them here, and are herding them toward the state line."

Hughes corked his canteen, keenly interested. "You mean . . . rustlers?"

"Looks like."

"You're joshing us!" exclaimed Todd.

I wish to hell I were, he thought, but shook his head.

"Should we ride back, tell Mr. Cahill?" Seth Thomas asked.

"Hell, no!" It was Jason C. Hughes who answered. "We go after them, right, old man? Kill some rustlers, now that's something nobody will believe back in Manhattan. This is just crackerjack!"

"We need help," Seth Thomas pleaded.

Hughes patted the stock of his Mauser. "We have all the help we need, right?" He pointed at the coiled lariat on Garrett's saddle. "Just like *The Virginian!*"

* * *

He could put his heart into this. Do a good job, Sam Cahill had told him, and Garrett planned on doing just that. Tracking rustlers filled his bill, even if the posse riding behind him wasn't up to snuff. Well, thirty years ago, he had ridden with posses about as worthless. Besides, at least Jason C. Hughes and Seth Thomas showed some interest in learning what it took to be a lawman.

"When do you think we'll catch them?" Todd asked.

Garrett shrugged. He had maintained a hard pace, but had slowed to a walk, as much for the sake of the dudes as the horses. Todd and Hughes had ridden up alongside him, and he cast a quick glance over his shoulder to see how far the other two had fallen back. Swearing softly, he drew rein to let Seth Thomas and Abraham catch up. The bay took the opportunity to graze, and Garrett leaned over and patted the gelding's neck.

"Then what?" Todd asked.

"Depends on the rustlers."

"Be like Steve in *The Virginian*, eh?" Jason C. Hughes grinned. "String 'em up."

He was glad Abraham had caught up and asked, "Do we rest now?" Because Garrett did not like Jason C. Hughes's question.

"No," he told Abraham, and kicked the bay into a trot.

You got an old man's memories. He coaxed his horse into an arroyo, leaning back in the saddle, wondering if those dudes would be able to make the climb down, but not really caring. *String 'em up.* Something the greenhorn had read in a damned book. Smiling when he had said it.

As a lawman, he had arrested plenty of rustlers, but couldn't remember anything about them, yet could never forget what had happened in Colorado when he had cowboyed. Those had been horse thieves, and they had hanged. He had helped *string 'em up.* Memories. Sometimes he hated them.

Thunderheads rolled over the mountains to the east. Garrett hobbled the bay, drew his carbine from the scabbard, and held a finger to his lips.

He pointed to Todd. "You stay with the horses. Keep them quiet. Rest of you, follow me."

Ignoring the stiffness in his legs, he moved up the hill and into the brush, smelling wood smoke, coffee, maybe even beefsteak. Near the crest, he dropped to his stomach and crawled the final few rods until he could look down at the line shack.

"I don't see any cattle," Seth Thomas said softly.

"No." But on the far side of the log cabin he could make out a black birch farm wagon, worn but useable, and five horses in a rawhide-looking corral behind the line shack, buttressed against sandstone formations that jutted out of the floor like tombstones. Smoke snaked from the cabin's stovepipe.

"How many times can that Mauser of yours shoot?" Garrett asked.

Jason C. Hughes withdrew a five-shell clip from

his jacket pocket. "As fast as I can work the bolt," he said with a grin. "I have plenty of ammunition."

"All right," Garrett said, "here's the way we play this hand." He handed his Winchester to Seth Thomas. "You head down to the corral, keep upwind of the horses. Hughes, you stay put right here where you got a clear shot at the door. Abraham, you come with me. Stay behind that rock yonder. I'll get to the well, then holler for them to surrender."

"And if they don't?" Jason C. Hughes asked.

"They'd better. None of y'all pull a trigger till I fire a round. Then just shoot over that line shack four or five times apiece, fast as you can. I want them to think I got an army of deputies out here."

"Hot damn!" Hughes shouted. "This is a hell of a lot better than shooting some elk!"

Garrett glared at him, and Hughes shrugged.

"Sorry, old man," he whispered. "You best hurry."

He had carried the Colt since the War of the Rebellion, an old cap-and-ball .44 that he had eventually converted to take brass cartridges. When he reached the well, he pulled the revolver, blew on the cylinder, eased back the hammer, and looked around him. Abraham crouched behind the rocks, Colt automatic in a sweaty hand. Seth Thomas knelt behind the corner post of the corral, the .30-30 aimed at the shack's roof. Up on the hill, sunlight reflected off Jason C. Hughes's Mauser, and Garrett smiled.

This might work, he thought, *and won't there be some stories told at the bunkhouse this winter. Lin Garrett brings in a band of rustlers with nothing but a bunch of dudes riding for him.* He fired a round into the air, then yelled, "I'm a federal marshal, and I got a posse surrounding you!" With a nod, he listened to the gunfire, keeping his eyes on Abraham, making sure the fool kid didn't accidentally shoot him again, and when the echoes died down, as Abraham slid another clip into the Colt, Garrett thought about the lie he had just told. Well, he had been a federal deputy some years back, and he did have something of a posse.

"Come out with your hands up!" he yelled at the cabin door. "Else we'll gun you sons of bitches down or burn you to a crisp!"

The door swung open, a mustached young man stepped out, waving a faded bandanna, saying, "Don't shoot no more!"

Immediately, Jason C. Hughes dropped him with a bullet through his leg.

"Damn it!" Garrett climbed to his feet, not even thinking that those other three rustlers might gun him down, yelling at Hughes. The horses loped around the corral, close to the poles, spilling Seth Thomas from his seat, and Abraham muttered something that sounded like a laugh.

"Hold your fire! And the rest of you sons of

bitches come out of that shack before we torch the damned thing!"

Inside the cabin, a baby cried.

"Aw," Garrett said, "hell."

"Listen, mister," the man with the mustache said through clenched teeth, "I got a sick wife and a baby. Nothin' to eat hardly. It ain't like you think."

Garrett drew a silk bandanna through the bullet hole in the meaty part of the man's thigh, then splashed whiskey over the wound. The man screamed and almost fell out of the chair.

"This is Triangle A land," Garrett told him. "You're squatting."

"I know that, but my wife took sick. Wasn't nobody here. Been tryin' to get to Lander. Matilda, that's my missus yonder, she's got a sister up there."

Garrett looked at the woman, feverish, lying on a cot, saw Seth Thomas bouncing the baby girl on his knee, and ran the man's story through his head once again.

Three riders stopped for the night, each with an extra horse, suggested he help them round up some cattle, said they'd pay him five dollars. He didn't know the stock was stolen, just thought he was helping out.

That part was a lie. They'd taken the cattle to a box canyon, worked the brands with running irons. No, this gent knew they were rustlers. But . . . well . . .

Garrett had thrown a wide loop in his younger days, too. Lots of cowmen had.

Once they had driven the cattle back here, the wounded man had said, the three strangers had left the winded horses in the corral, saddled fresh mounts, and ridden out with the cattle. Tracks Garrett had found told him that much was probably true. The three horses left behind were most likely stolen.

"You didn't suspicion them when they left their horses behind?" he asked.

The man grimaced. "Mister . . ." was all he could say, sweating heavily.

"You left your wife, sick as she was, and kid here?" Garrett asked him again.

"Matilda insisted on it. Said she was feelin' better. Wouldn't be gone more'n a couple of days, and five dollars is a lot of money to me." He bit his lip against the pain. "When I got back, Matilda had taken another bad turn. You gotta believe me, mister!"

"You butchered one of those steers."

"They let me. Give me a steer instead of money. Wife's sick. My girl's only eighteen months old. You tell me you'd let your family starve. I'll work off whatever I owe for the beef. And for the week I been at your cabin."

"You'll work it off, mister," Jason C. Hughes said from the doorway. "With a rope."

The man's eyes widened. "Look, I got a wife, a daughter, you can't—"

"Where'd your pards go?" Garrett asked him.

"They wasn't my pards. Just strangers."

"Their names?"

"I don't know. One called hisself Red. There was a tall one, about your size, went by the name of Ed. The other fellow was a Mexican. He never said much. Never heard his name that I recollect."

"Where'd they go?" Garrett asked again.

"Think they said Virginia Dale. They're in Colorado by now."

"Todd and me have the rope ready, old man," Jason C. Hughes said. "Let's string him up."

"Shut up," Garrett snapped. He started to stand, saw the rustler's eyes flash in warning, and Garrett reached for his Colt, turning, knowing he was too late, catching the blur of Mauser's stock as it slammed into his head.

A blacksmith pounded iron against an anvil inside his head, but Garrett forced his eyes open, tried to reach up and test the walnut-sized knot above his temple, felt the hemp rope tight against his wrists, and saw Seth-Thomas-Like-The-Watch-Company sitting in front of him, Garrett's own .44 pointed in his direction.

Beside him, the baby girl played with Garrett's spurs, spinning the rowel, laughing when the bobs jingled. The mother slept fitfully.

"Where are the others?" Just speaking caused Garrett's head to ache.

Seth Thomas glanced nervously toward the open door. "Todd and Abraham do whatever Jason says."

"Looks like you do, too."

The dude shook his head. "I . . . I didn't. Jason says it's law, the law of the West."

"It's murder."

"He stole your cattle."

"You won't get away."

Seth Thomas sighed. "I can't go against Jason, Marshal Garrett. His uncle is . . . well. And the man's guilty. You know that." Trying to convince himself of it, he swallowed. "Just like *The Virginian.*"

"It ain't nothing like that, boy. Them's words. This is real."

Outside, he heard laughter. Inside, the spurs chimed. Garrett nodded at the baby.

"Y'all going to hang her, too? And her ma?"

"No. I wouldn't let . . . uh. . . . Jason's a little . . . crazy. This is . . . well . . . the law . . . Western law."

"We strung up horse thieves when I wasn't that much older than you," Garrett said. "Biggest mistake I ever made in my life, and I've made a passel. You think about it." He closed his eyes.

When his eyes opened, he saw Seth Thomas squatting in front of him, pistol on the floor, opening the blade to a folding knife, and Garrett decided not all dudes were so damned worthless.

"Mister," Jason C. Hughes said with a drunken laugh, "get ready to be jerked to Jesus!"

Colt in his right hand, Garrett stood in the doorway, taking in the sight of the three dudes, drunk on whiskey, maybe drunker on power, the wounded rustler standing on a flour keg, a rope over his neck, looped around the branch of an ancient cottonwood.

And they saw him.

Garrett felt young, invincible, the way he had felt years ago, back when his life had a purpose. Abraham's hand darted for the automatic in its holster, and Garrett shot him. Todd had already turned and was running, and Garrett's second shot kicked up dust between his legs. The dude stumbled into the dust, crying, "Don't shoot me! For God's sake, don't kill me!"

Jason C. Hughes had grabbed his Mauser, working the bolt, cursing angrily. Garrett's third and fourth shots splintered the stock, and the heavy rifle dropped to the dirt. So did Jason C. Hughes, shaking his hands, groaning, then freezing as Garrett steadily drew a bead on the dude's forehead.

Garrett climbed out of the wagon, and turned back to face the woman and her baby, and her husband, resting inside the wagon. "Nearest town's Saratoga," he said. "Closer than Triangle A headquarters. Got some mineral baths there, and a doctor. Get you fixed up in no time." He looked behind him at Todd and Abraham, hands tied to the horns of their saddles, as tight as Garrett could manage, a stripped bed linen wrapped around the bullet hole in Abraham's side. "Got a jail, too."

"God bless you, Marshal," the woman said weakly.

"I ain't no marshal, ma'am. Not anymore." *What I am,* he thought, *is a damned fool.*

Smiling, he walked around the wagon and looked up at the driver. "You sure you can handle a team, Seth Thomas?"

"I'll try," the boy replied, and glanced uncomfortably at the flour keg and lynching rope.

"Get moving." Garrett went to his horse, gathered the reins, and swung into the saddle. He turned the bay and nodded at Abraham and Todd. "You boys follow the wagon. Try something foolish, I'll shoot you dead, or leave you like I'm leaving Jason C. Hughes."

"Old man!" Jason C. Hughes yelled. "You . . . I . . . my father . . . my uncle . . . we'll kill you. You cut me down!"

He nodded again, and the two dudes nudged their horses and followed the wagon up the trail. Garrett nudged his horse closer to Jason C. Hughes, perched precariously on the flour keg, the makeshift noose chafing his throat, his face flushed.

"You can't leave me here!" the dude said.

How he would love to leave Jason C. Hughes hanging, but, no, he'd just give the boy a scare, ride over the hills, let him sweat for ten minutes, maybe longer. *If I don't forget about him,* Garrett told himself. *My memory ain't what it used to be.*

"Don't rock that barrel too much, boy. You'll

wind up like Steve in Mr. Wister's book you've been so jo-fired about. That's what you wanted to see, ain't it? Well, you're about to get a real close look at someone getting strung up."

Clucking at his horse, Garrett trotted the bay after the wagon and his two prisoners, smiling, enjoying himself.

"Old man! Damn it, you get back here and cut me loose. Cut me down. Damn you, you better do as I say!"

Reining up, Garrett looked over his shoulder at Jason C. Hughes.

"Get back here, and cut me down!" the dude screamed. "Or you'll rue the day, old man!"

Garrett pushed back the brim of his hat. "When you call me that," he said, "smile."

Then he loped away.

Uncle Jeff and the Gunfighter

Elmer Kelton

Out in West Texas the old-timers still speak occasionally of the time my uncle Jeff Barclay scared off the gunfighter Tobe Farrington. It's a good story, as far as it goes, but the way they tell it doesn't quite go far enough. And the reason is that my father was the only man who ever knew the whole truth. Papa would have carried the secret to the grave with him if he hadn't taken a notion to tell me about it a little while before he died. Now that he's buried beside Mother in the family plot over at Marfa, I reckon it won't hurt to clear up the whole story, once and for all.

Papa was the oldest of the two brothers. He and Uncle Jeff were what they used to call "four-sectioners" a long time ago.

Lots of people don't know about Texas homesteads. When Texas joined the union it was a free republic with a whopper of a debt. Texas kept title to its land because the United States didn't want to take on all that indebtedness. So in later years

Texas had a different homestead law than the other states. By the time Papa and Uncle Jeff were grown, the state of Texas was betting four sections of land against a man's fee, his hope and his sweat that he would starve to death before he proved up his claim. It's no secret that the state won a lot of those bets.

But it didn't win against Papa and Uncle Jeff. They proved up their land and got the title.

Trouble was, their claims were on pasture that old Port Hubbard had ranched for a long time, leasing from the state. It didn't set well with him at all, because he was used to having people ask him things, not tell him. And there was a reckless streak in Uncle Jeff that caused him to glory in telling people how the two of them had thumbed their noses at Port Hubbard and gotten away with it.

It'd be better if I told you a little about Uncle Jeff, so you'll know how it was with him. I've still got an old picture—yellowed now—that he and Papa had taken the day they got title to their four sections apiece. It shows Papa dressed in a plain suit that looks like he had slept in it, and he wears an ordinary sort of wide-brimmed hat set square on his head. But Uncle Jeff has on a pair of those striped California pants they used to wear, and sleeve garters and a candy-striped shirt. He's wearing one of those huge cowboy hats that went out years ago, the ones you could really call "ten-gallon" without exaggerating much. The hat is cocked over to one side of his head. A six-shooter sits high on his right hip. The clothes made him look like he's on his way to a dance, but the challenge in his eyes makes him look like he's waiting for a fight. With Uncle Jeff, it could have been either one or both.

A lot of ranchers like Port Hubbard made good use of the Texas homestead law. They got their cowboys to file on land that lay inside their ranches. The cowboys would prove up the land, then sell it to the man they worked for. Plenty of cowboys in those days weren't interested in being landowners anyhow, and in a lot of West Texas four sections wasn't enough for a man to make a living on. It wouldn't carry enough cattle. And farming that dry country was a chancy business, sure enough.

It bothered Hubbard when Papa and Uncle Jeff took eight sections out of his Rocking H ranch. But he held off, figuring they would starve out and turn it back. Meanwhile, they would be improving it for him. When that didn't work the way he expected, he tried to buy it from them. They wouldn't sell.

Hubbard still might have swallowed the loss and gone about his business if Uncle Jeff hadn't been inclined to brag so much.

"He's buffaloed people in this part of the country for twenty years," Uncle Jeff would say, and he didn't care who heard or repeated it. "But we stopped him. He's scared to lay a finger on us."

Papa always felt Port Hubbard wouldn't have done anything if Uncle Jeff hadn't kept jabbing the knifepoint at him, so to speak. But Hubbard was a proud man, and proud men don't sit around and listen to that kind of talk forever, especially old-time cowmen like Port Hubbard. So by and by Tobe Farrington showed up.

Nobody ever did prove that Port Hubbard sent for him, but nobody ever doubted it. Farrington put in for four sections of land that lay right next to Papa's and Uncle Jeff's. It was on Rocking H country that had been taken up once by a Hubbard cowboy who later got too much whiskey over in Pecos and took a fatal dose of indigestion on three .45 slugs.

Everybody in West Texas knew of Tobe Farrington those days. He wasn't famous in the way of John Wesley Hardin or Bill Longley, but in the country from San Saba to the Pecos River he had a hard name. Folks tried to give him plenty of air. It was known that several men had gone to glory with his bullets in them.

A lot of folks expected to see Farrington just ride and shoot Papa and Uncle Jeff down. But he didn't work that way. He must have figured on letting his reputation do the job without him having to waste any powder. Papa said it seemed like just about every time he Uncle Jeff looked up, they would see Tobe Farrington sitting there on his horse, just watching them. He seldom ever spoke, he just looked at them. Papa didn't mind admitting that those hard gray eyes always put a chunk of ice in the pit of his stomach. But Uncle Jeff wasn't bothered. He seemed to thrive on that kind of pressure.

I didn't tell you that Uncle Jeff had been a

deputy once. The Pecos County sheriff had hired him late one spring, mostly to run errands for him. In those days the sheriff was usually a tax assessor, too. The job didn't last long. That summer the sheriff got beat in the primary election. The next one had needy kinfolks and didn't keep Uncle Jeff on.

But by that time Uncle Jeff had gotten the feel of the six-shooter on his hip, and he liked it. What's more, he got to be a good shot. He liked to ride along and pot jackrabbits with his pistol. Two or three times this trick got him thrown off a boogered horse, but Uncle Jeff would still do it when he took the notion. That was his way. Nothing ever scared him much, and nothing ever kept him from doing as he damn well pleased. Nothing but Papa.

If Tobe Farrington figured his being there was going to scare the Barclay brothers out of the country, he was disappointed. So he began to change his tactics. Farrington had a little bunch of Rocking H cattle with a vented brand, which he claimed he had bought from Hubbard but which everybody said Hubbard had just loaned him to make the homestead look legal. He started pushing his cattle over onto the Barclay land. He didn't do it sneaky. He would open the wire gates, bold as brass, push the cattle through, then ride on in and watch them eat Barclay grass. It wasn't the rainiest country in the world. There was just enough grass for the Barclay cattle, and sometimes not even that much.

Uncle Jeff was all for a fight. He wanted to shoot Farrington's cattle. Papa, on the other hand, believed in being firm but not suicidal. He left his gun at home, took his horse and pushed the cattle back through the gate while Farrington sat and watched.

"He couldn't shoot me," Papa said, "because I didn't have a gun. He couldn't afford a plain case of murder. When Farrington killed somebody, he made it a point to be within the law."

Farrington gave up that stunt after two or three times because Papa always handled it the same way.

After that it was little things. Steer roping was a popular sport in those days. Farrington always rode across Papa's land to go to Fort Stockton, and while passing through he would practice on Barclay cattle. It was a rough sport. Throwing down those grown cattle was an easy way to break horns, and often it broke legs as well. Farrington made it a point to break legs.

Uncle Jeff wanted to take a gun and call for a showdown. Papa wouldn't let him. Instead, Papa wrote up a bill for the broken-legged cattle they had had to kill and got the sheriff to go with him to collect. The sheriff was as nervous as a sheepherder at a cowboy convention, but Papa collected.

"Guns are his business," Papa tried to tell Uncle Jeff. "The average man can't stand up against a fella like Tobe Farrington any more than a big-city bookkeeper could ride one of Port Hubbard's broncs. You leave your gun at home, or one of these days Farrington'll sucker you into using it.

Second prize in his kind of shootin' match is a wooden box."

I reckon before I go any further I ought to tell you about Delia Larrabee. Papa might have been a little prejudiced, but he always said she was the prettiest girl in the country in those days. Uncle Jeff must have agreed with him. Papa met her first and was using all the old-fashioned cowboy salesmanship he had. But Uncle Jeff was a better salesman. It hurt, but when Papa saw how things were, he backed off and gave up the field to Uncle Jeff. Looking at that old picture again, it's not hard to see why Delia Larrabee or any other girl might have been drawn to my uncle. He was quite the young blade, as they used to put it.

Tobe Farrington had drawn a joker every time he tried to provoke a fight with Papa or Uncle Jeff. Stealing grass or injuring cattle hadn't done it. But when he found out about Delia Larrabee and Uncle Jeff, he realized he had found the way. The big dance in Fort Stockton gave him his chance.

Papa didn't go that night, or he might have found a way to stop the thing before it went as far as it did. But it still hurt too much to be around Delia Larrabee, knowing he had lost her. And he hadn't seen any other girls he felt comfortable with. Besides, he was tired because for two days he had been out with a saddle gun, trying to track down a calf-killing wolf. So he let Uncle Jeff go to town alone, though he made sure my uncle left his gun at home.

Tobe Farrington waited around till the dance had been a good while. That way, when he did show up he would get more attention. And get it he did. Folks said the hall fell almost dead silent when Farrington walked in. Dancers all stopped. Everything stopped but the old fiddler, and his eyes were so bad he couldn't tell a horse from a pig at forty feet. Farrington just stood there till he spotted Uncle Jeff over by the punch bowl. Then he saw Delia Larrabee sitting at the south wall, waiting for Uncle Jeff to fetch her some punch. Farrington walked over, bowed and said, "You're the prettiest girl in the crowd. I believe I'll have this dance."

Uncle Jeff came hurrying back. He had his fists clenched, but Delia Larrabee shook her head at him to make him stop. She stood up right quick and held up her hands as a sign to Farrington that she would dance with him. She knew what Farrington really wanted. To refuse him would have meant a fight.

But Farrington didn't mean to be stopped. When that tune ended, he kept hold of her hand and forced her into another dance. Uncle Jeff took a step or two forward, like he was going to interfere, but she waved him off. That dance finally ended, but Farrington didn't let her go. When the fiddle started, he began dancing with her again. Uncle Jeff had had enough. He hollered at the fiddler to stop the music.

By that time nobody was dancing but Farrington

and Delia Larrabee, anyway. Everybody else had pulled back, waiting.

Uncle Jeff walked up to Farrington with his face red. "All right, I'm callin' your hand. Turn her loose."

Farrington gripped her fingers a little tighter. "This is too pretty a gal to waste her time with a little greasy-sack rancher like you. I'm takin' over."

Uncle Jeff's picture shows that he had a powerful set of shoulders. When he swung his fist on somebody, it left a mark. Tobe Farrington landed flat on his back. By instinct he dropped his hand to his hip. But he had had to check his pistol at the door, same as everybody else. With a crooked grin that spelled murder, he pushed to his feet.

Delia Larrabee had her arms around Uncle Jeff and was trying to hold him back. "Jeff, he means to kill you!"

Uncle Jeff put her aside and looked Tobe Farrington in the eye. "I left my gun at home."

Farrington said flatly, "You could go and get it."

"All right. I will."

Farrington frowned. "On second thought, Barclay, it'd still be nighttime when you got back. Night's a poor time for good shootin'. So I tell you what. I'm goin' home. Tomorrow afternoon I'll come back to town. Say at five o'clock. If you still feel like you got guts enough, you can meet me on the street. We'll finish this right." His eyes narrowed. "But if you decide *not* to meet me, you better clear out of this country. I'll be lookin' around for you."

They were near the door, where the guns were checked. Farrington took his, strapped the belt around his waist, then drew the pistol. "So there's no misunderstandin', Barclay, I want you to see what I can do."

Thirty feet across the dancehall was a cardboard notice with the words FORT STOCKTON. Farrington brought up the pistol, fired once and put a bullet hole through the first O. Women screamed as the shot thundered and echoed.

Uncle Jeff waited a few seconds, till the thick smoke cleared. "Let me see that thing a minute," he said. Farrington hesitated, then handed it to him. Uncle Jeff fired twice and put holes through the other two Os.

Folks always said afterward that Farrington looked as if he had swallowed a cud of chewing tobacco. He hadn't realized Uncle Jeff was that good.

Uncle Jeff said, "*I'll* be here. Just be sure *you* show up." Right then he would have taken on Wild Bill Hickok.

He didn't go home that night. He knew Papa would argue and plead with him, and he didn't want to put up with it. He stayed in town with friends. Next morning he was out on the open prairie beyond Comanche Spring, practicing with a borrowed pistol.

Delia Larrabee had tried a while to reason with him. She told him she would go anywhere with him—California . . . Mexico—if he would just go, and do it right now. But Uncle Jeff had his mind made up. He would have done this a long time ago if it hadn't been for Papa. So Delia got her father to take her out in a buckboard in the dark hours of early morning to tell Papa what had happened.

"You've got to do something," she cried. "You're the only one who can talk to Jeff."

Papa studied about it a long time. But he knew Uncle Jeff. The only way Papa would be able to stop him now would be to hog-tie him. And he couldn't keep him tied forever.

"I'll try to think of something," Papa promised, "but I doubt that anything will stop it now. You'd best go on home." There was a sadness about him, almost a giving up. He sat at his table a long time, sipping black coffee and watching the morning sun start to climb. It came to him that Farrington was only doing a job for Port Hubbard, and all that Port Hubbard really wanted was to see the Barclay brothers leave the country. If it came to that, Papa had rather have had Uncle Jeff alive than to own the best eight sections in Pecos County.

He knew Jeff wouldn't listen to him. But maybe Farrington would.

Papa saddled up and started for the frame shack on Farrington's four sections. He still had the saddle gun he had used for hunting the wolf. He didn't really intend to use it. But there was always a chance Farrington might decide to make a clean sweep of the Barclay brothers while he was at it.

Not all the wolves had four legs.

Farrington's shack had originally been a line camp for Hubbard on land inside Papa's claim. When Papa took up the land, Hubbard had jacked the little house up and hauled it out on two wagons. The only thing left on the old campsite was a ruined cistern, surrounded by a little fence to keep stock from falling in. Papa had always intended to come over and fill it up, when he had time.

Now, he thought, *there won't be any need to fill it up. It'll be Hubbard's again.*

He saw smoke curling upwards from the tin chimney, and he knew Farrington was at home. "Farrington," Papa called, "it's me, Henry Barclay. I've come to talk to you."

Farrington was slow about showing himself, and he came out wearing his gun. Distrust showed all over him. His hand was close to the gun butt, and it went even closer when Papa's horse turned so that Farrington saw the saddle gun.

"It's past talkin' now, Barclay. There was a time we could've worked this out. But not anymore."

"We still could," Papa said. "What if we give you what Hubbard wants? What if we sell our land to him and clear out?"

Farrington frowned. "Why should I care what Hubbard wants?"

"We don't have to play games, Farrington. I know what you came for, and you know I know it. So now you've won. Leave my brother alone."

"You're speakin' for yourself. But your brother may not see it your way."

"He will, even if I have to tie him up and haul him clear to California in a wagon."

Farrington considered a while. "You make sense, up to a point. Pity you couldn't have done this a long while back, before I had spent so much time here. Now you might say I got an investment made. What suits Port Hubbard might not be enough to suit *me* any more."

"You want money? All right, I'll split with you. Half of what Hubbard gives for the land. Only, I don't want Jeff hurt."

"Half of what Hubbard'll give now ain't very much."

"All of it, then. We didn't have anything when we came here. I reckon we could start with nothin' again."

A dry and awful smile broke across Farrington's face. "No deal, Barclay. I just wanted to see how far you'd crawl. Now I know."

"You're really goin' to kill him?"

"Like I'd kill a beef! And then I'll come and put *you* off, Barclay. It won't cost Hubbard a cent. You'll sign those papers and drag out of here with nothin' but the clothes on your back!"

That was it, then. Papa turned his horse and made like he was going to ride off. But he knew he couldn't leave it this way. Uncle Jeff was as good as dead. For that matter, so was Papa, for he had no intention of leaving his land if Uncle Jeff died.

Seventy feet from the house, Papa leaned forward as if he was going to put spurs to the horse. Instead, he took hold of the saddle gun and yanked it up out of the scabbard.

Farrington saw what was coming. He drew his pistol and fired just as the saddle gun came clear. But Papa was pulling his horse around. The bullet went shy.

Papa dropped to the ground, flat on his belly. He had lessened the odds by getting distance between him and Farrington. This was a long shot for a pistol. It was just right for Papa's short rifle. Farrington knew it, too. He came running, firing as he moved, trying to keep Papa's head down till he could get close enough for a really good shot.

Papa didn't let him get that close. He sighted quick and squeezed the trigger.

Papa had shot a lot of lobo wolves in his day, and some of them on the run. Farrington rolled like one of those wolves. His body twitched a few times, then he was dead.

Papa had never killed a man before, and he never killed one again. He knew it was something he had had to do to save Uncle Jeff. But still he was sick to his stomach. All that coffee he had drunk came up. Later, when he had settled a little, he began wondering how he was going to tell this. Uncle Jeff probably never would forgive him, for he had wanted Farrington for himself. Papa would never be able to convince him Farrington would have killed him. Hubbard would scream murder, and it might be hard to convince a jury that it hadn't been just that. Men had been known to murder for much less than a brother's life.

Then it came to him: why tell anybody at all? Nobody had seen it. For all anyone needed to know, Farrington had just saddled up and ridden away. Gunfighters did that sometimes. Many a noted outlaw had simply disappeared, never to be heard of again. A new country, a new name, a new start . . .

Farrington's horse was in the corral. Actually, it was a Rocking H sorrel. Papa put Farrington's bridle and saddle on him, then hoisted Farrington's body up over the saddle. The horse danced around, smelling blood, and it was a hard job, but Papa got the body lashed down. He went into the house. He took a skillet, a coffeepot, some food—the things Farrington would logically have carried away with him. He rolled these up in Farrington's blanket and took them with him.

He worried some over the tracks, and he paused to kick dirt over the patch of blood where Farrington had fallen. But in the north, clouds were building. Maybe it would rain and wash out the tracks. If it didn't rain, at least it would blow. In this country, wind could reduce tracks about as well as a rain.

Papa led the sorrel horse with its load out across

the Farrington claim and prayed he wouldn't run into any Rocking H cowboys. He stayed clear of the road. When he reached his own land, he cut across to the one-time Hubbard line camp. There he dragged Farrington's body to the edge of the old cistern and dropped him in. He dropped saddle, blankets and everything else in after him. Then he led the sorrel horse back and turned him loose in Hubbard's big pasture.

Papa was not normally a drinking man, but that afternoon he took a bottle out of the kitchen cabinet and sat on the porch and got drunk.

Late that night, Uncle Jeff came home. He had been drinking too, but for a different reason. He had a couple of friends with him, helping him celebrate.

"Howdy do, big brother," he shouted all the way from the front gate. "It's me, little old Jeff, the livest little old Jeff you ever did see!" He swayed up onto the porch and saw Papa sitting there. "Bet you thought they'd be bringin' me home in a box. You just been sittin' here a-drinkin' by yourself and dreadin' seein' them come. But I'm here, and I'm still a-kickin'. I won. Farrington never showed up."

Papa couldn't make much of a display. "You don't say!"

"I *do* say! The whole town was waitin'. He never came. He was scared of me. Tobe Farrington was scared of *me*!"

Papa said, "I'm glad, Jeff. I'm real glad." He pushed himself to his feet and staggered off to bed.

Next day there must have been thirty people by at one time or another to congratulate Jeff Barclay. They didn't see Papa, though. He had gone off to fill up that old cistern before a cow fell in it.

It was told all over West Texas how Jeff Barclay, a greasy-sack rancher, had scared Tobe Farrington into backing down on a challenge. Folks decided Farrington was reputation and nothing else. They always wondered where he went, because nobody ever heard of him after that. Talk was that he had gone into Mexico and had changed his name, ashamed to face up to people after backing down to Jeff Barclay.

Papa was more than glad to let them believe that. Like I said, he kept the secret till just before he died. But it must have troubled him, and when finally he knew his time was coming, he told me. He kept telling me it was something he had to do to save Uncle Jeff.

The irony was that it didn't really save Uncle Jeff. If anything, it killed him. Being the way he was, Uncle Jeff let the notoriety go to his head. Got so he was always looking for another Tobe Farrington. He turned cocky and quarrelsome. Gradually he alienated his friends. He even lost Delia Larrabee. The only person he didn't lose was Papa.

Papa wasn't there to help the day Uncle Jeff finally met a man who was like Tobe Farrington.

Uncle Jeff was still clawing for his pistol when he fell with two bullets in his heart.

Uncle Jeff's four sections went to Papa, but he sold them along with his own—not to Port Hubbard. He bought a ranch further west, in the Davis Mountains.

And Delia Larabee? She married Papa. I was one of their six sons.

The Devil Doesn't Sleep

Deborah Morgan

Circuit Judge Mortal D. Stanton blasted into the courtroom on a gust of frosted wind and blowing snow. The likelihood of his getting back to civilization for the holidays was being rapidly buried—along with the train tracks east of the Continental Divide. He brushed snow from his buffalo coat, and traded it to the bailiff for judicial robes.

Judge Stanton fished his pocket watch from his vest, read it, scowled, then sat. As he propped the timepiece before him, his gaze swept the jury of twelve men. He thought how they looked more or less like every other jury that had helped him exact justice during his long tenure on the frontier. He glanced at the packed courtroom—no surprise there—before slamming gavel against wood. "Opening remarks, Prosecutor."

James Halsted scrambled to his feet. "Your Honor, gentlemen of the jury." The prosecutor was a middle-aged man of pale complexion with a belly gone to flab for lack of properly scheduled meals and his once-coveted morning constitutions. He had worked eighty hours a week, poring over every scrap of evidence and hearsay, since the defendant had been arrested for gunning down one of the town's most affluent citizens in his own home the morning of the Centennial celebration. Halsted hadn't enjoyed a moment in the bright light of day since.

"We will prove in this court of law that the defendant is nothing more than a criminal, hardened further with each act of murder performed, of which there have been many. I admonish you: Keep that in the forefront of your minds as you hear the claim of innocence that will be brought forth by the defense. We are here to exact justice on a criminal. A gunslinger. An assassin."

A murmur swept the crowd.

As the prosecutor painted broad strokes of the person he wanted jurors to believe they were up against, the young defense attorney reached over and patted the gloved hand of his client.

Lucinda Messenger sat unmoving, struggling against the emotions that threatened to pour forth in response to that simple gesture of compassion, that benevolent touch of the hand. How different her life might have been had she received such compassion in the beginning. She loosened the grip that she'd had on her left bicep—her only distinctive habit in a world anxious to learn her tells—and remembered what her attorney had promised: They would use the habit as part of her defense. It was perfect. From there, they had devised their strategy.

"Defense, your opening remarks," the judge said.

Matthew Gerber rose, reminded himself to keep his enthusiasm in check. This was his first big case, and he intended for it to mark his place in history. Western expansion was on the cusp of greatness, and he planned to be no small part of that greatness. The young man could have been a poster boy for Harvard. Not only had he been a star pupil at the college, but also a star on its revered rowing team.

But, Gerber had felt stifled by Eastern politics, and yearned for a larger field of play. It was his wife who suggested the move West, and he could not have been more pleased with his choice of a mate than at that moment.

He made a couple of long-legged strides toward the juror's box, and turned his clear blue gaze upon the crowd. "We have all read and heard the fantastical descriptions of the defendant." Gerber smiled. He was confident, animated. "Why, many Eastern newspapers have printed such magnificent reports over the past dozen years that no less than fifteen dime novels have been written about that Dastardly Dame of the Wild West: Lucy Angel." As he spoke, he strolled back to the table, reached into his satchel, and withdrew three of the small books. He fanned the stack, held it up for all the audience to view. They were here for a show, and he was prepared to give them one. "No doubt, you've seen these illustrations—a buckskin-clad woman of Amazon stature carrying four pearl-handled Colts, three derringers, and two Remington rifles."

This solicited a chuckle from the audience.

Young Matthew Gerber felt at ease. He had mapped his journey to freedom for Lucinda Messenger down to every possible turn in the road, every detour that might be thrown in his path, every highwayman the prosecution might have hidden along the route.

"The prosecution will have you believe that the larger-than-life Lucy Angel is, indeed, this gentle, petite woman with the kind eyes seated before you.

"Mrs. Messenger wishes to address, here and for all, the sensational stories that have clung to her skirt hems for more than a decade. She will tell you the truth behind these tales"—he waggled the books before the jury—"so that no doubt about her just ways might cloud your judgment.

"She will tell you that she killed the man for whose death she is on trial."

The crowd wasn't sure it had heard correctly. Many turned questioning glances or outright statements to their pew mates.

"And, she will tell you that he was not the first."

This last threw the room into turmoil. Some called out support, some shouted for justice, some even applauded. All were on their feet.

Judge Stanton pounded gavel to oak repeatedly, aware that he must act swiftly, or be tethered to this post presiding over the case till hell froze over. Even if the Devil slept straight through the harsh winter, the task would take weeks if not contained with an iron hand. And, everyone knows that the Devil doesn't sleep.

Stanton bellowed orders, his baritone reverberating off marble and glass and paneled walls. "Sit and close your mouths now, or be found in contempt."

Within seconds, the tick of the clock could be heard from the back wall. The judge exhaled, looked at the lawyers. "No character witnesses, no circus acts, no histrionics. Cut it to the bone. Am I understood?"

"Yes, Your Honor," both said in unison.

The judge surveyed the crowd. "If you people want a show, you can hire Barnum."

Matthew Gerber dodged the boulder in the road, and edited the final sentence of his opening statement before delivering it. "Gentlemen of the jury, your honorable Judge Stanton, Lucinda Messenger will tell you that she has killed. Our defense lies in the reasons why."

The judge told prosecution to call its first witness.

Halsted rose, tossing a last, regretful glance at his numbered list of those who had said they would testify. "Your Honor, we call Mrs. Asa Calloway."

Lucinda studied Kathleen Calloway as she approached the bench and placed her hand on the Holy Bible held forth by the court clerk. Once an abused wife who had walked in fear of her own shadow, The Widow Calloway now appeared to be a woman of confidence—even, one might say, a happy woman. Nothing like the woman Lucinda had met in the Calloway mansion July past.

"State your name for the court."

"Kathleen Calloway, widow of Asa Calloway."

"Mrs. Calloway," the prosecutor said, "Please relate to us the events of July fourth."

"My husband—may God rest his soul—was running for city mayor. Every citizen of the town knows that, of course. The evening of the third, he discovered that an error had been made on the flyers made up at Mr. Larkin's print shop. Since Asa needed them for the opening ceremonies on the Fourth, he sent word to Larkin to print corrected ones and have them delivered first thing. As you know, my husband was a particular man."

"The point, please," said Judge Stanton.

Mrs. Calloway cleared her throat. "It was an intense morning. My husband was understandably anxious. By the time Mrs. Messenger arrived with the corrected flyers, he told her that she was almost late.

"I had sent the maid on errands. I was the one who showed Mrs. Messenger into Asa's library. Of course, I had no idea she was a murderer."

"Objection!" Gerber was on his feet.

"Sustained. Madam, stick to the known facts."

The prosecutor said, "Mrs. Calloway, what do you

want to tell the court about your relationship with your husband?"

"I loved him according to everything the Good Book teaches. True, Asa had a temper, but I knew how to cope with that."

"Did you ever fear for your life?"

Kathleen Calloway studied a white handkerchief that she held firm in her grasp. After a moment, she looked up. "No. Fear and faith cannot coexist."

The prosecutor nodded to the witness, then to Judge Stanton, before returning to his seat.

The judge said, "Mr. Gerber, your witness."

Gerber approached. "Admirable statement, Mrs. Calloway."

"A true statement, young man."

"Mrs. Calloway, did your husband raise a hand to you in the presence of Mrs. Messenger?"

Mrs. Calloway's mouth went slack. She fiddled with the handkerchief. "He did not strike me."

"But he threatened to, did he not?"

"Idle threats." She tossed her hand, and the kerchief flapped like an injured bird.

"The marshal's report from that day documents that you had a black eye and a cut lip when he arrived on the scene."

"That was six months ago, but I suppose it is possible." She chuckled nervously. "I must admit that I have never been a graceful woman. Likely, I had walked into a door."

"I see. Shall we call your doctor to the stand to report how many times you have walked into doors, or fallen down flights of stairs, or stepped off porches, or fallen from—"

"Get to your point, counsel." The judge glanced toward the window. The snow had picked up. His pocket watch read 10:40.

"You were a long-time victim of abuse, were you not, Mrs. Calloway? Over the years, your husband had broken your nose twice, cracked several ribs, dislodged teeth, broken your arm. Can you deny these reports?"

She waved the handkerchief, its symbol of surrender lost on her. "That did not give her the right to kill him. With God's grace I had things under control. I was a submissive wife, according to the teachings of the gospel. I prayed for my marriage every night, and I arose every morning and forgave my husband. I set breakfast in front of him and asked God for a good day. Most days, God gave me that. Mr. Calloway meant nothing by what he did, and he was quite sweet and genuine when he apologized. He always apologized. I felt loved then, and I knew my prayers were being answered."

She dabbed at tears as she continued. "It is quite upsetting for all this—our private life, our way of working together—to be brought out publicly. And, it is her fault for meddling."

"What did you say to her that day, when you returned to the room?"

"I-I don't recall."

"Was anyone else present?"

"I'm not sure. Our maid might have returned by then."

"Thank you." Gerber turned to the judge. "Your Honor, I call to the stand Esther Knowles."

"Objection!" Halsted cried. "The maid is my witness."

The judge said, "How many witnesses do you have?"

"Minus my character witnesses, two."

"Gerber?"

"One, Your Honor."

The judge nodded. "Overruled. I don't care who talks to her first, just get it done."

The women scrambled, and as Mrs. Calloway stepped down, Esther Knowles was sworn in and put on the stand.

Gerber said, "Tell me about Mrs. Calloway's habit of cooking breakfast."

"She only did that after they had fought the night before. I always knew when Missus had been beaten—even if Mister hadn't left marks—because she would take over the breakfast duties in the kitchen."

"Do you recall what she said after Mr. Calloway died?"

"Yes, sir." The woman sneaked a sideways glance at her employer.

Gerber said, "Madam, you are under oath to tell the truth."

"Yes, sir. Mind you, she was in a sort of daze. I had just returned from the mercantile and set my basket in the kitchen when I heard the gunshot. I was standing in the doorway of the library when she said, 'I have often wondered whether my life would be better if he just died.'"

The gasp that escaped many a female lip—including Lucinda's—left no doubt that several had entertained similar thoughts.

"Halsted, your witness."

The prosecutor mentally sifted for something with which to dilute the maid's story. "Mrs. Knowles, did you ever see the deceased physically abuse his wife?"

The maid studied a moment. "No, sir. But I—"

"Did you see the deceased physically assault the defendant?"

"No, sir."

"Nothing further."

Halsted returned to his station with clenched teeth.

"Gerber?"

"Your Honor, I call Lucinda Messenger to the stand."

Lucinda took a deep breath and exhaled, then stood and walked for what seemed like miles toward the court clerk waiting with Bible in hand. She was glad she had chosen her gray wool suit with its lined cape. The extra warmth was comforting.

She looked up at the judge. "Do I need to remove my gloves? It's awfully cold in here."

He was touched by the tenderness of her voice. "No, ma'am," he replied.

The clerk said, "Place your left hand on the Bible, raise your right hand, and repeat after me."

Lucinda simultaneously raised her right hand and positioned her left hand over the words *Holy Bible* stamped in gold on the cover. Tentatively, she lowered her left hand, while her mind superimposed a picture from her past. The past and present jumbled together, and she saw a Bible slammed against a pulpit, heard her own voice instructing an old woman, heard the old woman repeating I solemnly swear, I solemnly swear . . .

"Mrs. Messenger? Mrs. Messenger?"

"I'm sorry, Your Honor," Lucinda stammered, remembering where she was. "Yes, I solemnly swear."

She took the seat indicated by Mr. Gerber, and clamped her right palm around her left forearm as if she could hold back the venom that life tried to pump into her veins.

"Is there something wrong with your arm, Mrs. Messenger?" The attorney's tone of concern seemed genuine.

She paused. "It is from the bite. Rattlesnake."

The judge leaned forward. "Rattlesnake? When was this?"

"At our homestead. My husband threw it on me."

The crowd gasped.

Gerber studied the reactions of judge and jury. "Your husband threw a rattlesnake on you? What led up to that terrifying act?"

Her eyes welled, and it was as if the courtroom floated in a mirage. Do not cry, she admonished. It wasn't easy, being forced to go back to the origins of her altered path. She closed her eyes and willed her mind back there, back to that place. . . .

Hiram Messenger dragged his feet, stirring dust as he approached the house. The wind in turn swept it away as it had swept away the dirt that had covered the seeds from his spring planting. After it had finished with that, it swept the seeds away, too.

He was almost past the blacksnake when he made out its form. It was coated with a fine silt, just as he was.

He didn't bother brushing off his clothes before throwing open the door and entering the soddy. He sniffed, then cursed. "What the hell's burning?"

Lucinda, standing in front of the cook stove with pistol in hand, swung around and shot him a look. She'd never thought the prairie would get to her. She'd never anticipated day upon dreary day of nature pounding at you, days when she couldn't regulate the cook stove to bake a pan of biscuits, days when her unkempt hair would hang like wet rags from a clothesline on a windless day. She wondered whether windless days still existed. Somewhere, perhaps.

"Heard the pistol shots," Hiram said. "Didn't know but what you'd called yourself quits."

"You call me that enough for both of us."

He grunted. "Someone has to. You won't face

anything for yourself. I'm surprised you had the gumption to kill that snake. Where was he?"

"He fell out of the rafters, landed in your supper." She used the gun as a pointer. "I tried to haul the pot out the door, but the snake was swirling and flailing so much, I couldn't. I fished it out with a poker, but it wriggled off the poker and slithered toward the bedroom. When it—"

"Shut up, woman, and put down that gun. I'm not some damned female you can complain to."

"Huh. Find me another woman foolish enough to stay out here and I'll gladly complain to her. No doubt she would be looking for the same thing, having been dragged to these Godless plains."

"I said shut it." He bolted toward her, hand raised.

She flinched.

He dropped his arm, told her she was lucky he didn't have the strength today to give her what she deserved. He glanced toward the bedroom, saw the snake's severed head, the pool of blood. "How many cartridges did you waste killin' it?"

She ignored the question. She'd heard it so many times before, how they couldn't waste anything. He never acknowledged her gun skills—or didn't realize them, so assured was he that she was worth no more than the threadbare calico she wore. If her husband had had any clue about her ability with firearms, he might have kept his haranguing to himself. Particularly while she had a pistol in her grip. "Would you close the door?"

Hiram took his seat at the table. "Not till the stench of burned supper is gone. And you'd better have salvaged somethin' for me to eat."

She gave him the stew, then dug the centers out of the charred biscuits and gave him most of those, too. For her own supper, she drizzled a ladle of broth over the rest of the salvaged centers.

The man who sat across from her acted more animal than human lately, and she wondered whether this prosperous life out West was affecting him as much as it was her.

Hiram Messenger wasn't the man she'd married. At least, she thought he wasn't. In truth, she hadn't taken time to get to know him beforehand. She had wanted adventure, and Hiram had said all the right things to get her attention. They had climbed aboard his wagon and headed West immediately after the preacher had declared them joined.

She realized, too, that she wasn't the woman Hiram had married. This savage land changed a person, she knew that now.

Of late, she had speculated over whether Western cities might offer more. She'd suggested that to Hiram, but he was bound and determined to be a farmer. A sod-buster. Lately, though, the changes she had seen in him had been more disturbing. Instead of mending straps or sharpening plow blades during the evenings, he sat and stared. He stared for hours at her while she cooked and scrubbed and mended and fought off rodents and snakes and peered out windows for Indians and checked latches on doors.

A rattlesnake slithered across the threshold and toward the small pine table where they sat.

Lucinda yelped, flew from her chair, and grabbed the gun. Hiram seized the snake, moving quicker than she'd ever seen him move. "Only one way to cure your fears, woman. Throw you into the pit." He flung it toward her.

The snake sank its fangs into her left arm. Hot pain shot toward her shoulder. She beat at the reptile with the pistol. It let go, dropped to the floor and slithered toward the man.

"Shoot the damn thing," he ordered.

"What kind of an animal are you?" she shrieked. "Who does that to a person?" She was dead anyway, she was sure of it. She aimed the pistol at the man and squeezed the trigger.

He dropped.

She turned the gun on the snake and fired. Its severed head slammed up against the wall, leaving its body twitching on the floor.

She jerked loose her apron strings, used them as a tourniquet, and grabbed a butcher knife. . . .

A woman called out from the back of the crowded courtroom. "How did you survive that snake?"

"I shot him," Lucinda said before she fully remembered where she was.

Every female in the gathering applauded.

Judge Stanton brought down the gavel. "Order!"

Gerber smiled. "I believe she means the bite, Mrs. Messenger. The venom?"

"Yes, of course. An old Indian couple found me unconscious, made a poultice—I do not know what was in it—and I eventually recovered.

"I remember thinking that I would use the third bullet on myself, if the poison became too much to bear. Working fast, I cut a cross, drew out the blood."

"What happened then?" asked Gerber.

"I went south to start a new life."

Judge Stanton peered at his pocket watch, then at the clock. "Now is as good a time as any for a recess. Court will reconvene at one o'clock. Sharp." He emphasized the last word with the gavel.

When they returned, there wasn't a woman left outside the courtroom for twenty miles. Spotting his wife among the spectators, one of the jurors sprang to his feet. "Mrs. Billings, who is minding the store?"

"Mr. Billings, you're the one who insisted on having seven children to help with the work. It's high time they gave their worn-out mother a break."

Laughter swept the courtroom.

Mr. Billings bowed elaborately. "No one deserves a break more than you do, my dear."

The second round of laughter was tamped down

by the judge's gavel. "Mrs. Messenger, please take the stand. I remind you that you are still under oath. Gerber, proceed."

"Your Honor?" Halsted said.

"Prosecutor?"

"If it please the court, I would like to question the defendant regarding her statements prior to lunch."

"Granted."

Halsted grabbed his own set of the dime novels—many more than those exhibited earlier by Mr. Gerber—and eagerly approached the witness. He indicated the cover of the one on top. "Mrs. Messenger, do you recognize these weapons?"

Lucinda studied the image. "I know that the long-barreled ones are rifles, and—"

"Madam, are these images of your weapons?"

"No, they are not."

"Do you carry a weapon?"

"Only the tiniest of derringers in my reticule. A lady alone cannot be too careful in the wilds of the West."

"Mrs. Messenger, do you deny that you are indeed Lucy Angel?"

"I have used that name."

"I mean to say, are you the Lucy Angel portrayed in these books?" He shook the stack in her face.

"Step back, Counselor," the judge said.

When Halsted retreated, Lucinda said, "Since I have not read them, and since I have not to my knowledge been interviewed by"—she leaned forward to get a better look at the cover—"J. B. Pendleton, I would have to say that I am not."

"How, then, do you account for the fact that *Lucy Angel: Rattlesnake Slayer of the Lone Prairie* is the same story you shared with us this morning?"

Lucinda's lips parted in surprise. "I'm afraid I do not know. The only time I ever used the name was wh—" She interrupted herself, looked from Halsted to her own attorney.

Gerber nodded slightly.

Halsted seized the lifeline. "When, Mrs. Messenger? Who knew you as Lucy Angel?"

"I had traveled to San Francisco," she said, "where the only acceptable work I could find was in a café too near the docks. I was walking home one night when a drunk accosted me. I wounded him with my derringer, and was taken to the jailhouse. There, I spent several hours answering questions for an officer who said he needed as many facts as possible for his report.

"I recall now, he commented more than once on the fascinating account of my life. I told him there was nothing fascinating about it, that I was only trying to survive.

"But," she concluded, "surely the character in those books isn't me."

"Surely, it is." To the judge, Halsted said, "Nothing further at this time."

Another fork in the road, Gerber thought. His strategy included plans to reveal the story behind the Lucy Angel of novel lore, even though he had not let his client in on the particulars of that strategy. Halsted had beat him to the punch, but Gerber felt confident he could turn it to their advantage. "Mrs. Messenger, were you aware of your reputation as a female gunslinger before we began preparing your defense?"

"No, and frankly, I am still a bit stunned by it all."

"Why, then, did you change your name when you moved?"

"At first, I was frightened, alone. After I left the homestead, I thought about the name Messenger. That led to Gabriel, the archangel who delivered a message. I had delivered the message that a barbarian posing as a man should not physically, mentally, verbally, and emotionally abuse the helpmeet God had blessed him with. And, I vowed to God that if I ever found another female being treated that way, I would help her.

"By the time I arrived in Texas, I was going by the name Lucy Gabriel."

"When you were sworn in, I couldn't help but notice your reaction to the Bible."

"Not to the Bible. Rather, to its abuse."

"So"—Gerber reached for the court's Bible—"this particular book did not cause your distress?"

"No." Lucinda watched her lawyer raise the Book. She stiffened. She knew how difficult it would be to tell the story, yet she must. If people weren't made aware of sin, how could they possibly prevent it in the future?

"What did, then?"

She spoke, and as she did, she thought her words sounded distant, muffled, as if uttered through an oppressive haze of southern heat. . . .

The boardinghouse was run by a retired school marm named Ruth Porterfield, who welcomed Lucinda with open arms. The two women bonded quickly, as is the way of women. Ruth helped Lucinda find work as a housekeeper at the town's largest hotel, and it didn't take long for the newcomer to settle into the pace of the bustling Texas community. After a few weeks, she had her new life nicely tacked down.

One afternoon, Lucinda returned to the house early from work and found Mrs. Porterfield seated at the kitchen table, crying. A newspaper was spread open before her.

"Ruth?" Lucinda touched the woman's shoulder. "What's wrong?"

"I'm sorry, dear." She blotted her face with her apron. "I cry when I get angry. Always have. It's an irritating trait."

"I think it shows compassion. Now, tell me, what has you in such a state?"

Ruth stood, and jabbed her index finger into the paper, smudging the ink. "Them."

Lucinda skimmed the article about an evangelist coming to town to lead a tent revival.

"The nerve of the townsfolk, allowing him to come back here."

"You mean The Reverend Malachi Thompson? I don't understand."

Ruth told Lucinda about questionable events surrounding the reverend's visit the year before. She had witnessed signs of a vile relationship between the man and his young granddaughter who traveled with him.

"Did you attend his services last year?"

"Two or three, before I reported him. No one believed me. They now think I'm a crazy old woman. Before he preaches, the little girl sings. Did I tell you? Prettiest voice I've ever heard. I would like to hear that again." Ruth stared out the window, her expression wistful for a moment. "Damn him," she shouted as she slammed her palm against the table. "Damn him to hell."

Lucinda had never heard a woman curse before. She promised Ruth that she would be on the alert.

What Lucinda observed of the reverend and his granddaughter over the next few days could easily have been seen as benign affection—if she hadn't had those depraved thoughts planted in her head by Ruth.

On the third day, Lucinda realized that she had not transferred the linens from the supply closet on the hotel's fourth floor to the one on the second. The manager in turn had warned employees not to disturb the reverend in the afternoon when he was preparing his evening sermon. Lucinda decided to retrieve the linens while the reverend and his granddaughter were in the restaurant.

She was in the closet directly across from their room when she heard their voices. She decided to wait. Once they were in their room, she would descend the back staircase in plenty of time to finish her tasks.

The reverend said, "Claire, you were a good girl in the restaurant, very respectable to the others."

"Thank you, Grandfather."

Lucinda smiled, questioned whether Ruth's imagination had run away with itself.

The reverend unlocked their door and stepped aside for the girl to enter.

Lucinda held her breath, listening for the door to close. Just before she heard the latch click, though, she heard the reverend say, "Claire, honey, I think it's time you earned yourself a new bonnet."

The man's insinuating tone struck Lucinda and she sank to the floor. She thought she was going to be sick.

At length, she rose and smoothed her apron. She had not survived her own ordeal to turn her back on this child. She had found strength, and she must use that strength for those who were weak.

She was astounded at how quickly the answer came to her. She left the linens, silently descended the back staircase, and walked briskly to the boardinghouse.

"I knew it," exclaimed Ruth when Lucinda confirmed her fears. "What should we do?"

Lucinda said, "I have a solution. In order to protect you, though, I will not share it. Swear you will tell no one."

"I solemnly swear. You can trust me."

"I must move fast. Is your rifle any good?"

"The best, why?"

"No questions. Where's the tent set up?"

Ruth told her.

"I need your buggy."

"Done. Joe over at the livery will fix you up, just like he did for our picnic last month."

The tent's canvas looked stark, almost ghostly, as it waited in the afternoon heat for the hope-filled attendees who would begin arriving at dusk. The sides were rolled up and tied in order to take advantage of the evening breeze.

Lucinda surveyed the area, studied angles, fine-tuned her approach. When she had everything in order, she returned to town to dress for the meeting.

"I am channeling The Almighty Himself!" he bellowed by way of introduction as he brought the Bible down with a mighty force against the oaken lectern.

The Reverend Malachi Thompson was all hellfire

and brimstone that night, adding to the thick, hot air that hung in the tent like a pall when the breeze died. Slamming fist against pulpit, slamming the Bible, he stomped the plank platform upon which he stood.

After a while, he settled into his message and people—women, mostly—ducked out of the long meeting to go do their business or tend fussy infants. More time passed, and here or there a man would quietly leave, returning after a few minutes. Nearly two hours into the service, Lucinda slipped out of the tent and headed down the path toward the outhouse she had been told was for the womenfolk.

It was nearly pitch black out, and Lucinda's widow's weeds helped her blend into the darkness. She moved slowly till her eyes adjusted.

She surveyed the area around her and determined that no one else was on the path. Backbreaking work on the homestead had strengthened her, and she thought how it was all part of the armor God had provided her. For the second time that day, she climbed the tree.

Two dark leather straps held the Winchester to the top of a branch, one securing the barrel, the other holding the stock in place. With fluid movements, she unclasped the front strap, pivoted the barrel, drew a bead, held her breath, and squeezed the trigger.

The reverend slumped forward against the podium,

then slid out of sight behind it. During those seconds, as a stunned congregation watched the scene play out before them, Lucinda refastened the strap, dropped to the ground, and ducked into the outhouse.

After a moment, she heard the sounds of someone approaching. When he was almost upon her, she stepped from the privy.

"Ma'am? Pardon, have you seen any men out here?" The man was out of breath.

"Men?" She brought her hand to her throat. "Did I come to the wrong—?"

"No." He waved off the notion. "Nothing like that. The reverend's been shot."

"Shot? Are you sure?"

"Yes, ma'am. Any men spotted out here?"

"No, I haven't seen any men out here."

"Well, you shouldn't be out here alone. I'm taking you back up to the tent."

She nodded, felt an odd comfort as he gripped her arm just above the two scars.

Someone coughed.

Lucinda jumped, surveyed the courtroom. The silence echoed.

Her attorney was still standing there, and she tried to shake the feeling that she had been in a trance or a deep sleep.

"Are you prepared to move on?"

She nodded.

"Please relay the events of the morning of July fourth."

"Mrs. Calloway answered the door, and I noticed immediately that she had been injured. She smiled slightly, though, and allowed me into the foyer. I explained that her husband wanted to see the flyer correction before the crates were unloaded.

"I waited while she announced me, and heard how unkind he was toward her."

"Do you recall what he said?"

Lucinda nodded. "He told her that she knew not to enter his library and that he would handle the problem himself. Then, it sounded like he sprang from his chair, and Mrs. Calloway made a little . . . yelp, I suppose is how I would describe it. The door flew open, she rushed past me, and her husband bellowed for me to come in."

Lucinda's pulse pounded in her ears. She fought the urge to grip her arm.

"Take your time, Mrs. Messenger," Gerber said as he sent a look to the judge that dared him to rush the woman at this stage of the trial.

She exhaled. "He was putting on his jacket as I entered the room, but I saw that he wore a shoulder holster over the left side of his chest."

"Did you notice whether it contained a gun?"

"Yes, sir. It did."

"Continue."

"I was upset over what I had heard, and didn't want to even be in the same room with him. I handed him the print proof, and said that Mr. Larkin would have the boxes sent to the park gazebo, as originally arranged. I excused myself, but he rudely told me that I had not been dismissed, and that he would be allowed the courtesy of my silence while he verified the correction.

"My heart was pounding hard enough, I suspected he could see it shaking my body."

"Were you afraid of him?" asked Gerber.

"Not at first. I saw him as someone who wanted to be in control, to have the upper hand. I have seen many women like Mrs. Calloway, and I believe God has given me a voice for those women. Therefore, I confronted the man. Before I knew what had happened, he had grabbed my wrists and wrenched them, forcing me onto his lap. I tried to struggle, but he was more than twice my size. He laughed then, and said he wished he had a feisty woman instead of that—I'm sorry, Mrs. Calloway—that milquetoast he had been saddled with.

"He let go of my left wrist with his right hand, and clamped it around the nape of my neck. I put up a real struggle then, started to cry out." Lucinda brought her hand to her throat and swallowed. "That's when he grabbed my throat. I fumbled for the gun. I thought that if I could scare him with it, he would back off. As I pulled the gun loose from the clip, and pivoted the barrel toward him, it went off. I had no idea it was one of the new double-action pistols."

"Thank you, Mrs. Messenger, nothing further."

"Halsted?" said Judge Stanton.

Halsted approached, thinking how he had never seen the likes of this case. Remarkably, the woman seemed innocent of the crime for which she was on trial. Yet, she had admitted to other killings. Rather than cover up the rumors—the legend of Lucy Angel—who was most assuredly the woman seated before him in the witness box, the defense had looked it boldly in the face and attacked it. If the strategy works, Halsted thought, I must try it.

Today, though, he had a job to do. He said to the defendant, "Do you deny that you have blatantly taken the livcs of three men?"

"Yes."

"Yes? But—"

"None, sir, were blatant. All were in defense."

"Were there more than three?"

"Objection! Irrelevant."

"Sustained."

"Three, then. Nothing further."

Judge Stanton glanced at his watch. 2:45. He should have just enough time to make the 4:15 train. "Closing statements, gentlemen."

Halsted drank water from the glass—more than anything, it was a means of collecting himself—and approached the juror's box. "This woman has appeared before you today and admitted to killing three men. Murdering them. She even had the audacity to share her lawless ways with a writer.

Gentlemen, I implore you. Do not allow her feminine wiles, her notions of some cosmic justice to sway you. She could have asked for help from the authorities. She could have walked away. She could have remembered her place as a lady and avoided confrontation. Lastly, she could have minded her own business, and not interfered in the privacy of marriage. Be mindful of our laws when you govern this case."

Matthew Gerber waited for Halsted to sit before he addressed the jury. "Gentlemen, the real victim in the case set before you is our very own defendant, Lucinda Messenger. She did not kill Asa Calloway because of his repeated abuse to his wife. She shot him in self-defense when he, like an animal, physically attacked her. You have seen what hanging a man does to his throat. Imagine, if you will, the beefy hands of Asa Calloway around the slender throat of Lucinda Messenger. If she had not acted swiftly and with a cool head, she surely would not be here now to relate her story.

"Do not allow the prosecution to make you believe that this woman is anything less than a survivor, a champion of the weak, an angel of mercy."

Gerber clasped his hands on the rail of the jury box. "God placed Lucinda Messenger in harm's way to help those in need. Who was she to question that calling? Could any one of you have left a child to the devices of a barbarian hiding behind the Word of God? You could not. There is a greater justice in having saved that child.

"Does any among you condemn her for defending herself against a husband so cold-blooded that he would throw her into the viper's pit?

"Those nightmarish events gave her the strength not to be a victim when she was brutally attacked by Asa Calloway."

The jurors deliberated for only twenty minutes.

Judge Mortal D. Stanton brought down the gavel with vigor.

The foreman of the jury handed a folded slip of paper to the bailiff, who in turn handed it to the judge.

Stanton opened and read the slip. "Will the defendant rise?"

Lucinda Messenger and her attorney stood.

"Gentlemen of the jury, what say you?"

The foreman rose. "Your Honor, in the matter of the territory versus Mrs. Lucinda Messenger, we find the defendant not guilty."

The crowd whooped. The women sprang to their feet and applauded (save Kathleen Calloway, who fought her way through the press of people and out of the courtroom).

Judge Stanton said, "Mrs. Messenger, you're free to go. Court dismissed." One more strike of the gavel, and he was gone. Many years later, long after he had forgotten about clocks and trains, the Lucinda

Messenger trial would form the centerpiece of his memoirs.

The crowd scattered. Lucinda lowered herself back into the chair.

Matthew Gerber confirmed that she was all right before making his way toward the cluster of reporters waiting in the foyer. He had no way of knowing that among the cluster was one J. B. Pendleton, scribbling across the top of his pad a title for his next book: *Lucy Angel and the Devil of Destination Point.*

After another moment, Lucinda breathed a sigh, then stood and turned. Two women faced her, smiling tentatively. The younger one's eyes glittered with hope as the older said, "Mrs. Messenger, would you care to join us for tea?"

Lucinda's eyes welled. "That is so kind of you. Yes."

They linked arms. The older woman said, "Your dear lawyer should keep those reporters busy enough that we can sweep you right out of here."

"Is it true that you carry one of them derringers?" asked the young woman.

"Of course. As I said, a lady alone cannot be too careful."

"I need to get me one." The young woman's brow wrinkled. "Men seem to have guns everywhere upon their person, have you noticed?"

Lucinda Messenger nodded, but it didn't concern her. She wondered whether the men of the world would ever understand the power of women united.

As the three walked down the street, they were joined by one woman, then another, and another.

Two blocks behind them, a little girl watched. She pointed to the trail of women and exclaimed, "Mother, look! May I follow the Pied Piper, too?"

Destiny's Gun

Jory Sherman

Old Thad Fergus drove his wagon into the Superstitions once a month, sometimes more often, to haul supplies up to Morgan Wilson's place. He pretty much knew what Morg needed, because he had learned to keep track of the days and how much flour, tobacco, salt and such Morg used in a month's time. And, if Morg ran out of something or needed something, he would ride one of the horses he broke to Thad's and give him a list on a slip of paper he kept in his adobe shanty. It was always the same slip of paper. Thad would return it with the goods he bought and Morg would tuck it away in one of the cubbyholes in his rolltop desk. The paper was getting pretty worn and crinkled, but it served its purpose. Morg was a man of few needs.

Thad rumbled up the rocky, twisting road to Morg's, not because it was time to deliver any goods, but because the day before, when Fergus went into town,

Lily Baskin had given him a letter to deliver to Morgan. She had said it was urgent, which overrode all of Thad's objections.

"I ain't no mailman, Lily, and you know Morg wants to stay clean away from you."

"I know, Thaddeus," Lily had said, "but I really need this delivered to him. Right away. It's very urgent."

"He might tear my head off. Morg's got more bad moods than a wet cat of late and I don't like to bother him."

"Thaddeus, don't make me beg."

The way she stood there in the somber light of Arena's General Store, he knew he couldn't refuse her. She was trying to hide her face behind one of those accordion fans the Mexes sold in Taos. But he could see the bruises on her face, the dark crumples of skin at the corners of her eyes she had tried to powder away. She had so much powder on her face, she looked as if she had been leaning over a flour bin when the wind was blowing her way.

"I hope this don't mean trouble for Morg, Lily. You know he's done his best."

"I know. I-I just can't say any more right now. I'm so scared I don't know where to turn."

"If you put it that way, Lily—"

"I do. Thank you, Thaddeus. And hurry. Please."

She had given him the letter and then left the store, running like a scared antelope to her buggy, and whipping her horse out of town like she was trying to outrun the devil himself. Thad wasn't old, but everybody called him "Old Thad" because he looked old and he seemed old. He was like the hills that footed the Superstition Mountains, weathered, craggy, thorny, homely, and, perhaps, wise in the way a tree is wise, having lived through quakes and thunders, rains and floods, burning winds and snowy winters. Thad had lost his wife some five or six years ago, but stayed at the place they had built when they both came to prospect for gold. They had built dry rockers, combed the mountains, camped by the creeks, made knife slits in the corners of horse blankets, stretched them across the streams, tied each side to bushes, trees or rocks so that the wool would collect particles of gold in its wiry mesh. They had eked out a living, but had never discovered the bonanza everyone believed was hidden somewhere in those brooding mountains.

Now, he kept a few goats because he liked their company and the milk the nannies gave. The kids were pets who nuzzled his clothes with their mouths and noses, trying to find the plugs of tobacco he chewed and always had to hide from them. He raised hogs, too, Poland Chinas, and made more money off them than he had ever garnered from the edge of black dolomite in his pan, or from a rocker or placer. People stayed away from Old Thad's place because of the swine stench, and that suited him just fine. People, he had long ago decided, were a whole lot dirtier than hogs and twenty times meaner. His hogs had no smell, it was just their offal that gave off a stench and such odors were not exclusive to pigs.

A dust devil danced across the plain, scattering tumbleweeds, chewing them up, flinging twigs and rocks from its dervish vortex and whipping its own winds as it swirled in an aimless cavort toward no specific designation. Old Thad, in a reflexive action, ducked his head and pulled his hat on tighter. He spat a flume of tobacco from the side of his mouth and rattled the reins to speed up the horse before he was caught in the path of the spinning spout.

A red-tailed hawk rose from behind a low hill and sailed along an invisible line, its neck and head craned back and forth as its golden eyes scanned the ground below for prey. A vagrant gust of wind caught his pinions and nearly flipped him over, but the bird swung its tail feathers for purchase and righted itself, bending its wings to skid out of danger. Its high-pitched *scree scree* pierced the silence and floated off into a desolate emptiness that seemed never to have known a footfall, whether animal or human.

The pale yellow sun wobbled behind the dust, as if temporarily blinded and the heat waves vanished like ghostly waterfalls in the sudden hush. Old Thad topped the slight rise and followed the winding road into a funnel created by two low ridges. Morgan's place was at the end of a corridor where the ridges almost converged to create a box canyon. The spread had belonged to Morgan's father, who died shortly after the war, alone and destitute. Morg's mother had passed away in childbirth and he had never known a mother's breast. He had grown up among men, his father and brother Billy, until he was as hard as a hickory stump and awkward as a newborn colt around women.

In the wake of the dust devil, the air turned crystal clear, almost as if someone had set a freshly washed bowl over all of it. The Joshua trees stood like mendicants all around, their arms raised in supplication to the blue sky. The stately stalks of yucca, their blooms arranged like yellow concho belts hanging on store pegs, stood like sentinels. All about him, off the road, the cholla bristled like exploded muffs of delicate lace, so beautiful, yet as lethal to the touch as surgeons' scalpels, so sharp they'd slice through a child's hand if any dared to touch.

Thad entered the walled tunnel to Morgan's homely patch, that lonely stretch where he always felt as if an Apache might be on either ridge, looking down on him, his face painted for war like some hideous harlequin in an Edgar Allan Poe story. Traversing that stretch gave Thad the bitch-willies—every blamed time.

He started whistling and rattled the reins just to hear some sound in that desolate emptiness. A pair of mourning doves whistled past, twisting and turning in the air like feathered darts, and then disappeared at the narrow end of the funnel, a pair of dusky gray phantoms, vanishing from an old tintype of rocks and hills and empty sky.

The place looked deserted, but Thad knew Morgan was there. He set the brake after he pulled up in front of the adobe hut, with its thick thatched roof, a porch made of whip-sawed lumber and live oak poles. The door, as usual, was open a crack. A hollow gourd hung from one of the porch posts and a wooden wind chime, dangling from a rafter at the edge, clinked an out-of-rhythm tuneless melody. Morg's horse whickered from the pole corral as Thad walked over to the lean-to with its three walls of weathered lumber. He rounded the corner to the open side that faced a field of sparse grass that had to be planted every spring, a mixture of seeds that was different each year, as if real Kentucky bluestem, gama and grama could grow in such hostile country.

Morgan was covered in blood when he stood up to greet Thad. He held a bloody knife in his hand.

"You look like you been in a knife fight, Morg."

"Little early, aren't you, Thad?" He squinted into the light and lifted his boot, the one that was holding down the black colt with the blaze face and three white stockings.

"Yep, got a message for you. I see you done gelded that little foal out of Lady Rose. You coulda waited 'till I come up."

"Seemed a good time. Cool morning." He reached down, picked up a bottle of alcohol and poured it on the colt's open sac. The colt rose up on all fours as if it had been scalded and romped from the lean-to, flicking its tail up and down, switching it back and forth like a semaphore wigwag.

Thad laughed. "Some uses salt," he said.

"Star would just lick it off," Morg said, whipping his hands on his denims. He wiped the knife, too, and slid it back in the sheath on his belt.

"That what you named him? Star?"

"Yeah. You name things, you can tame 'em. That one's going to give me trouble when I go to break him. He's wild as a March hare."

"I want to be up here for that."

"Let's go sit on the porch after I wash up. Got some *tepache* in the big *olla* should be ready to drink."

Thad licked his lips. "You use pineapple or banana?"

"Banana. Sort of. Plaintain, the man said it was."

"That's what I smelled in that crate I brought up last month. Wondered what it was. Shipped from Georgia or somewheres."

"California, Thad."

"Yeah, California."

They both laughed.

Morgan worked the pump and filled the trough in front of the house. Sinking his arms in the water he splashed his face and rubbed his arms. He wiped off with a towel hanging from a nail on one end of the trough.

They walked up to the porch where there were two chairs—Mexican made, hard on a man's backside, but tolerable for a half hour or so.

"Before you go in and get that *tepache*, Morg, you better read this. It's from Lily."

"I'll read it directly." Morgan took the note and slipped it into his shirt pocket, smearing one side with a thin stripe of blood.

He returned in a few moments with two tin cups. Thad was already sitting in one of the chairs, filling his pipe. Morgan handed him a cup, sat down and took a sip of the brew. It was sweet and cool. It wouldn't get a man drunk from the beer in it, but it would give him a pleasant buzz if he drank enough of it. Morgan never did.

"Let's see what Lily has to say. Not more trouble, I hope."

Thad said nothing while Morgan pulled the note out and read it. His face did not change expression.

Neither man spoke for several seconds.

"Poor Lily," Morg said.

"It's that no count husband of hers, ain't it? Andy Baskin."

"What makes you say that?"

"Her face looks like it's beestung where it ain't wearin' purple bruises. She didn't say it, but I know Andy beat her pretty bad."

Morgan swore under his breath. "I've got to go down to the Junction."

"Big mistake, Morg."

"I know." He paused, staring off at the periwinkle sky with its wisps of clouds floating above the rocky hills. His brow furrowed as if he was wrestling with his thoughts. He sipped the *tepache*, perhaps to cool the fires raging within him. "I've got to run Andy off, Thad," he said, finally. "Or kill him."

Thad let out a low, keening whistle. "He won't run off. Not as long as he's got likker in his belly. And he's keepin' the Estrella Cantina in business, whores and barkeeps both."

"The sonofabitch. Lily's too good for him."

"You always knew that. Ever since . . ." Thad's voice trailed off, but Morgan knew what the old-timer was talking about.

"I should have let Andy drown," Morgan said.

Thad finally lit his pipe and puffed on it, spewing out plumes of smoke from his nostrils and lips. "Yep. You should have. You saved the bastard's life. And it nearly cost you your own, Morg."

"That's what started it, I reckon."

"Oh, yeah Miss Lily was so grateful she fell head over heels in love with you."

"Something I regret."

"You couldn't stop it, no more'n you could help savin' Andy Baskin from drownin' in that flash flood."

"Do you believe in fate, Thad? Destiny?"

"Is there a difference? I don't know. Which is fate? Which is destiny?" He drew smoke into his lungs, let the smoke drift slowly from his mouth.

"They might be the same thing. But I always thought fate was something that happened to you, whether you wanted it to or not."

"And what about destiny?"

"I don't know. I guess I thought destiny was

something written down, like in a book, and you couldn't change it. Destiny was where you had to go, and fate was what happened to you along the way."

"I never gave them things that much thought, Morg."

"No, but I have. A lot."

"How come?"

"Ever since Lily told me about Andy's brother, Norman. She told me that was what was always eating at Andy, what made him drink. What made him mean."

"Well, I know his brother was killed in the war. Nothin' special 'bout that. A lot of men died, women, too, both Yankee and Rebel."

Morgan stood up, walked to the porch edge and grabbed the post next to the steps. His horse whickered and a pair of doves sliced the air beyond like a pair of gray missiles hurled from a silent cannon. A quail piped a fluting call from its perch on a yucca on one of the small hills.

"The way Lily said it, Andy talked his brother Norman into taking his place on picket duty one night. A Rebel sniper shot Norman, killing him dead. Andy never got over it."

"What's your point, Morgan?"

"Andy knew if he'd gone on picket that night, he would have been the one to take the bullet, the one to die. So, he blames himself for his brother's death."

"Well, he ought to give thanks to his brother for his own life, you ask me."

Morgan turned and sat back down in the chair. He drained a good draught of the drink in his cup and his eyes misted. "You might be able to cheat fate, Thad. For a time. But you can't cheat destiny."

"What are you getting at, Morg? I don't cotton much to superstition myself."

"Andy Baskin cheated fate twice, I figure. But maybe he was destined to die both times."

Morgan finished his drink and stood up. He started toward the door.

"Where you goin'?" Thad asked.

"I'm going to strap on my Colt and ride down to the Junction."

"I got a ham for you. I'll fetch it and be on my way. Here's my cup. Mighty good drinkin', Morg."

"I'll beat you to town," Morgan said, taking Thad's cup from him, and then disappeared inside himself, as if entering another world Thad would never know.

Morgan was leading a wagon train out of Fort Apache when they got caught in a thunderstorm in Salt River Canyon. He yelled at the drivers to get their wagons to high ground. They all got out except for Andy and Lily Baskin, who were in the hindmost wagon. Andy's horses spooked when a lightning bolt struck a hundred yards away. He lost control and the horses broke the harness, got tangled up in the traces. Morgan raced back and dragged Lily from the buckboard seat, carried her over to another wagon. He was riding back for Andy when a wall of water surged down the canyon.

It struck the wagon and threw Andy into the maelstrom.

"My husband can't swim," Lily screamed.

Morgan jumped from his horse and dove in after Andy. When he grabbed him Andy fought, smashing Morgan with his fists as the water hurled them down the canyon. Morgan nearly drowned. Finally, he strangled Andy until he passed out, then dragged him to the bank. They were knocked back down into the swirling waters and tumbled along until Morgan was able to grab a branch sticking out of the bank. He hauled himself and Andy up. He had swallowed water and was coughing blood by the time the others found them. Andy came to, and hugged Morgan while Lily wept and hugged them both. Morgan had water in his lungs, developed pneumonia and nearly died.

Lily visited him every day he was in the infirmary, and fell in love with him. She forced Andy to settle in Apache Junction so she could be near Morgan. He saw her marriage crumbling and told her to leave him alone, get back to her life with Andy. But Andy knew he had lost her, and started drinking. He was a freight hauler so he got by with the drinking as long as he showed up for work, drunk or sober.

Lily had tried to stay away, but she was heartbroken when Morgan rejected her. "No matter what you think of me," she told him, "I love you, only you, and I always will."

"Andy needs you, Lily."

"No, he's just a drunk, and he hates me now, for falling in love with you. I know he feels betrayed, but we've done nothing wrong."

"And we're not going to," Morgan told her. "I have nothing to offer you."

"Except yourself," she said. "And that's all I want."

He had tried to forget her, but the truth was that he had fallen in love with her.

He forced himself to wait it out. Andy was a loose cannon on deck in that marriage and he was bound to blow hell out of it sooner or later. When he heard that Andy had struck her one drunken night when he was in a rage, he almost walked back into the thick of it. But he didn't. What they did in their marriage was none of his business, he told himself. Lily would either leave Andy, or he would kill her. And that was that.

Now, though, Morgan realized that Lily had been living in hell and he blamed himself. He should have taken her away from Andy six months ago when she expressed her love for him. He should have forced the issue, driven Andy out, and taken Lily to get a divorce.

But that went against his grain. He did not like to meddle in other people's lives. Now, after being alone for the past six months, avoiding town as much as he could, he realized that he loved Lily, loved her deeply, and the beatings Andy had given her for the past two months had gotten worse, by all accounts. There was no longer a marriage there, he was sure. And she was in trouble, deep trouble, or she wouldn't have sent Thad out with that note.

The house was silent when Morgan tied up at the hitch rail. He walked up the path to the porch, his heart filled with dread. He knocked on the door and called out her name.

"Lily? You there, Lily? It's me, Morgan."

Silence.

Then he heard a low moan. He tried the door. It was open. He walked in.

"Lily?"

"In here, Morg," she said, her voice so weak he could barely hear it. He had never been in her home before, but he saw how clean and neat it was in the front room—the women things and the man things in separate places, doilies on the divan, rifles on wall racks, paintings on the walls, a vase of flowers, a big masculine chair, a dainty table in a corner, out of the way. The room smelled of rose water or lilacs, and, underneath, the faint tang of whiskey that lingered despite the perfumery.

She was lying on the bed in a small room. He knew that was not their bedroom, but a spare one that he guessed had been her sleeping quarters for some time.

"Oh, Morgan," she sobbed. "You came. I knew you would. I prayed you would."

She hid her face from him, holding up her

bruised arms so that he had to pull them down to look at her.

He did not recognize her.

Both eyes were swollen nearly shut. She had an egg-sized dark lump on one cheek. Her mouth was smashed, the lips cracked in several places. There was an ugly gash on her chin. More bruises on her neck.

"Andy do this to you?"

"Y-yes," she said. "He-he's gone, but he-he said he'd kill me when he got back. Oh, Morg, I don't know what to do."

"I'll take you over to Doc Carrington's."

"No. I can't see anybody like this. Look at me."

"He's a doctor, Lily. You need medical attention."

"Andy would kill me if I told anyone. He warned me not to go to see Doc Carrington."

"He's not going to hurt you anymore, Lily. I promise. Come on, you're going to see the doc. I'm going to the Estrella."

"Wh-what are you going to do?" she asked.

He breathed in hard.

"I'm going to let Andy drown," he said softly, and the room went quiet.

By the time Morgan left Doc Carrington's, it was dark. But he had stayed long enough to find out that Lily had no broken bones. Carrington said she might have some internal bruises and he would keep her there in the infirmary overnight, at least. She was in pain and the doctor gave her sedative powders. Morgan squeezed her hand before he left and cringed when she winced. He gave her a small peck on her forehead and her hazel eyes sparkled with bright golden and copper lights.

The cantina stood alone at the edge of town, on the road to Mesa. The sign on the false front read CANTINA ESTRELLA in red letters. Beneath it was affixed a wooden star, its silver paint faded to a dull pewter. Horses stood at the hitch rails on three sides. Music blared through the colored lamps that lined the windows and hung from the ceiling. It was a large adobe that had once been a trading post, burned down and rebuilt after the Mescaleros and Chiricahuas had been driven east past Fort Apache. Morgan wrapped his reins at a hitch rail in back and walked in the front door after he stood there a moment, looking through the batwing doors at one of the colored lanterns. He stepped inside the smoky room to the rippling arpeggios of a guitar, the rattle of a trap drum, and the bugling of a cornet from the bandstand at the back wall.

The tables were all full, the long bar nearly so. Painted Mexican women sat on the laps of ruddy-cheeked men, their bright skirts shouting the pageantry of the occasion. A man sang one of those sad Mexican songs about love and betrayal and death, a *son huasteco* that had men and women weeping at its plaintive story.

Morgan moved to the near end of the bar where

he saw an open spot. He kicked aside a brass spittoon and put one boot up on the brass rail. A beefy, squat bartender glided toward him, wiping the tears from his eyes.

"Mezcal," Morgan said.

The man replied in Spanish. He put a shot glass on the bar and poured it full of the amber liquid. A worm slid from the spout into Morgan's glass.

"Ah, *el gusano*. I buy you the next drink, eh?"

Morgan nodded. He did not touch the glass, but scanned the bar, looking for Andy's face among the bobbing balloons under straw and felt hats. There were ranchers, wranglers, horse thieves, gamblers, and owlhooters everywhere he looked. They all turned away when they saw his piercing glance.

He didn't see Andy right away and he started to lift his drink when a man near the middle of the bar turned his head toward him. Morgan saw the flash of recognition in Andy Baskin's eyes. The look turned savage in an instant as Andy's lips curled up in a hostile snarl. He lifted his arm and pointed to Morgan, as if he was silently accusing him before a jury in a court of law.

Morgan set the drink down and stepped away from the bar. He dropped his right hand to the Colt .45 on his gunbelt and lifted it from its holster, then let it fall back gently.

A thousand thoughts moiled up in Morgan's brain, stumbling over each other like a pack of clubfoots at a three-legged sack race. He didn't come to kill Andy, but the man looked as if he was ready to fight. He didn't look drunk, but he had enough liquor in him to give him the courage he didn't ordinarily possess.

Morgan nodded at Andy in a friendly manner, then held up his glass as if inviting him to share a drink.

Andy picked up his glass of beer and swaggered toward Morgan. Several pairs of eyes tracked him. Morgan set his glass down again and stepped to the corner of the bar. Andy was armed. He was a big man, with the strong arms of a teamster, a bulging neck, thick heavy eyebrows, and a sloping forehead that jutted out like a ledge over his eyes and nose.

"You wife-stealing bastard," Andy shouted in a loud voice.

The music stopped abruptly and chairs scraped the dirt floor. Not a glass clinked, not a playing card whispered as the room went silent and every man and woman in it froze into puppets who all stared at Andy Baskin, then at Morgan.

"Buy you a drink, Andy," Morgan said amiably, loud enough for the whole bar to hear him.

"You ain't buyin' me no drink, you no-good bastard. You stole my wife Lily from me and I'm callin' you out."

A woman let out a breath in a long sigh.

A man cleared his throat.

"Andy, you don't want to do that. You might regret it."

"I regret you takin' Lily from me, you no-good sonofabitch. Now, step out and I'll damn sure spill your thievin' blood, Wilson."

One of the Mexican barkeeps reached down and lifted a sawed-off scattergun from behind the bar. Morgan held out his hand to the man and shook his head. Then he stepped into the open. Men peeled away from the bar like bats fluttering from a cave wall and all the bartenders ducked down. Several tables near the bar emptied and left a deserted arena.

"Andy, you don't have to do this. I didn't steal Lily from you. You beat her to a pulp and she's in the infirmary."

"You stay out of my life, Wilson."

"You leave town and I will. Tonight."

Baskin's face contorted in rage.

"I ain't leavin' nothing, you sidewinding bastard."

All of Morgan's thoughts untangled and his mind was a placid lake, calm and serene. For a split second, he had the feeling that he had been there before, in that very place, facing off with Andy Baskin. Maybe it was in a dream, but he knew everything at that moment. He knew what was going to happen and he knew he couldn't stop it. The hairs on the back of his neck prickled, but inside, he was as steady as a mule pulling a plow.

Andy struck for his pistol. His hand lashed downward, his fingers folded around the grip and he bent to the side slightly as he jerked his hand upward, freeing the pistol from its holster.

A collective gasp filled the room.

Morgan slipped his Colt from its sheath. His draw was smooth and fast. He thumbed back the hammer before Andy cleared leather and he took deliberate aim as a look of disbelief crawled across Andy's face.

Morgan squeezed the trigger, felt the pistol buck in his hand. He heard the explosion as if it came from some faraway war and, through the smoke and the orange fireflies of burnt powder, he saw dust puff up on Andy's shirt just as a hole appeared right where his heart lay underneath his skin. Andy cleared leather and hammered back in that last instant. His finger squeezed the trigger and the bullet dug a hole in the dirt a foot from his boots. Then the pistol slid from his hand as blood gushed from the hole in his chest. He took a half step, then pitched forward, fell facedown. Blood pooled up and then the flow stopped. There was a dusty film over the blood.

Morgan turned to the barkeep nearest him.

"You take him to the undertaker's and I'll pay whatever it costs. And if any man here says anything but self-defense, I'll come hunting him. *Claro*?"

"*Claro*," chorused the bartenders and a half dozen men standing nearby.

Just then, Thad walked inside. "Wagon's outside," he said. "I'll take the deceased to the undertaking parlor, if one of you will give me a hand."

"You're a good man, Thad," Morgan said. "Put it on my bill."

Morgan walked over to the bar, downed the glass of mescal and left a ten dollar bill on the bar. He walked to the doors without a man stopping him and stepped out into the night.

Lily chased the black colt a hundred yards before she caught him with the loop of her lariat. She pulled the rope taut as Morgan had taught her, and walked up to Star and put her arm around his neck. Then she pulled a lump of sugar from her apron pocket and held it in the flat of her palm right under his nose.

Star bent his neck and nibbled at the sugar cube, then worried it through rubbery lips until it disappeared. Morgan could hear it clack against the colt's teeth as he tumbled it around inside his mouth.

"Oh, he's so darling, Morg. I just love him. Don't sell Star after you break him, please. I want him."

Morgan smiled. He looked up at Thad, who was sitting on the top rail. Thad smiled at him and nodded in silent approval.

"He's yours, Lily. Anything you want, Mrs. Wilson."

"You won't hurt him when you break him, will you?"

"Nope. When I finish with Star, he'll be gentle as a lamb."

"Just like you," she said and her face softened. She took the rope from around Star's neck and the colt didn't run away.

"See?" Morgan said. "You've got him half broke, just like me."

She laughed and Morgan drew in a breath that filled his lungs and his heart. He looked up at the hazy forms of the Superstitions, at the blue, cloud-flocked sky and knew that life was good and his destiny was working out all right, too.

He glanced at Thad, who had been a part of it and was averting his gaze like some modest old maid embarrassed by Morgan's show of intimacy.

Morgan pulled in a breath, swelling his chest.

As for Fate, it had not been too unkind either.

As Good as the Bad

Ken Hodgson

Lonnie Landers stopped in front of the batwing doors of the Concho Pearl Saloon. He nervously shuffled his hobnail boots on the boardwalk, trying to muster up the courage to enter. After several moments, he stuck his right hand into a pocket of the faded and tattered overalls he wore. The reassuring feel of cold metal gave him the needed grit. He swung open the doors and stepped into the smoky interior.

No one at the bar gave the simple-minded son of Doc Landers widow more than a passing glance. The hulking boy often ran errands to earn money.

Lonnie fixed his gaze on a rear table occupied by three men, two of which he knew and were the objects of his quest.

"Mister Handleys, sirs," Lonnie sputtered. "I hear you find people."

Dallas Handley, known as the deadliest bounty hunter in Texas along with his father, looked up and nodded. "Most all of the folks here in San

Angelo know that, son," Dallas said. "Why do you ask?"

Lonnie could only swallow hard while squeezing the metal in his pocket.

Barney Handley turned to the third person at the table, a trail-dirty man wearing a Texas Ranger star who was obviously tired and in need of a shave. "The boy has difficulty with words on occasion."

"That's a trait I can admire," the ranger said. "Especially here in West Texas."

Lonnie cut off Barney's reply. "I know you only find people for money. I have money." The boy laid out a lone silver dollar along with some small change in front of Dallas. "I saved all of this. There's ten dimes, twelve nickels and a dollar. I can count good."

Dallas Handley's mood turned serious. "Lonnie, just who do you need found?"

"My ma an' my sister, sir. They took them this morning."

The three men seated at the table exchanged knowing glances.

"Who took your folks, boy?" Dallas asked.

"There was five of 'em. I was down at the river takin' a catfish off a bank line when they come up to the house. I heard a shot when they killed my dog. Then Ma and Sarah started screamin'. I didn't know what to do. I didn't have a gun or nothin'. Then they put my Ma and sis on horses, tied their hands with rope and took 'em away. I don't think the bad men even saw me."

Barney said, "If they had, they would have shot you quick as they did your dog. The ranger here was dropping off wanted dodgers on this gang because he believes they might be moving our way."

The Texas Ranger scooted his chair back and stood. "I'm Captain Carson Kelly out of Austin. The gang of outlaws that hit your place is most likely the bunch we've been after for some time. Slade Black and his gang of cutthroats have a tendency to raid in these parts, rob banks and kill anyone they run across. Then they head to Mexico where they lay low for a spell." Carson hesitated. "For the past year or so they've started kidnapping women. Got away with well over a dozen now."

Dallas lowered his brow. "First I've heard about them kidnapping women." He looked up at Lonnie and chose his words with care. "Any idea what becomes of them?"

"They're never seen again, that's all we know for certain." The ranger continued, "Slade and his gang robbed a bank in Abilene four days ago which brought the reward for the lot of them up to six thousand dollars. That much money gives those scum enough value to cause them worry."

Dallas stood. "Lonnie, we know your folks are close by and also where they're heading. Don't you fret, we'll saddle up and be nipping at those outlaws' heels right soon. Your ma and sister will be all right."

Lonnie looked at the money on the table. "I can get some more money."

Dallas walked around the table and placed an arm around the boy's shoulder. "You take your money and go home. The law will pay for our services."

"I don't got no home no more," Lonnie said.

The two bounty hunters along with the ranger were silent for a while. Finally Captain Kelly said, "Let's ride. We have a manhunt on our hands."

The fires of a desert sunset were painting the western sky blood red when the Texas Ranger and two bounty hunters rode south of San Angelo, following a winding trail along the Concho River.

"Slade and his gang's not bothering to cover their trail," Dallas remarked. "A train would be harder to follow. They either don't think the law's after them or are arrogant enough to believe they can kill any that are."

"Attitudes like that make for troublesome outlaws," Captain Kelly said. "Most folks were church raised and have at least a tatter of conscience. That upbringing causes a man to hesitate before pulling a trigger. When men get mean enough to kill without even blinking, pursuing them is dangerous as messing with nitroglycerine."

"Nitro doesn't have a six thousand dollar bounty on it," Barney said.

Dallas Handley squinted into the glare of a dying sun. "I learned a long time ago that a dead outlaw is worth the same as a live one. They're also a lot less trouble to bring in. What concerns me are the women."

"I didn't want to talk in front of the boy," Carson said. "The word is a rich Mexican bandit by the name of Gregorio Cortez has a hideout just south of the Rio Grande that's almost the size of a town. He pays big money for white women to work in his saloon. They're quite a draw for business. Most of those poor gals don't last too long. That's why he's always in need of fresh stock."

Barney said, "If that's a fact, the good news is Slade will be forced to deliver prime merchandise."

The captain nodded. "That makes it likely those little gals won't be harmed until they get sold and Cortez gets his hands on them."

"Let's see to it that don't happen," Dallas said.

The Texas Ranger rode in silence for several minutes, then looked over at Dallas. "I've been chasing after outlaws for so long I've learned to save getting a crick in my neck by knowing when there's someone behind me. Without turning around, I'm guessing there's a big kid riding a horse on our heels."

"Yeah," Dallas replied. "He's been following us now for a solid half hour. Your neck can be spared the pain. He's also wearing a gun he's come up with somewhere."

"Wave him on in," Carson said with a shrug. "On

a manhunt anyone with a gun that'll shoot in the direction of the bad guys is always welcome."

A few minutes later Lonnie was riding alongside the three lawmen. They had expected the big, simple-minded boy to have teary eyes along with a distressed disposition; they were wrong. Lonnie had a stern set to his jaw and a narrowness to his eyes that the experienced manhunters recognized as determination born of seething hate. They also knew the youngster would be prone to rash actions no matter how stern their orders might be.

"My sister's name is Sarah," Lonnie said. "She is fourteen years old. Ma's name is Millie, she's thirty-five years old. I'm good with numbers, but most folks don't think I'm good at much of anythin'. They call me an idiot."

Dallas Handley said, "Lonnie, people can be plenty cruel. No one here thinks you're an idiot. Your pa was a mighty fine dentist and it was a sad day when he died of lockjaw. Your poor mother has had a lot to endure and everyone in San Angelo knows how hard you work to help out. These outlaws we're after are mean as rattlers, and we don't want you to get hurt."

Lonnie slapped a calloused hand to the pistol holstered on his right hip. "There's only five bad men. I got twenty-six bullets includin' what's on this belt. I'm gonna get my family back with ammunition to spare. It's costly to buy an' there's rabbits to be hunted later." He added proudly, "This was my pa's gun. It's a good one, too."

Captain Kelly noticed the gathering shadows. "Let's make camp for the night. From the stride of Slade's horses, they're moving plenty slow and easy. Besides, I'm tuckered as a wh—a barkeeper a week after a cattle drive hit town."

"There's sure no moon coming out," Barney said. "It'll be black as the ace of spades tonight. Slade an' his bunch will be forced to hunker down, too. Let's make camp while there's still enough light to separate firewood from rattlesnakes. We're still a fair piece from Mexico. An early start in the morning should have us caught up to that passel of outlaws by noon or so."

The West Texas sky had darkened to a sooty gray when the four men scooted rocks around a flickering fire to use as seats. Reflections from the yellow flames danced off nearby mesquite leaves like fireflies. In the distance, a pair of hoot owls welcomed the newborn night with their eerie songs.

Barney gritted his teeth and cradled a Sharps rifle in his lap when he sat. "Not too many years ago, those owls would have been Comanche. That sound still gives me the willies."

Captain Kelly filled a battered coffeepot from a canteen, dropped in a handful of grounds, then placed it as close to the fire as possible. "There's still a few raiding parties of Comanche warriors about that don't know they've lost the war. Just last year the rangers wiped out over a dozen renegades and buried that many settlers—or more."

Barney winced. "Oh, *that* news will cause me to sleep like a baby tonight. Thanks a heap for the unwanted and unneeded information."

Dallas grinned as he added dry sticks to the fire. "Dad, the captain is just funning you. There hasn't been a single Indian raid in these parts for months."

Lonnie Landers broke the prattle when he said, "How many Indians are out there? I can count up all of our bullets."

"There's no Indians, boy," the ranger said. "I was only joshing 'em." His demeanor turned serious. "Do you know how to use that gun on your hip?"

"I watch people good. There's six holes for six bullets. I got six more in my belt. You pull back the hammer each time you shoot, an' point it like a finger. My pa showed me how to line the pointy thing at the end of the barrel with the notch at the rear to make the bullet go where it should. I can hit what I aim at."

"You ever actually *shot* a gun?" Dallas asked.

Lonnie shrugged. "Never wanted to waste the ammunition. It's costly you know."

Barney lowered an eyebrow. "If I heard you right, you have *six* shells in that gun. Most everyone only loads five, which leaves the chamber under the hammer empty. This way, if you drop the gun or snag a tree, it won't go off and shoot you in the foot or leg."

Lonnie gave a firm look. "I don't drop *my* gun." Then he settled down by the fire, leaned against a tree and began snoring.

Captain Kelly shook his head. "Five outlaws to kill, two women to rescue, and now we've got a kid packing a gun who's never even shot one to watch after. Manhunts in this part of Texas are always plenty interesting, providing a person lives through 'em."

"We always aim to entertain," Barney said, then began to chew on a piece of jerky. Tomorrow was going to be a long day.

An orange orb glared down from a cloudless blue sky, causing heat waves to shimmer on the distant hills like nervous swarms of insects when the four horsemen rode across a barren section of sand and cactus.

"Not a speck of cover," Dallas remarked. "At least that works the same for the outlaws."

"From the tracks, Slade and his bunch are still lollygagging. There's a stage road crossing not far to the south. We should cross it shortly. From there on the country is mighty rugged," Barney said.

The Texas Ranger pointed to a narrow column of smoke. "I'm guessing there *was* a way station for the stages right about there."

"Crap!" Dallas exclaimed. "That's the Frasier's

place, Joe and Lizzy"—he hesitated—"and their two young boys—"

"Let's ride," Barney said. "But likely we're too late."

The stench of burning flesh was nearly overpowering. All four manhunters stayed in their saddles. There was nothing anyone could do.

"I'm hoping they were kind enough to shoot those people first," Kelly said. "They herded the goats and dairy cow into the cabin with them folks, and torched it with coal oil. Then dumped what coal oil they didn't use into the water tank to keep us from giving our horses a drink. Those bastards really *need* killing."

Dallas wiped smoke from his eyes. "Wasn't planning very hard on bringing any of them back alive. Not now for sure."

"Bounty hunting is like fishing, got to catch 'em before we clean 'em," Barney said. "They aren't far, we know that for certain."

Lonnie Landers kept squinting into the sun while staring off to the east.

"We've been fools," Captain Kelly yelled. "Slade's bunch knew we'd stop to check out the burning way station. Get down! They're coming at us from both sides."

Barney stayed in the saddle long enough to fire his Sharps. An answering scream of pain from behind a lone greasewood bush spoke that at least one outlaw was out of the fight.

Black smoke puffed from the end of a rock fence

and the Texas Ranger tumbled from his saddle to crash onto the dry ground.

Dallas fired three times, bringing down the outlaw behind the fence when he was foolish enough to peek over it to see if his shooting was accurate.

"There's another," Lonnie said, "back of the windmill." He pulled his pistol, took a few seconds to aim carefully, then sent a hot slug of lead square between the outlaw's eyes just as he peered around the rock tank at the windmill's base. "One bullet, one dead bad man."

"This might be all of 'em," Dallas said, scanning the area while holding a cocked pistol.

Barney climbed down from his horse to see how badly the ranger was hurt. He was surprised to see the lawman sit up, holding a rifle with a shattered stock and cursing up a storm.

"The bastard went and ruined my Henry," Carson fumed. "I've had this gun since I was a pup. I was pulling it from the scabbard when a bullet went and smashed it. Damn, I hate it when things like this happen."

"If that slug had demolished your innards same as that wood stock," Barney said, "you'd have something to *really* complain about. I'd venture you had best not miss church Sunday. Now grab up a gun that ain't busted. There's more desperados about and you've rested long enough."

A few minutes later, Dallas came striding back from behind the rock fence that served as a corral.

"There was just the three of them. Their horses are tied under those trees yonder."

"That will leave Slade Black plenty shorthanded," Carson said. "You can bet your hole card *he* wasn't one who got shot."

"Gratified *you* ain't among the casualties," Dallas said to the ranger. "It appears either you were mighty lucky or those outlaws weren't. Anyway, we need to move on. Slade's not going to wait around long when his boys don't show up."

"Most likely they're holed up in those rocks along the road to the south," Barney said with a head wag to the distant hills. "Mexico's not a far piece from here."

The ranger stuck the remains of his beloved rifle in the scabbard and mounted his horse. "They tried flanking us and it nearly worked. What do you say we return the favor?"

"Dad and I will circle east," Dallas said. "You and your good luck can come in on them from the west."

Barney put a foot in the stirrup of his horse then turned to his companions. "Did anyone notice we seem to be short a big galoot of a kid wearing overalls?"

"He knows his family's close and he's already killed a man," Barney said. "The boy's not all that smart to begin with, but he should've waited."

Captain Kelly said, "There's nothing we can do to stop him now. We have no choice but to go ahead with our plan of attack and hope the kid plugging that outlaw between the eyes like he did was no accident."

"There's been too much jawing already," Dallas said. "Let's ride."

Lonnie Landers caught the glint of sunlight off steel about a quarter mile ahead, near the rocky ledge of a low mesa. He tied his horse to a stunted mesquite, then pulled his Colt and placed a fresh bullet into the cylinder to replace the one he had fired. "Two bad men, six bullets." Then he bent low and scurried to where he had seen the reflection.

Thick patches of cholla and prickly pear cactus forced him to take a circuitous course to his destination, which caused him to come out above a long flat ledge of rock that protruded over the road below. Lonnie flattened against the sandstone like a lizard when he saw his mother and sister along with two men holding rifles.

Luckily, the desperadoes were focused intently on the road to the north. It was obvious they were still expecting their companions to come riding up.

Lonnie could see that both his mother and sister had their hands tied in front along with thick sticks of wood fastened across their backs, holding the elbows behind them. The outlaws were obviously experienced in transporting captives.

Lonnie gritted his teeth in anger. He knew he had to fight down the urge to simply run in shooting.

The outlaws could easily kill one of his family before he could shoot both of the bad men. The situation called for calm. Lonnie took a deep breath, then another. He could do this, he *had to.*

"Drop that gun or die!" a voice boomed behind Lonnie Landers.

The startled boy did what would turn out to be the last thing the renegade expected. He dropped to the ground and rolled over, still hiding his pistol. Then he fired two quick shots into the man's middle.

"There were *three* bad men," Lonnie said with odd calm. "I got four bullets now."

"Did you get him, Slim?" a voice boomed from the mesa.

Lonnie crawled over to the dead outlaw and removed the man's hat, then placed it on his head and stood.

"I killed 'em." Lonnie hollered. He was proud of his idea, but knew it would only buy him some short time.

The boy made it to within a hundred feet or so of the remaining two outlaws before one of them noticed who he actually was and sent a hot slug of lead singing past Lonnie's right ear.

Lonnie was rattled now. He had never been shot at before. He pulled his Colt and fanned three quick shots into the closest outlaw, killing him instantly. To Lonnie's amazement, the last desperado only glared at him and smiled an evil, snaggle-toothed grin.

"I'd say you're out of ammo, button. I know you shot five times." The big man slowly reached for his gun. "I plan to gut shoot you. That's a slow, painful way to die, but you caused me problems. No one causes Slade Black problems without payin'."

Lonnie carefully pointed his Colt at the leader. A brief gaze of disbelief washed across the outlaw's face less than a second before a black hole appeared between his eyes. A cloud of black powder smoke kept Lonnie from seeing his startled foe stumble back and fall from the cliff onto the road below.

"I don't drop *my* gun," Lonnie said. Then he holstered his Colt and set about untying his family.

The sun was sinking low in the west by the time all of the dead outlaws had been loaded into the back of a freight wagon taken from the burned way station and the horses hitched for travel.

Millie Landers sat on the front seat of the wagon daubing at teary eyes. Sarah had yet to stop shaking, but thankfully, both women were unharmed.

Barney climbed onto the wagon to drive it back to San Angelo. He nodded toward Lonnie who was alongside the wagon on horseback. "You ought to be plum proud of him, Missus Landers. Lonnie not only saved the both of you, but he done in four wanted men with a mighty big price on their heads.

The captain said there was two thousand dollars on Slade, the others were only worth a thousand each, but that comes to five thousand which Lonnie will be paid."

"Lordy," Millie said between sobs. "I never dreamed of that much money. Things have been awfully tough for us since my husband passed away."

Lonnie Landers grinned and patted the handle of the gun on his hip. "Folks always said I wasn't good for much of anythin'. They were wrong. With a gun I'm as good as the bad."

Barney Handley glanced back at the bloody cargo in the wagon and spat a wad of tobacco onto the dirt road. "I reckon that's the truth." Then he flicked the reins, starting the wagon creaking slowly to the north, heading for San Angelo and home.

Inferno

William W. Johnstone

with J. A. Johnstone

Frank Morgan smelled the smoke before he saw it. That was a mite unusual, but he was riding upwards through a ravine at the edge of the Cap Rock, and that restricted his view of the landscape.

When he reached the top of the ravine and came out on the prairie, he saw the smoke, sure enough. Big billowing clouds of the thick gray stuff rolled across the Texas plains, driven by a hard wind that threatened to pluck the hat from Morgan's head. He reached up to hold it on as a frown settled on his weathered face.

The fire was coming toward him, leaping across the prairie at dizzying speed. It was still about a mile away, he figured. He could see the southwestern end of it, but the wall of flames and smoke stretched off to the northeast farther than he could see.

Note: This story takes place before the events in the Last Gunfighter novel *The Drifter*.

Morgan had a good horse under him, a hammer-headed dun that he had been riding for a while. It took him only a second to realize he could gallop hard to the west and get safely out of the way of the blaze.

The settlement that was smack-dab in the fire's path didn't have that option.

Even with the threat that faced him, Morgan paused for a moment at the sheer horror of it. The flames were eight or ten feet tall and devouring ground at a terrifying rate. He could see some of the townspeople scurrying around like ants, panic-stricken by the fire's inexorable approach. Some of them clustered around the public well, hauling up buckets of water to fling onto the buildings in the futile hope they might turn back destruction. Others leaped onto horses and fogged it out of there, escape their only thought. Still others tried to load a few belongings onto wagons, buggies, and buckboards, bartering time to flee against their possessions.

Poor stupid bastards, thought Morgan. Everything they had, including maybe even their lives, was about to be snatched away from them through no fault of their own, and there really wasn't a damned thing they could do about it.

He didn't have to worry about anything except saving his own life. He turned his horse and heeled it into a run, leaning forward over the dun's neck as he urged it on to greater and greater speed.

The wind shifted a little in Morgan's favor. That

took away any chance the fire might blow on past the settlement without destroying it. Not that there had ever been much of a chance to start with.

Morgan looked over his right shoulder and saw that he was getting clear of the danger. He kept the dun running hard for another few minutes, just to be sure another sudden wind shift wouldn't send the flames in his direction again. It wasn't long before he was well clear, and could rein in and turn his mount. He watched as the blaze reached the town and the gray smoke turned black and billowed even more as the buildings went up, one after the other.

Morgan could have just ridden on. There was a reason he was known throughout the West as The Drifter. Ever since he had gotten a reputation as a fast gun, when he was just a young man, he had been on the move most of the time, always riding, never staying in any one place for very long. At first, maybe he had been searching for happiness. But as man after man fell to his blazing speed and unerring accuracy with a Colt, every opportunity to settle down ultimately had been lost. So now in middle age Morgan drifted, one of the last of his breed, seeking only to be left alone. Wanting only not to have to kill yet another snot-nose punk out to make a name for himself.

So it was an unaccustomed impulse that sent him riding into the ruined settlement after the fire had roared on through it and finally burned itself out when it reached the edge of the Cap Rock, the time-eroded escarpment that divides the High Plains from the rest of Texas.

Morgan had come to a stagecoach road that cut a path through the charred landscape and followed it into town . . . or rather, into what was left of the town, which wasn't much. The walls of the adobe buildings were still standing, but their interiors were burned out. The frame buildings were gone, right down to the ground, except for their foundations and the occasional partially consumed timber. Inside the buildings were just heaps of ashes. The conflagration must have been incredibly hot. It looked like what Morgan had seen during the war—towns that had been bombarded by artillery and then set afire.

The people who had gotten out in time were trickling back in, on foot, on horseback, or in wagons. They wandered around, dazed, staring in disbelief at what was left. Morgan saw burned bodies lying here and there, which accounted for the sickly-sweet stench in the air. The wind had finally fallen still, too late to save the settlement, and an eerie quiet lay over the scene, broken only by a faint crackling from the places where some of the ruins still burned.

That hush was shattered by a harsh, incoherent scream, followed by a woman's agonized voice. "Gone, all gone!" she cried. "The boys, too! They're dead! Dead! You son of a bitch! You son of a bitch!"

Morgan turned his horse and saw a middle-aged woman pounding frenzied punches into the chest of a man who stood there looking stunned as he absorbed the punishment. Stocky, with thinning white hair and a neatly-trimmed beard, his expression was that of a man who'd been shot in the gut. He looked like he was dead and just didn't know it yet.

Frank Morgan had seen that expression all too many times. He hadn't liked it then, and he didn't like it now.

"Your fault, your fault, your fault!" the woman screamed at the man as she continued hitting him. He made no attempt to stop her. Finally, grief overwhelmed her and she fell to her knees, then toppled over onto her side and lay there in the ashy dust, covering her face with her hands as she sobbed.

The man finally became aware of Morgan sitting on the dun a few yards away. He looked up at The Drifter and asked in a dull voice, "Who're you, mister?"

"Just a fella who's passing through," Morgan said. Despite the hard shell he usually cultivated around him, he wasn't an unfeeling man. He went on, "I'm sorry for your loss. For all the losses here. I saw the fire coming, but there was nothing I could do to help."

The man shrugged. "Wasn't nothin' anybody could do once the fire was lit."

"You mean once the fire started, don't you?" Morgan asked with a frown.

"Nope." The man shook his head. "That fire was started a-purpose." He looked around at the destruction surrounding them. "My wife's right. This is all my fault. I founded this town. I was the mayor. This was my *home*, and I burned it down."

The man's name was Al Bowman. He sat in the shade of a still-standing adobe wall and nipped at the bottle Frank Morgan had taken from his saddlebags and given to him. Bowman made a face at the raw bite of the whiskey.

"I'm not really much of a drinkin' man. And while I appreciate it, mister, I got to say it don't help much."

"Nothing will but time," Morgan said as he hunkered on his heels in the shade.

Bowman shook his head. "Not even that'll do it. Some things can't be forgive or forgot. My wife lost our home and three of our boys. Tell me how time's gonna help that."

"You lost your sons in the fire?"

"Three of the four. I grabbed the youngest and went lookin' for the other three, but I couldn't find 'em nowhere. They were off somewhere in town. You know how boys are, always underfoot except when you're lookin' for 'em."

Morgan nodded.

"God, it tore my heart out to leave without 'em," Bowman went on in a choked voice. "But them flames were practically on top of us already, and there was nothin' else I could do." He took another swig of the whiskey. "I tell you, though, mister, I'm already startin' to wish I'd stayed and died with 'em."

Morgan shook his head. "One more death wouldn't have done anybody any good."

"You don't know, mister," Bowman whispered. "You just don't know."

Morgan had no answer for that. Nobody knew what was in another person's heart. Instead he said, "What you said earlier about it being your fault . . . even if somebody set the fire, it wasn't you, was it?"

"No, but I caused it. It wouldn'ta happened if I hadn't done what I did. I told the Locklin brothers to get out of town. I got a posse together and we cornered 'em with shotguns in the saloon and told 'em to get out of Flat Rock. We had the drop on 'em, so they didn't have much choice. But Steve Locklin said nobody talked like that to the Locklin brothers and got away with it. He said we'd be sorry." Bowman heaved a sigh. "I reckon we are."

Locklin . . . Morgan recognized the name. Steve Locklin and his brothers Asa and Rance all thought they were slick on the draw, and they had the kills to prove it. Their arrogance and greed had led them to become outlaws, and they had murdered and plundered their way across the Lone Star State. The Texas Rangers had been on their trail for a while, but the Rangers were spread thin and the Locklin brothers had fast horses as well as fast guns. They had escaped from every trap the lawmen had tried to set for them.

"Jed Ainsley came foggin' in just as the smoke started to rise," Bowman went on. "He was ridin' into town for supplies from his spread northwest of here. He spotted Steve Locklin with a torch, settin' fire to the grass. The wind was so high Jed knew the fire would come straight for us, so he took off hell-for-leather to warn us. The Locklins saw him and opened up on him, and Jed caught a bullet. He kept on anyway. Of course, it didn't make a bit of difference. Poor son of a gun died for nothin'." Bowman gestured vaguely to a blackened corpse that hardly looked human anymore. "There he lays, over yonder."

Morgan's jaw tightened. He wasn't a man given to brooding and pondering, but this was a rare occasion when he felt himself torn inside. Nothing was more feared by frontier folks than a prairie fire, and one look around Flat Rock was enough to see why. Anybody who started such a blaze, especially through resentment or even carelessness, was lower than dirt in Morgan's eyes. The fury he felt when he saw what had happened there warred with his long-ingrained desire to be left alone and continue drifting.

"They wasn't our blood, you know," Bowman mused, breaking into Morgan's thoughts.

"What?"

"The boys. They was adopted, I guess you'd say. We took 'em in to raise when they was orphaned, because nobody else would. Our own kids are grown and gone. But that didn't matter to my wife. She loved 'em like they were our own."

"You saved one," Morgan pointed out.

"Yeah, but . . ." Bowman couldn't go on. He made a choking sound and just shook his head.

Morgan rubbed his jaw. Clearly, no words he could say were going to offer any comfort to Al Bowman, and the whiskey wasn't helping, either.

So he did the only other thing he could.

"You know where I can find these Locklins?"

Bowman's drooping head came up as he frowned in surprise. "You ain't . . . you ain't thinkin' about goin' after them, are you, mister?"

"Anybody left alive in this town who's up to the job?"

A bitter laugh came from Bowman. "There was nobody here who was up to that job even when everybody was still alive."

"You don't want them to get away with this, do you?"

"God, no! But I didn't think there was anything anybody could do."

Frank straightened to his feet. "Maybe I can."

Bowman blinked as he looked up at Morgan, a dark shape with the afternoon sun behind him. "Who are you, mister?"

"Name's Frank Morgan," The Drifter said.

Bowman's breath hissed between his teeth. He scrambled up. "Morgan! You mean you're Frank Morgan, the gunfighter?"

"Some call me that."

"What are you doin' in this part of the country?"

"Passing through, like I told you," Morgan said. "Now, can you tell me where to find the Locklins, or not?"

Bowman rubbed his mouth as a look of desperate hope came into his eyes. "I've heard rumors that they're hangin' around a road ranch and stage station about ten miles north of here, on the trail to Lubbock. Place called Vinegar Hill. Don't ask me why; there ain't many hills in these parts."

Morgan nodded and said, "Much obliged," as he turned toward the dun, which stood nearby waiting patiently with its reins dangling.

Bowman took a quick step after him. "Wait a minute. Are you really goin' after 'em?"

Morgan looked around at the burned town. "I figure if I don't, it's liable to stick in my craw."

"Then I just got one request of you, Mr. Morgan . . . take me with you."

Morgan's mouth tightened as he gestured toward the woman who had finally gotten up and was wandering around aimlessly in circles. "Don't you think you ought to be comforting your wife?"

"She don't want no comfort from me. She just wants things back like they were, and that's somethin' no man can do. Nor God, either, I reckon. Like the Good Book says, the movin' finger has writ, and the page is turned. All that's left now is settlin' the score."

"It's your choice," Morgan said. "I don't tell any man how to live his life."

"I don't care about livin'," Bowman said. "Just dyin'. I want to be there to see it when those damned Locklins cross the divide."

Morgan swung into the saddle. "Up to you to keep up, then," he said as he turned the dun and prodded it into motion, heading north out of Flat Rock.

He figured Bowman would give up the damn fool idea, but he had underestimated the man's determination. When he looked back a few minutes later he saw that Bowman had gotten hold of a horse somewhere and was riding after him, bouncing awkwardly in the saddle. Morgan shook his head and slowed the dun so that Bowman could catch up to him.

When he did, Morgan saw that Bowman had a revolver stuck behind his belt. He gestured toward the gun and asked, "Where'd you get that?"

"Made the town marshal give it to me. He didn't care anymore. Said he was ridin' out and never comin' back. I thought I might need a gun. I thought I might help you."

Morgan bit back a curse. The last thing he needed going up against three gun-wolves like Steve, Asa, and Rance Locklin was some grief-stricken townie "helping" him. For a moment he seriously considered reaching over and walloping Bowman. The best thing might be to knock the man out until his showdown with the Locklins was over.

But there was a look of such pathetic eagerness in Bowman's eyes that Morgan couldn't do it. He didn't think Bowman was going to find what he was really looking for at Vinegar Hill, but short of violence, the man wouldn't be stopped now.

"When we get there, stay out of the way," Morgan said. "This is my kind of work, not yours."

"I'll only take a hand if I need to," Bowman promised.

They rode the rest of the way in silence, because really, what was left to say? When they came in sight of the low, rambling adobe building with the sod roof, Bowman said, "That's it. That's Vinegar Hill." He leaned forward in the saddle. "And those horses tied up in front belong to the Locklin brothers! I recognize them."

"Last chance to go home, Bowman," Morgan told him.

Bowman shook his head. "Got no home to go to. Not after today."

The men inside the road ranch either heard the horses or saw them coming. They ambled out the door and spread out—a sign that they knew what they were doing. The skinny one with the buckskin jacket and the long, tangled hair under a flat-crowned brown hat moved over to the water trough and propped his left foot on it. The short one who was about as wide as he was tall crossed his arms over his massive chest and leaned back against the wall beside the door. The third man, about as tall as the skinny one but heavier, with a dark mustache drooping over his mouth, went the other way and stopped by the corral fence. He had a Winchester cradled in his arms.

Steve, Asa, and Rance, in order from right to left, Morgan thought. He had never crossed trails with them before, but he had seen their pictures on enough reward dodgers tacked to trees. Kill-crazy scum, the lot of them, especially Steve. The other two might callously gun down somebody in a robbery, but only Steve was loco enough to set a fire that he knew would destroy an entire town.

"Howdy, mister," Steve called. Grinning, he gestured toward Bowman. "You know you got a turd followin' you?"

Asa made a rumbling sound, and after a second Morgan realized that it was laughter. "I never knew a turd to ride a horse before," Asa said.

The most practical and pragmatic of the brothers, Rance said, "Who are you, mister, and what do you want?"

Never taking his eyes off them, Morgan dismounted without answering. He wanted to be on solid ground. As he faced them, he said, "You'd be the Locklin brothers, I reckon."

"That's right," Steve acknowledged. "You got the advantage on us, friend."

Morgan shook his head slowly. "I'm no friend to snakes like you."

Steve's arrogant grin disappeared as he lowered his left foot to the ground and dropped his casual pose. He wore two guns, fancy ivory-handled pistols. Asa was a two-gun man, as well, wearing them butt-forward in cross-draw rigs that hung from bandoliers crossed over his broad chest. Rance had a Colt, too, but he was best with a rifle, Morgan recalled. He made it a habit to know as much as he could about men he might have to face in a showdown one day. It came in handy.

"You some kind o' lawman?" Steve demanded. "Texas Ranger, maybe?"

"Lawman?" Morgan repeated. "Not hardly. Just an hombre who doesn't like what you did today."

"You mean burnin' out Turdface and his friends?" A bark of laughter came from the man. "Hell, they had it comin'. They shoulda known better than to run the Locklin brothers out of town. That's just like spittin' into the wind." Steve laughed again. "And that was some wind earlier today, wasn't it? I never saw flames move so fast in all my borned days."

"So you don't deny what you did?" Morgan asked.

"Deny it? Hell, I'm *proud* of it! It ain't ever' day that a fella can destroy a whole damned town!"

Slowly, Morgan nodded. He said, "You know, Locklin, I haven't enjoyed killing most of the men I've killed. But I think I'm going to enjoy killing you."

Steve's face twisted with anger and hatred.

"That's mighty big talk for somebody who won't even tell us who he is. I think you're nobody! I think you're just one more stupid bastard who's got it comin' to him!"

Suddenly, Rance spoke up in a worried tone. "Steve, I think I know who this hombre is! I've seen pictures of him! He's Frank Morgan!"

"Morgan!" Steve's eyes widened with surprise. His hands stabbed toward his holsters. "Gun the son of a bitch!"

Then it was like it always was, as time seemed to slow down for Frank Morgan. With the speed that was as natural to him as breathing, he drew and fired. His first bullet tore out Asa's throat, because he had heard that despite his bulky build, Asa was the fastest Locklin brother. He pivoted, crouching as he shifted his aim, and pumped a slug into Rance's chest, driving him over backward. The rifle in Rance's hands cracked, but the barrel was already tilted skyward. Morgan shifted smoothly, anticipating Steve's shots, and sure enough, a pair of slugs whistled through the air where Morgan's head had been an instant earlier. His Colt came to bear on Steve . . .

But before he could pull the trigger, more shots roared close by. Bullets pounded into Steve Locklin's body, making him do a jittery little dance as he backed up to the adobe wall behind him. Al Bowman walked forward, the gun in his hand blasting two more times as he turned Locklin's face into a ghastly crimson smear.

"*You* had it comin'!" Bowman cried in a tortured voice. "You!"

Morgan hadn't even seen the man dismount. All his attention had been focused on his opponents, not this unlikeliest of allies.

Bowman stopped shooting and lowered the gun as Steve Locklin's corpse slid down the wall to come to rest propped in a sitting position on the ground. "He's dead, isn't he?" Bowman said.

"Considering that's his brains and blood all over the wall, I'd say so," Morgan replied. "I told you to stay out of it."

"I didn't think you were gonna get him in time. I thought he was going to kill you."

Bowman could tell himself that all he wanted to, Morgan thought. The man might even believe it. It didn't really matter.

Morgan punched the empty loads out of his Colt and slid fresh cartridges into the chamber. "Well, it's done with," he said without looking at Bowman. "You can go back to your wife and boy now. Make something out of what's left of your life, Bowman. That's all I can tell you."

"You're not comin' back to town?"

Morgan shook his head. "No reason to. Like I've told you, I'm just passin' through." He pouched the iron and took up the dun's reins.

"I tell you, there's nothing for me to go back to." Bowman looked at Steve Locklin's body and shuddered. "It doesn't change a thing. Not a damned thing. *He* started the fire, but I'm still to blame for what it did."

Morgan turned the horse. You couldn't talk to a man in the state that Bowman was in. He'd have to find his own way out.

"Thanks, Mr. Morgan!" Bowman called when The Drifter was about fifty yards away. "Thanks for your help! And Mr. Morgan . . . there's one bullet left in this gun!"

Morgan's head jerked up as the shot rang out over the plains. He twisted in the saddle and looked around in time to see Al Bowman's body slump to the ground.

So he had a reason to go back to the settlement after all. He lifted Bowman's body, draped it over the saddle of the horse the man had ridden to Vinegar Hill, and took him home.

When he lowered the body to the charred ground at the feet of Bowman's wife, the woman looked at it for a long moment and then spat on it. "It was his fault," she said. "All his fault. Big man who had a job to do. Had to run those outlaws out of town. He had it comin'."

Morgan was getting damned sick and tired of hearing that.

As he rode out of Flat Rock, leaving the devastation behind him, he thought that within days sprigs of green grass would begin to poke up out of the ground where now there was nothing but ashes. Just nature's way of showing that it truly didn't give a damn what happened to people, Frank Morgan reflected. The world would turn, the rain would fall, and the grass would grow, no matter how much suffering the folks who lived there had to endure . . .

And the only ones immune to that pain were those who had nothing left to lose.

Like the man called The Drifter.

Waiting for Mr. Griffith

Tom Carpenter

Once Eloise Griffith decided to kill her husband there wasn't much to do except wait until he returned home. She sat in her rocking chair beside the open parlor window of her small house on Fourth Street, with a double-barreled shotgun on her lap. She rocked slowly as she talked with her sister, Jane Burton, who sat in an embroidered chair that had belonged to their mother and held a derringer in her chapped hands. They had stopped talking almost an hour ago when they took their seats in anticipation of the return home of Big John Griffith. They watched their neighbors float by on the dusty street, propelled by a light wind that swirled and eddied gently, as if looking for someplace to go.

Jane leaned forward to touch her sister's eye, but stopped and leaned back in her chair. The fresh swollen bruises on Eloise's face reminded Jane of a bowl of plums. A scab beside her sister's left eye looked like someone had darned a black sock with red thread.

"Here comes the sheriff," Eloise said. She looked down at the shotgun in her lap. She watched Otis Pomeroy ride by on his buckskin horse. "He looks tired."

"Hungover, no doubt," Jane said. "The old fool."

"Maybe," Eloise said. "But it still was sad news about his wife."

Jane said nothing as she watched the sheriff plod out of view. Then, "It smells like rain."

Eloise nodded. "Clouds are gathering over the Hualapais." Beyond the rooftops across the street, a thickening wreath of gray clouds rested atop the granite peaks and pine-covered slopes of the mountain range to the east. Somewhere between there and here, her husband was making his way back home. When he walked in that front door, she would shoot him with both barrels.

Big John Griffith looked up at the gathering clouds. His back ached from putting a shoe on his horse. The cattle he'd been moving to this pasture switched their tails and mooed, as if they knew a storm was coming.

"Better get a move on," Big John said to his horse. He stowed his tools in his saddlebag and hoisted himself into the saddle. The knuckles of his right hand ached. He could feel the raw skin through his glove. "I shouldn't have hit her," he said to his horse. The horse nickered.

"I could use a drink." He reached back into his saddlebag and pulled out a pint bottle. He hesitated, then twisted off the cap and took a big swig that drained the bourbon to the last drop. He tucked the bottle back in his bag and let the warm flush run through him like water. "She shoulda kept quiet." He nudged and swung the horse around to the trail down the mountain and home.

Jane rose from the chair. "I'm going to fix some tea. Would you like some?"

Eloise shook her head without turning away from the window. "No thank you." She touched her swollen cheek. "I think I have a loose tooth."

"Let me see." Jane leaned over her sister. "Open wide."

Eloise tried, but the effort made her yelp.

Jane said, "Come in the kitchen with me and we'll rinse your mouth with some warm salt water."

Eloise clutched the shotgun. "What if he comes home?"

"Then we'll kill him in the kitchen," Jane said. "Now, come on. You don't want to lose a molar."

The sisters carried their weapons through the parlor to the kitchen. Eloise sat at the table in the chair facing the hallway. Jane put a kettle on the stove and lit the fire. She sat at the table where she could see the hallway and the back door.

The light through the back window had softened. Daylight was fading.

Eloise said, "It'll be dark soon. He didn't take anything for staying out all night. He'll be back." Her voice trembled. She raised the shotgun from her lap and put it on the table. "It looks like part of a water pump or some piece of a steam engine."

"Except for the triggers and those barrels," Jane said. "Do you want to trade?" She held up the derringer.

Eloise studied it for a moment. "No," she said. "It's his shotgun. I'll use it."

Big John let his horse pick its way down a steep section of the trail. He leaned back heavily against the angle of descent and rocked with the motion of his horse. "I gotta stop hitting her," he said. "But she argues. Goddammit. Won't let it be. I know what the hell I'm doing, goddammit. She doesn't know."

The trail leveled and he squared himself in his saddle. The whiskey made him thirsty. "We'll stop at the stream," he said. "And get a little water." He nudged his horse along.

The stream seeped from a fissure in a granite ledge. Aspens and ferns marked its location. The aspen leaves trembled on the breeze raised by the clouds gathering overhead. Big John climbed down and led his horse to water. While the horse drank, he climbed a few yards upstream and knelt where the stream flowed through a rock bowl. He cupped his hands and drank several times.

Jane poured warm water into a cup and added a palm-full of salt. She stirred it. "Come over to the sink," she said. She gave the cup to Eloise who swished the water in her mouth, moaning slightly. When Eloise finished they returned to the kitchen table. The parlor looked dark and cold in the fading light, but there was still sunlight in the kitchen.

They sat quietly. The shadows lengthened in the room.

"I saw John shoot the Baxter boys," Jane said.

Startled, Eloise said, "You never told me that. After all these years, why didn't you tell me?"

"You hadn't married him yet, and at the time I never thought you would," Jane said. "So, I just didn't say anything. Then when you surprised everybody and married him, I thought, what good would it do?"

"I was teaching school in Chloride," Eloise said. "I didn't see it happen. I heard about it."

"Everyone heard about it," Jane said.

"So, you actually saw it?"

"I did."

"Why didn't you come forward during the inquest? There were no witnesses."

"What John said was the truth," Jane said. "I didn't want to get involved. I suppose if John had lied about what happened, then maybe."

"So it was the Baxters' fault?"

"I was doing laundry for Mrs. Higgins. She was sick at the time, dear old girl. I had come by that morning to lend her a hand. So, I was hanging clothes in her backyard when I saw John stopped in the street by the Baxters—Lyle and his big brother Tyrone."

"They were mean even as kids," Eloise said.

"It was their old man, Hoyt, who did that to them," Jane said. "He was a bastard. Anyway, the boys sort of blocked John in the street. They were shouting something about him firing them—he was a foreman on the Ritter ranch at the time, I think. Anyway, Tyrone grabbed for John's arm and he stepped back and hit Tyrone in the face with his fist. Lyle rushed forward and tackled John and knocked him to the ground. With John flat on his back wrestling with Lyle, Tyrone started kicking at John's head. He kicked his brother about as often as he kicked John until Lyle rolled off John clutching his broken nose. Lyle was so angry, yelling and cussing, he reached into his back pocket and pulled a pistol. John was carrying a gun, too. He pulled it from his holster and shot Lyle in the chest. Lyle dropped like his legs were kicked out from under him. Tyrone reached for a knife tucked in his boot and John shot him in the chest, too. John got to his feet and leaned over Tyrone who was writhing on the ground. I could hear him gasping for air. John said something I couldn't hear, then shot Tyrone in the head."

Eloise brought her hand to her mouth. "My goodness. And nobody saw it?"

Jane nodded. "It was the middle of the morning, and happened so fast. Folks didn't come running until after the gunshots. John waited for the sheriff and turned himself in."

"Nobody knows you saw it happen?"

"One person does," Jane said. "John."

"John?"

"After he shot Tyrone, he stood up and sort of looked around. He saw me watching him. We looked at each other for a moment, neither of us moving, until somebody came running up to John and he turned to explain what had happened."

"All these years and he's never mentioned it?"

Jane shook her head. "Nope. Not a word."

Where John drank the shadows had thickened. He took one last sip from his cupped hands, then rose from his knees and picked his way through the rocks back to his horse. He checked his cinch and poised to climb back into the saddle when he heard a horse approach. He hadn't seen anybody on the mountain all day. There wasn't anybody who had any business on his part of it, anyhow. Not even Leo Black. John eased back to the ground and stood beside his horse. If he needed it, his rifle in its scabbard was within reach.

"Hello, John," Leo Black said, as he rode into view from the lower end of the trail.

"What are you doing up here, Leo?" John said. He put his hand on his horse's rump, near the butt of his rifle. He patted the horse gently to keep it still beside him.

"Been checking my herd," Leo said. He reined to a stop and crossed his arms on his saddle horn. He didn't smile. "Getting late."

"What did I tell you would happen the next time I saw you?" John said.

Leo grinned. "That was the whiskey talking."

"Whiskey didn't say nothing, you cheating bastard. I said it."

"I told you before, John, I didn't cheat you."

"Then where's my herd?"

"They were mavericks, John, and you know it."

"They were eating my grass. Drinking my water. They were mine, goddammit. Mine."

Leo sat up. His hands slid back and hung loose, his right one near his pistol butt. "John, we've been friends for a long time. Twenty years. We've been in business together, for God's sake. I didn't cheat you and I didn't steal from you, you crazy bastard. Now calm down and let's talk about it."

John's horse flinched. "I said I'd kill you the next time I saw you, by God, and I mean to do it."

Eloise rose from the kitchen table with the shotgun in her hands and returned to her seat by the window in the parlor. Jane followed her with the derringer in her apron pocket.

"It's getting dark," Eloise said.

Jane said, "You sound worried."

Eloise said, "He wasn't always mean. I don't think he raised a hand to me for the first six years of our marriage. Maybe it was because we didn't have children."

"It's the whiskey," Jane said. "He's always been a drinker. It just got worse over time. I've seen it happen, even if you haven't. The whiskey made him mean. Crazy."

"He's a good man," Eloise said, "in a lot of ways."

"He's no good if he hits his wife."

"I think it was the trouble with his ex-partner Leo," Eloise said. "He's been so angry about it, thinking that Leo had cheated him."

Jane said, "Everybody's been talking about how John threatened to kill Leo."

Eloise looked at her sister. "I know. It's terrible. Leo was John's best man at our wedding." Eloise thought about that for a while. "It's my fault he hit me. I got so tired of John ranting about killing Leo, I just finally screamed and told him to do it then and get it over with, for goodness sake, so we can stop talking about it."

"Last night wasn't the first time he hit you."

Lamps were lit in windows across the street. Eloise rose from her chair and carried the shotgun across the room to the cabinet where John kept his rifles.

Jane watched her unload the shotgun and place it carefully in the cabinet and close the glass door.

Eloise lit the lamp on the table in the parlor. Its light filled the room with a warm yellow glow. "He'll be hungry when he gets home," she said, and went into the kitchen.

Jane listened to her rattling pots and pans. She looked out the window toward the dim silhouette of the mountains. She shook her head and went into the kitchen to help her sister with the meal.

It was full dark when they heard boots on the front porch. They didn't expect the knock on the door. With Jane close beside her, Eloise opened the door.

Otis Pomeroy held his hat in his hands. His badge glowed in the light from the parlor.

Eloise said, "He's killed Leo Black."

"Afraid not, ma'am," the sheriff said. "It's the other way around."

The First Ride of Monday Happenstance

Russell Davis

Bran Farrell once told me that what you do isn't always a reflection of who you are, and that a man is known less by the company he keeps than by how he keeps his word to his company. "Even when you've got nothing but broken-down boots and a bare mouthful of spit, you've still got your word," he said. "You look to keeping that first, and the rest will take care of itself."

He was right about that, as he was about so many other things, and these words you are reading is how I'm keeping my word to him. I promised I would tell my story—it mattered to Bran, for reasons I can't fathom—so in these last days of my life, I'm setting pen to paper and keeping my word. Maybe you can suss out why Bran thought my story was so important.

Of course, you've never heard of Bran Farrell, and that was the way he wanted it, but in so many ways, my story starts with him. He was the kind of shootist that never made the papers or the dime novels, but if you listened close to the old trail stories you might hear a whisper of his name. A whisper and that was all. Bran didn't like attention and didn't want to be known as a gunman. He always said that being known was the fastest way to die when a man earned a living like he did. Bran didn't fear the hangman's noose or the lawman's badge, no sir. Mostly, he feared having to live with a reputation that made every damn fool west of the Appalachians want to try and shoot it out with him.

Anyway, my story starts with him, but the story that comes before that . . . well, Bran always said that it didn't matter where I come from, but I should stand proud all the same. I was born on the grounds of Wilton House, a massive tobacco plantation near Richmond, Virginia, just before the end of the Civil War. My parents, who were both slaves, named me Kojo Ajali, but when Mrs. Randolph tried to make sense of it from what my parents told her, she took to calling me Monday Happenstance not long after she insisted I learn to read. It's not exactly accurate, but close enough, and it seemed to tickle the funny bone of most everyone who heard it. I guess some names are like reputations—they just stick. Bran always said that Monday would serve me better than Kojo and for the most part, he was right about that, too.

This is the story of how I took my first ride and how I met Bran, and the first real lesson I learned about being a free man . . . and a shootist.

* * *

The horse was a swaybacked old mare, with a splotchy gray coat and a mane that looked like someone had trimmed it with a butcher knife while they were drinking. I studied her carefully, trying to look beyond the swayed back and general air of age and neglect. What I saw was actually promising. Her eyes were clear and her ears swiveled to the sound of my voice, which told me she was paying attention. Her hooves were in good shape, though she needed a new set of shoes.

I picked up her feet and she responded to the barest touch, lifting them one by one and standing patiently. Her legs were solidly formed.

"She's a good 'un," the livery man said. His name was Herman Carter. Everyone called him Cart. He was a middle-aged man who was balding and didn't bother to wear a hat to hide it.

"Mr. Cart, sir," I said, "she's a broken-down old quarter horse. She doesn't have fifty miles left on her, let alone fifteen hundred or more."

The old man nodded in thought. "Maybe so, Monday, my boy. But she's got a good head on her shoulders and won't eat much."

I snorted. "No, I don't suspect she will. Dead horses eat very little."

Mr. Cart slapped his knee and guffawed. "You always did have yourself a fine sense of humor, my boy. Tell you what. I can let her go for ten dollars. That's what the knacker was going to pay me anyway."

I thought about it for a moment, then said, "How about ten and you throw in that old saddle I saw on the rack next to your office?"

Mr. Cart's eyes scrunched up in thought as his hands took out his tobacco pouch and made a roll-your-own almost of their own accord. "I suppose I could see you take her and the saddle for twelve," he finally said. "I'll even toss in a bridle and a roping rein, so you've got something to pray with."

I couldn't help but laugh. When you're on a horse with your hands clasped around the saddle horn and the reins trapped between your fingers, folks will say you're not riding, but praying. When a horse takes off with you, that's a fine time to get religion. "All right, Mr. Cart," I told him. "Twelve dollars, it is."

"I'll get you a receipt, Monday," he said. "When are you leaving?"

"Tomorrow morning," I replied. "First light."

"You know you're crazy, don't you?" he asked. "What are you going to do out there?"

I shrugged. "I'll make my way, I guess. I hear tell that there's lots of work for a man good with horses." That was the one skill I had, having been assigned to work in the stables from the time I was old enough to earn my keep. On the plantation, folks said I could ride or break anything with four legs that wasn't a cougar and at one time I'd tried to prove it by riding a cow. As it turned out, folks were wrong—at least as far as the cow had been concerned.

Cart looked at me for a long moment, then nodded. "Maybe, my boy, but don't you forget something. The war is over and the slaves are free, but there's plenty of folks who still think a colored man is a nigger."

"No, sir," I said. "I don't suppose they'll let me forget it."

He chuckled again. "No, they won't." He headed toward his little office, limping on one leg that had been broken two years earlier when a horse rolled over on him. "Let me get you that receipt and saddle."

"Mr. Cart, sir," I said, following in his wake. "What's the horse's name?"

"She don't have one," he said. "Least not one that I know of. I've always believed that if a wise man waits a bit, a horse will name itself."

"If she drops dead beneath me, I suspect that will be a sign, too."

He laughed again and said, "Oh, indeed. Then you'll know for sure that her name is Daisies."

"Daisies?"

"As in pushin' up," he chuckled.

I followed him into his little office as the knowledge sunk in that I'd bought my first horse and I was really leaving Richmond. I was seventeen years old, and the next day, I would ride out and head west, looking for a new life for myself.

The one I had in Richmond had died the week before, when I'd buried my momma in the slave graveyard next to my father, who'd died the year before that. I didn't have anyone else for kin.

I didn't know what I'd find, but I was determined to try. I wanted to be something and I knew that in Richmond, I'd never amount to more than a servant.

Out west, they said, there was land and opportunity for everyone willing to work hard.

It was only later I found out that they meant opportunity for everyone *but* a nigger.

If there are worse places to be broke with no prospects in the winter than the sandhills of western Nebraska, I don't know where they are. Winter had closed in hard on the plains, and every ranch had closed up tight for the season, turning most of their hands loose to fend for themselves until spring. I'd been on my own for six months and despite my skill with horses, I'd only found day-to-day work in out of the way places where no one was likely to see me working.

And the best wages I could get were half of what other hands were making.

My last paying job had been more than a month ago and as winter closed in, I found myself holed up in an abandoned sod house, hoping no one came back to reclaim it. It wasn't a great shelter, but beat sleeping outside with the teeth of winter in full snarl. What little I had in supplies was quickly disappearing and my horse, who I'd named One Foot—as in one foot in the grave—wouldn't last ten minutes out in a full blow like the one that was coming in as night fell.

I stared into the lean fire I'd made out of dried buffalo chips and realized that things were bad and going to get worse unless I found some work or a better place to hole up in for the winter. These thoughts were occupying my mind when I heard the sound of horse near the front entrance. It wasn't covered with anything more than a moth-eaten buffalo robe, but unless One Foot had gotten loose and moved to the front, there was another horse out there.

For a moment, I wished I owned a gun, but there wouldn't have been much point to it. I had never owned one, and for the most part, they always seemed to invite trouble. I stepped over to the robe and moved it aside just in time to get a face full of snow and see a man topple out of his saddle and land in a heap at his horse's feet.

I ran to him as quickly as I could, and knelt down, wondering if he was dead. I'd no sooner peeled the scarf away from his face, when his eyes snapped open and I heard the distinctive sound of a gun being cocked. "I have no problem with killing you, mister," the man's voice rasped.

I lifted my hands up in surrender. "No, sir," I said. "I don't reckon you do."

The man stared at me for a long moment, then released the hammer and holstered the gun. He moved slowly, and his voice was tired when he said, "Can you help me inside? I could use some rest and I'll pay you for the trouble."

"Yes, sir," I said. "Just hold on a moment."

I've always been strong—when you spend your life wrestling with horses that weigh more than a thousand pounds, you'll put on muscle like a banker puts on fat—and I had no problem getting my arms beneath him. When he started to protest that he just needed help, I simply lifted him off the ground. "Rest easy, sir," I said. "You don't weigh all that much."

The man grunted something under his breath and I carried him inside, then laid him down on the battered cot I'd placed next to the dying fire. He groaned a bit and gritted his teeth, then relaxed with a tired sigh.

"I'll go and put up your horse, then we'll see what we can do about your injuries," I said.

The man closed his eyes and kept silent, so I turned and went back outside, into the storm. The truth was that in the dim light of my little fire and the burning nubs of the two candles, I had seen that the man was seriously wounded. It looked to me like he'd been shot at least two times, and had lost a lot of blood. His face was white as a sheet.

For all I knew, he'd be dead before I could get his horse put away.

I moved his horse around to the back of the house, pulled off the saddle and other tack, as well as the man's bedroll and saddlebags, then turned the animal into the makeshift corral I'd built. He quickly moved beneath the shelter of the lean-to and One Foot calmly moved aside to make room for him. I felt bad that I didn't have anything to feed him, but at least he could rest up, which was more than it looked like I would get to do. I shouldered the man's belongings and carried them inside.

Whoever he was, the man had either fallen unconscious or asleep while I was out in the storm dealing with his horse. I tossed his gear into one corner and stood by the fire long enough to warm up a little bit. A very little bit, as I couldn't waste what few buffalo chips I had left on myself. The man might need them to survive the night.

I moved the stubby candles closer to him, and filled a chipped basin with icy water and the cleanest rag I could find. The lighting was very poor and the candles flickered, barely able to stay lit in the drafty air. I could see my breath and the ragged breath of the man, and I hesitated for long moments to remove his buffalo-robe coat, let alone his clothing, so I could try and deal with his wounds.

The man hitched an awkward breath and his eyes flickered open. "Don't . . . hesitate, mister," he said. "If you can get the bullets out and pack the wounds . . . I might live yet."

"I'm sorry, sir," I said. "I don't have much to work on you with. Not even a rag really."

He nodded weakly and waved a hand in the direction of his gear. "There's plenty of bandages and anything else you'll need. Help yourself." His eyes closed again and I wondered if he was asleep or simply resting.

It didn't matter, I supposed, and moved to look

through his bedroll and saddlebags. Compared to my own poor existence, the man was a treasure trove of affects, all carefully packed away. I found a good knife—my own was dull and I'd lost my sharpening stone in a late fall flood—as well as bandages and a pint of decent whiskey. He also had coffee, corn dodgers, a partial side of bacon, and other foodstuffs. If nothing else, we wouldn't starve tonight.

In one of the saddlebags, I found a lantern and a small flask of oil. I filled the lantern and lit the wick, trimming it back carefully, but pleased with the additional light. I set the bandages and the knife on the makeshift table, then peeled off the man's coat and shirt.

He'd been shot twice, once in each shoulder. The wounds looked messy and ugly, and blood leaked from both of them. I lifted him and found that neither bullet had gone completely through his shoulder. I took up the knife and poured a little of the whiskey on the blade, then took a firmer grip on the bone handle.

I'd never done this before, though I'd seen my momma do it on a couple different occasions. It appeared to mostly be a matter of using the blade to dig into the wound and lever out the bullet. I pried the tip of the knife into the first wound, ignoring the fresh spurt of blood and began to dig. The man said nothing, but I felt his entire body tense beneath me and I knew he was in pain. The tight muscles around his jaw and the muffled groan were the only other signs of discomfort he gave.

I worked as quickly as possible, and to me it felt like I was digging in the man's shoulder for at least an hour, but it was more like ten minutes. I felt the tip of the knife wedge beneath the bullet, then levered it free. The wound was bleeding freely by then, but the worst was over. I poured more of the whiskey into the hole, soaked a bandage in it, then applied it to the wound. I added a dry bandage on top, then turned my attention to the other shoulder.

The wound on the other side was not quite as bad and the bullet came out faster. As before, the man said nothing, simply gritted his teeth and waited. I had to admire his toughness and his ability to endure pain. Finally, it was finished, and I covered him back up with the buffalo coat and built up the fire again.

He shivered beneath the coat for a while, dozing, then opened his eyes. "How long"—he coughed and started again—"how long have I been here? What time is it?"

I shook my head. "I don't know, sir. You've been here maybe an hour and half or so. I don't own a watch, so I don't rightly know the time."

He grunted. "Can you make us some coffee?" he asked. "Maybe warm up some of those biscuits and . . . I think there's a tin of soup in the bags."

"Sure enough," I said. "Though it'll take a while. The fire's not very hot and if we want to keep it going until the sun comes up, I have to go easy. I'm almost out of buffalo chips."

"Damn," he said, struggling to rise. "Lend me a hand up, will you?"

I moved to help him sit upright and heard him suck in his breath painfully. "You should rest, sir," I said. "Those wounds are nasty."

"Tell you what," he said, leaning gratefully against the wall. "You call me Bran, instead of sir, and I'll call you by your name instead of mister. In a short time, we aren't going to need any formalities."

I wasn't completely certain what he meant, but I told him my name. "Monday," I said. "Monday Happenstance."

He laughed, then grimaced. "That's a hell of a handle someone put on you," he said, offering his hand. "Bran Farrell."

We shook hands, and I noticed that despite his wounds, his grip was strong.

"Now," he said, "how about that coffee, soup and biscuits?"

I set to work, wondering how I'd come to be holed up in a Nebraska sodhouse in the middle of a winter blow with a wounded Irishman, then decided that my momma had been right. People meet for a reason, and as I stirred the soup, I thought long and hard about what reasons could have brought Bran Farrell to this place at this time.

I didn't have to wait long to find out.

Bran put his tin mug down with a tired sigh, and leaned back against the wall once more. "So,

Monday," he said. "I suppose I should tell you what's coming next."

"What do you mean?"

"Well, if I've got my time right, in about three hours, the sun is going to rise and the last bits of this storm will blow off to the east. About an hour after that—maybe less—the three fellas that did this to me are going to be showing up here."

"Why are they after you?" I asked him. "Are you an outlaw?"

He chuckled. "Not exactly," he said. "These days, I'm working as a bounty hunter, though I admit that sometimes it's hard to tell the difference." He looked into the dying light of the fire for a moment, then shook his head. "No, Monday, I'm not an outlaw, but the men that are coming are . . . and they mean to kill me."

His eyes stared hard into mine, and I noticed how green they were. Green and cold, like a pine tree after a deep freeze. "And if they find you here, they'll kill you, too," he added.

"Why would they kill me?" I asked, fear sweeping through my body. "I-I don't even know them."

"You wouldn't have to know them," he answered. "They're just ornery and cussed-mean. It doesn't help that I already killed their brother, and if things had gone a little differently, they'd be just as dead as he is, and I wouldn't be in this fix."

"What happened?" I asked, fascinated in spite of my fear.

"Sometimes, Monday, the best plans go to hell simply out of random chance. I found 'em holed up in a little shack south of here, and crept up nice and close. I knew if I waited, one or more of them would step outside and I could take them with my rifle, easy as picking potatoes, but not half as much work." He sniffed and spat, aiming for the fire and almost making it, then shrugged.

"To make a long story short, the first one came out and I took my shot. He dropped like a stone. About that time, the others came boiling out of the shack like a swarm of angry bees, and I figured everything was right as rain—until the snow shelf I was laying on gave way beneath me and tumbled me halfway down the hillside. I lost my rifle on the way and took these hits trying to get back to my horse."

"How do you know they're still after you?" I asked. "Maybe when you got away they went back."

He shook his head, a sad expression crossing his face. "They'll be here," he said. "Men like these don't stop until they're dead."

I thought on Bran's words for a bit, then said, "What did they do?"

"You mean what crime?" he asked.

"Yes, sir," I said. Sir is a long habit, and I haven't been able to break it my whole life.

"Cattle thieves," he said, his voice short and sharp, masking his faint accent even more. "Ranchers down on the border with Kansas are offering a good bounty. One hundred dollars a man."

I whistled. That was a lot of money, if one could survive to collect it. Considering my current job prospects—or even the prospect of eating again soon—I was willing to try. "I don't know much about guns," I said. "I don't even know much about fighting. But if you'll share the bounty, I'll try to help you get those men."

Bran's eyes widened a bit, then he said, "Good lad!" and for a moment, his Irish came through loud and clear. Then he cleared his throat roughly. "I'm not going to be much good in the fight," he admitted, "but if we work together, I think I know a way we can end this right quick."

"What do you need me to do?" I asked.

"Well, Monday," he said, "are you any good with horses?"

I shivered inside Bran's buffalo coat and wondered what I was doing, sitting on his horse and waiting for the sun to come up and the outlaws to show themselves. Bran's plan was fairly simple. They would arrive and look the place over, not seeing his horse, but knowing *someone* was in the soddy. When they got down from their horses, he would call out to them, drawing them closer, and when the moment felt right, I was supposed to ride down on them, wearing his coat, his hat and shooting one of his guns.

In the confusion, my job wasn't to shoot anybody, but to run off their horses. Bran said he'd take care of the real shooting after I almost dropped the revolver he'd handed me. "Just shoot in the air and make a racket," he said. "Stay as low as you can and try not to get shot. I'd feel bad."

"Me, too," I said.

The first gray edges of sunrise were staining the eastern horizon and the last few, stray snowflakes were drifting down as the storm clouds moved east. I was thankful the wind had died down as well, as it made listening for the muffled sound of hooves on snow a bit easier.

"In some ways," Bran had told me, "the waiting is the worst. Your mind will get to thinking on all sorts of things, but you just put them away and stay focused. That's the difference between a living shootist and a dead one, you know. A willingness to ignore all those things a-clamorin' around in your head so you can do what needs to be done."

"I'm not a shootist!" I'd said.

A long moment of silence passed, then he said, "Not yet, maybe. But I've got a feeling you will be." He'd pushed aside the robe hanging in the doorway and said, "Now get into position and don't forget what I've told you or being a shootist will be the least of our worries. We'll be *shot* instead."

So I sat on Bran's horse and waited and listened, trying to do as he'd instructed and ignore the voices in my head. One telling me to ride out and never look back. A competing voice that suggested if I did that—and Bran somehow survived—I'd be looking over my shoulders for a great many days to come. And the other voice, which sounded like my mamma, that said, "Ain't nobody who makes a livin' with a gun that can sleep good at night." As it all turned out, she was right about that, just like Bran was right about so many things he said.

The muffled sound of shod hooves on fresh snow startled me out of my thoughts, and I felt my body tense in fear. They were coming and it was too late to do anything but hope Bran's plan would work. If it didn't, I thought, at least I wouldn't be cold anymore. Not that dead was much of an improvement.

I gently coaxed his horse in a wide arc, moving away from the sound of the horses to place myself to the side and somewhat behind them. They weren't being particularly cautious, and no sound came from inside the shoddy.

I eased into a shadowy overhang of snow and rock, praying the horse would keep silent and the riders' attention would be focused elsewhere. First one, then the other two swung down from their saddles, and though I couldn't make out the words, I could hear the low mutter of their voices. One of them broke away from the group, moving toward the back of the sod house. *That* wasn't in the plan, but there wasn't anything I could see to do about it.

Suddenly, one of the men drew his gun and shouted, "Farrell? You in there, you damn bushwacker?"

"No one in here but us bushwackers!" Bran's voice called out. "What took you so long?"

"Lost your blood trail in the storm," the man replied. "Guess you know we're here to kill you for what you done to Charlie."

"Charlie was a thieving scoundrel just the same as you," Bran replied. "He got what was coming and so will the rest of you, unless you ride out of here."

The man laughed long and loud. "Oh, to hell with it," he called. "Let him have it, boys!" All three of them opened up with their guns, the loud sounds of gunfire echoing in the morning air and causing their tired horses to begin shuffling nervously.

I didn't wait to see what would happen next, but laid low over the horse's withers and put my heels to him. He shot out from beneath the overhang like a white bullet and I was on them before they even knew I was there.

I fired wildly into the air, not aiming, nor even trying to hit anything, but riding straight for their horses, who bolted in all directions, leaving the men cursing and swearing and taking potshots at my back as I rode up and over the closest snow-covered sand dune.

I hit the top and spun around, prepared to make another charge, suddenly aware that I was alive . . . alive and breathing and that everything felt just right as the sun peaked out from beneath the clouds and illuminated the scene below in yellow and orange light. It was a Nebraska sunrise and even in the worst winter, those can be damn pretty.

Bran stepped out of the cabin, a revolver in each hand, as I looked back on the situation. "You never were very damn smart, George," he said.

The men spun back around, firing in a panic, and Bran killed them both with what appeared to my eye to be ridiculous ease. While their own bullets kicked up snow and sung in the air, he took his time, and fired one shot from each hand at almost the same moment. They were dead before they'd hit the ground, the blood from their hearts steaming crimson in the air.

Bran's shoulders sagged, and I knew that exhaustion and his wounds had taken their toll. I nudged the horse back down the hill to lend him a hand, when I saw the third man creep out from behind the house, moving in the shadows and intent on doing to Bran what he'd done to his brothers.

I didn't stop to think about it. I lifted the revolver and fired, feeling it buck in my hands. The man screamed once—a sound of despair and pain that I will never forget—then fell over backward, even as Bran spun to see what happened.

His eyes took in the scene and he nodded at me in acknowledgment. "That," he said, "was their brother William. The smart one."

"Smart?" I asked. "He looks dead to me."

"Smart to try and take me from behind," he said. "That's pretty much how most anyone who's good with a gun dies, Monday. They get shot in the back."

"It's not much of a life, is it?" I asked.

"No," he admitted. "But it's ours."

I stepped down out of the saddle and offered him back his revolver, but he shook his head. "No, Monday, you keep it," he said. "If you're going to be a shootist, you'll need it."

"Is that what I am now?" I asked. "A killer?"

"No," he said softly, moving toward the sod house and looking worn out. "But someday, that's how people will think of you. It comes with the job, my boy, but you'll know it's not true."

"It isn't?"

He stopped in the doorway and shook his head. "No, it's not. A killer ain't no better than a rabid dog or a crazy person. He kills for no reason or any reason. What we do is different. We kill when we choose to, consciously, and while we may do it for money, we have to live with our choices. A killer doesn't have to."

I nodded in understanding. "I guess you should go inside, Bran. Get some rest. I'll clean up this mess."

"Sounds fine, Monday," he said. "I'm plumb wore out, to tell you the truth."

"Makes sense to me," I said, noticing that one of his shoulders was bleeding again. "You should get a fresh bandage on that."

"I will," he said, turning to go inside, then he stopped once more and looked back at me. "Good ride, Monday. A damn good ride."

The morning air was crisp and cold and held a

leftover bite from the storm, but it felt clean to me. Despite the death and the blood, I was starting a new journey and a new life, and in my bones, I knew it was right.

It was right for me and that would have to be good enough.

There would never, I knew, be a lack of opportunities because of who I was or the color of my skin. All that would matter would be my ability to think and to use my revolver better than the killers and criminals Bran and I would hunt down.

Yes, I thought, dragging the dead men behind the sod house. It was right.

Ricochet

Don Coldsmith

ric•o•chet: a rebounding from a flat surface, as of a cannonball from the ground. To skim, as a stone, along the surface of water. To strike and fly onward . . . *Webster's Encyclopedic Dictionary*, MCMLII.

In more modern usage, there is also the hint of a projectile improperly fired, unsafely or carelessly. If such a misguided bullet strikes a hard object such as a solid wall, a tree or a boulder, it may fly in a totally unexpected direction, usually with an ominous whine, changing as it flies, but suggesting unpredictable evil.

The old medicine woman sat, watching the riders approach. She knew that was not good. Only the day before, two riders had stopped to rest their horses. They had carefully avoided giving their names, but she knew they were fugitives. . . outlaws. Today's riders must be pursuing them, even onto the Cherokee land.

To most citizens of the Cherokee Nation those men would be considered traitors. They were pursuing young men of their own nation for minor infractions, under the pay of the government. Not the government of the Cherokee, who owned that part of what the whites would later name Oklahoma, but the government of the Territory. To sell out their own people for pay. *Aiee*, such a shame!

Her mind drifted back, further than she would like to admit. She recalled that she had always had visions of the sort of man she would marry. Strong, brave and handsome, of course; a good provider. At least, he would become one.

Little Bear had seemed to fit exactly her desires as a husband. They were drawn together when they were only a few winters old. In a group of children at play, they would always drift together.

Both sets of parents were pleased, and long before most youngsters began to notice the attractive differences in their developing bodies, the two were fast friends. Even so, they were quite competitive. Until the girls began to feel the need for children and a family, the youngsters at play were, from all appearances, attracting attention by way of athletic skills. Housekeeping would come a little bit later, along with children.

In this way, Flower and Little Bear were assumed

to be an established pair. Even before their bodies and physical development occurred, they seemed destined to be together. A glance across a group of children at play always seemed to result in a silent exchange of emotion and of pleasurable possibilities between the two.

It lasted past the maturing of adolescence. Their childhood friends grew and married, and people began to wonder about them. Was there no urgency to be together?

In truth, there was, though they never realized it until it was too late.

Little Bear had traded for a colt, one of extreme agility and potential. He had decided to train it specifically for the father of his wife-to-be, the gift which symbolically would compensate her parents for the loss of a daughter. (Many times this has been misunderstood by the whites. It appears to be an act of "buying" the wife.)

Sometimes the spirits are cruel in their deadly sense of humor, it is said. The colt intended to be the gift, with its training almost complete, slipped and fell, rolling over across Little Bear's head and neck. It was said that the spectators nearby could hear the popping of the bones.

Flower never fully recovered from her loss. She refused to change her name, but for all practical purposes she became "the one-who-cries."

* * *

She realized it had boiled down to a point where young men of the People were ready to betray their own, for small amounts of the white man's money as rewards for their treachery.

She shook her head sadly. This had been a beautiful place to locate her modest house, built by the young sons of her relatives. Its spirit felt right, and her heart was good in this place. Across the meadow there was a wooded area, where she could gather many of the herbs that would be useful in her healing profession.

Close to her dwelling, the grass had begun the summer growth, and was as tall as her knees, except for the pathways created by use. She had planted in one area, a few herbs and cuttings of plants, useful in her healing. She was highly respected among her people—*The* People.

By autumn some of the native grasses would be taller than a man's head. That fact probably had an effect on the timing of these "Rangers" in the pay of white men. It would not be long until the tallgrass prairies would be grazed by the white man's spotted cattle, instead of buffalo. She sighed deeply and stepped to the doorway to greet the visitors.

Three of them. She had counted correctly, even at a distance. She had always, since her childhood, been noted for her visual skills. She had never been quite certain where that gift of keen eyesight stops and the vision of things not seen begins. It was considered a blessing by most of the People. But they, of course, were not aware of the responsibility which is linked to such gifts, the gifts of the spirit. These, she had realized quite early, are often more of a curse than a blessing.

She already knew, even from that distance, the riders were young men of her People. Not only because the area had been assigned to them, but by the way in which they handled their horses. It was not easy to describe, but it was there—the slight difference that could be traced to the training methods of the People.

It did not take long to evaluate the newcomers and realize the situation. The young men had been given some authority by the whites.

There were those among the People who had lost all respect for these young warriors. They had sold their heritage as children of the People, for the questionable status of working for the whites as "deputies." But to young people, the winning of respect is important. To them, it seemed a shortcut to such status.

She shook her head sadly.

She thought she recognized one, by his resemblance to his father at a similar age. But that was unimportant just now.

Their leader rode his horse across her well-groomed dooryard. Without the respectful attitude that would be expected toward his elders, the young man swung down and looped his horse's reins over the rail on the porch.

Yes, she was certain now. This was the son of one of the men of her own generation—the same haughty attitude, the lack of respect for a woman . . .

He took off his hat, a white man's hat, and wiped the sweat of his forehead on his sleeve.

"Woman," he snapped, "we're chasin' a couple of outlaws. I want to know, did they come past here, and you'd better not lie to me."

She had not intended to lie, until he spoke. The two previous riders had been polite, respectful, and pleasant in their enjoyment of the food she had provided for them. She wondered how this young man's mother would react to his disrespect.

The other two riders swung down and left their horses ground-tied by dangling reins. Certainly these young men were hardly comparable to those who had passed a day or two ago.

She spoke carefully. "I seem to recall a man or two passin' by."

"When?" he snapped.

"A day or two ago."

The horseman reached out and grabbed a loose fold of her buckskin dress—an absolute taboo in their culture, to lay hands on a woman.

"Don't you try to lie to me!" he warned.

She could hardly believe that a man of the People could behave in this way. Obviously, too much influence of the whites.

She drew herself up proudly. "Your mother would be ashamed of you!" she accused.

A wave of anger swept across his face, but he

seemed to realize that his attitude was not productive. "My mother is no concern of yours," he snapped, but without the rage he had shown. "When did they pass here?"

"Many people pass here," she reminded him cautiously.

His anger was rising again, but she could do little about that. Maybe another approach, she thought.

He seemed to ponder a moment, and changed his attitude a bit. "Forgive me. I am trying only to do my duty."

"And what is that?" she answered, using a softer tone.

"I am a marshal," he explained, obviously trying to impress her. "We are pursuing an outlaw. Now, did anyone pass this way in the past day or two?"

"Many might pass," she said vaguely. "I saw a rider yesterday."

The questioner's attitude changed again, almost instantly. She sensed that there was a personal bitterness between the fugitive and this determined marshal. There must be bad blood between them. She also sensed that the two other riders were not totally in sympathy with the leader. She tried again to show cooperation, but decided it was no use.

"Well, I hope your mission is satisfied."

"It will be!" he predicted. "There will be a bullet-hole in someone's head. Right here!" He pointed to a spot between his eyebrows.

"Well, what will be will be," she snapped.

But she was uncomfortable. This must be a grudge

situation, the reason for which she could not guess, and did not really care. But she saw no reason for one in authority to have already *decided* to kill.

She looked out across the grassland in the direction they were headed. The early growth of the grasses was nearly tall enough to hide the red stone boulders which were scattered across the plain. They were all rounded from centuries of being rolled and scrubbed by wind, water, and drifting sand. A bit taller, and this season's growth of the grass would effectively hide them, as it happened every season.

She did not understand why her thoughts would turn in this direction. Well, no matter, she decided.

"Fix us some food, woman!" the leader ordered.

She nearly refused, but that would prove nothing.

They ate hurriedly and moved on. The two underlings expressed their thanks but their leader merely nodded.

It was two days later that the three passed by again, heading back the way they had come. The leader's body was tied, facedown, across his own saddle. They stopped for water and she offered food, as was the custom.

"You found the men you sought?" the medicine woman asked. The answer was obvious.

"Yes. Our leader was hit by a bullet, right there! It was as he said." The man pointed between his own eyes. Both men were acting strangely, and more than a little frightened.

"What is it?" she asked.

The answer was a bit slow, but one of the men finally blurted it out. "It was a bouncing bullet. No one can tell where they will fly."

"Yes, I know," she said thoughtfully. "But I had not thought of it. He pointed the way, himself!"

If a miracle seems to support the honest efforts of someone whose heart is right, why would one want to argue? Some things are not meant to be explained. Let them think as they wish. And maybe . . . could it be?

It is said that the spirits have a sense of humor. Who has the experience or wisdom to question their ways?

Note: This story is based on an actual incident in the Cherokee nation. Names have been changed, but the ricochet is a valid part of the story.

Bounty Hunter

John Duncklee

Jake Dunn stood in the middle of dusty Brewery Gulch in Bisbee with the smoking .45 Colt Peacemaker in his right hand pointed downward. The acrid smoke wafted up to his nose as he looked toward the crumpled figure of Virgil Vickers. Virgil had weaved his way from the Copper King Bar, seen Jake approaching and pulled his Smith & Wesson out from its holster and pointed it at the deputy. Jake hesitated momentarily, but when Virgil pulled the trigger on his revolver, sending a bullet into the street in front of Jake's feet, Jake pulled out his revolver and made a bloody hole in Virgil's chest. He was dead before he hit the street. Jake stood looking at the result of the incident.

Virgil Vickers was the first man Jake Dunn had ever killed.

Several days later the sheriff asked for Jake's badge because Virgil Vickers had been the son of a prominent rancher. He had also been the twin brother of Amy Vickers, Jake's sweetheart. In spite of carrying Jake's child, Amy told him she never wanted to see him again.

As he sat in the Copper King Bar a friend suggested that he become a bounty hunter. Instead of trying to find work in Bisbee, Jake saddled his sorrel horse, packed his mule, and headed to Tucson.

Not only did Jake Dunn try the occupation of bounty hunter, he found the line of work interesting and profitable enough to keep him in food and lodging even when there was a scarcity of wanted posters. Through the years he chased cattle and horse thieves, train and bank robbers, and several hardcases that were wanted for murder. Through it all he had still killed only one man, Virgil Vickers. He never returned to the Vickers Ranch near Bisbee. Occasionally he wondered about the child that was supposed to be his. Time had a way with Jake Dunn, and it healed the sadness and disappointment he had felt so strongly the day he rode his sorrel horse out of Bisbee with his pack mule behind, loaded with all his belongings.

Many years later, he found himself in Ehrenberg by the Colorado River. Jake sat in an old wicker-backed rocking chair watching the deputy fill out the affidavit. Jake was entitled to the two hundred dollar reward for capturing Henry "Hank" Elliot.

After trailing the murderer for two months, Jake had finally caught up with him in the Red Rose Saloon in Ehrenberg on July 4, 1898. Elliot had gunned down a storekeeper in Prescott while in the middle of an armed robbery.

"Well, Jake, here's your affidavit," the deputy said. "Seems like pretty low wages for two months trackin' that killer."

"I've got a low overhead business, Alden. Aside from riding through the country seeing all the sights, the only real work is when I catch up with the jasper I'm following."

"I got this in the other day," the deputy said. "You might be able to make another two hundred if the escapee didn't make it into Mexico yet."

Alden Kane handed the wanted poster to Jake. As the bounty hunter looked at the poster, the deputy began trimming his fingernails with his pocketknife.

"It's not every day a lifer escapes from the Hell Hole," Jake remarked. "Yuma's just a three-day ride. I reckon it might be worth a try."

Jake spent the night in a hotel, enjoying the bath and meal cooked by someone else besides himself. Early the next morning he saddled the stocky sorrel gelding, packed the mule, and was headed south toward Yuma before the sun had given a glimmer of light to the eastern sky.

* * *

Jake's work had taken him to Yuma often enough that he had become well acquainted with the town on the banks of the Colorado River. But, as was his custom, he did not mingle much with the local populace so he could maintain his anonymity. He paused and watched the ferry, hauled by cables, as it made its way across the river. The summer heat at three o'clock in the afternoon baked the arrowweed along the river and the ground that always seemed thirsty. The river gave the air a heavy level of humidity. Jake removed his hat, and wiped his sweaty brow with the sleeve of his shirt. Plunking his hat back on his head, he continued his way into Yuma, a town that had already proven to be a bawdy and bustling settlement between Arizona and California. He rode toward the center of town.

Jake first stopped at the sheriff's office. J.T. Moran had held his office for several years and was a better politician than law officer. Jake was well acquainted with J.T. from meetings with him when Jake tried to glean information about wanted fugitives with rewards for their capture.

J.T. sat, leaning back in his chair, with his polished boots on the top of his cluttered desk. "They didn't miss Hammond until the day after San Juan's. We went out with a couple of the prison guards to see if we could pick up some sign. Most of those escapees head for Mexico, but we didn't find a single track goin' south from the dunes. It was the same with the Quechan trackers. They couldn't find a sign of him."

"Do you think he headed to California?"

"I did until someone found a body dressed in prison stripes hung up on a snag by the river."

"Who was it?"

"It wasn't Hammond. The warden went over to the morgue and said he'd never seen the man before. There was a hole in his chest. Didn't look like a bullet, more like an arrow, but the Indians around here haven't stirred up nothin' for a helluva while."

"Is the body still at the morgue?"

"No tellin'. You'd have to go over there and see for yourself. They might have planted it already since there wasn't any identification on it."

"Let me get this straight," Jake said, removing his hat and scratching the top of his head. "This body was dressed in prison stripes. Whoever he was wasn't an escaped prisoner, and it looked to you like he was killed by an arrow to the heart."

"That's all I can help you with, Jake. If I knew anything more you'd have it. I'd just as soon you went off after Hammond rather than me trying to find him. The man's a lifer. At least he was a lifer until he flew the coop. Since the Quechan trackers came up with nothing there's two hundred bucks dead or alive on his head."

Jake left the sheriff in the same position he had found him. The man in charge of the county morgue told him that the hole in the corpse was definitely not made from a bullet. The edges of the hole had been lacerated when whatever it was that killed the man had been removed.

"Do you still have the body?" Jake asked.

"You're lucky. If you'da come tomorrow it would have been six feet under."

The mortician led Jake back into a storage room where he pointed to the corpses awaiting burial. "The fellow you're wantin' to see is over on the end."

He beckoned Jake over when he had uncovered the corpse's face. "We didn't have any identification so we're plantin' him with the clothes he come in with."

Jake looked at the dead man's face and recognized him as a petty confidence man who made a living selling bogus deeds and such. He had once seen a wanted poster but the reward had not been enough for him to fool with. He decided to say nothing to the mortician and allow the man, Henry Waters, to be interred without any further inquiry.

The warden of the Arizona Territorial Prison rose from his chair, and greeted Jake with a warm handshake. "It's good to see you, Jake. I'll bet you're here to start after that escapee, Hammond."

"You're right as always, Warden. From what I can gather, Hammond's got about a week's start on me."

"That appears to be the case. What can I do to help?"

"I'd like to see a photograph that is better than the one on the poster. Do you have one?"

The warden stepped over to a file cabinet, opened the drawer, and leafed through the files. "Here it is. Benjamin Hammond." He opened the file, and sorted through the papers. "Here's the official photograph that's on the poster, and here's another taken out on the dunes while the construction crew was working."

Jake looked at the two photographs intently, fixing the images of Ben Hammond in his mind. "Would you mind if I took this one on the dunes with me? I'll send it back when I catch him."

"If I know you, I'll have Hammond and the photograph back shortly."

"Thanks, Warden." *I just hope he isn't spreading around his good opinions of me. The last thing I need is to be a well-known bounty hunter.* "With almost a week on me Hammond is probably long gone. But, I've found them when they had a couple of months between them and me. Have you seen that corpse at the morgue?"

"Yes. The sheriff asked me to go over to see if I could identify the dead man. He had Hammond's clothes on, but he sure wasn't Hammond. Beats me who it is."

"I suppose we can conclude that Hammond changed clothes with the dead man before or after he was killed by the arrow."

"That sounds reasonable, Jake. Good luck finding

him. I was surprised to learn he had escaped. Hammond seemed to be a model prisoner."

Jake thought about the death wound made by an arrow and decided to visit a band of Quechan Indians he knew well. He wanted to find out if the arrow had been one of theirs. It had been four years since he had saved the Quechan headman's daughter from a wild bull that was charging toward her along the river. He had managed to swing the girl behind him as he spurred his horse in front of the bull. Upon arriving with the girl at the village the headman had shown his gratitude with a weeklong feast. Jake looked forward to seeing the Quechan again.

By the enthusiastic reception given him by the Quechan it seemed like he had been absent four weeks instead of four years. The headman told Jake about two Quechan boys that had killed a priest because they remembered the old stories about the Spaniards visiting and killing their ancestors. Then, when told to return and retrieve the holy man's mule, the boys, hiding in the tall arrowweed along the river, had encountered a very much alive holy man riding the mule. When they returned to their village they reported their findings to the headman.

Jake Dunn felt confident with his research, and rode south to the Gila River several miles east of its confluence with the Colorado. He found Ben Hammond's camp and had a definite picture of the mule's tracks. He liked tracking. He thought of it as the best part of bounty hunting. He had always depended on surprise in capturing his prey rather than using his Peacemaker. During the many years he had spent bounty hunting after killing Virgil Vickers, Jake Dunn had never again killed a man.

On his second day away from the Quechan village, the sun was casting its smallest shadows when Jake spotted the windmill at a ranch headquarters. The faint mule tracks in the dried silt at the crossing showed him that Hammond had crossed the river, and then returned to the trail. The sorrel hesitated momentarily at the edge of the running water. Jake jabbed his sides slightly with his spurs, and the horse stepped quickly into the current. The mule balked at the water's edge, but the lead rope wrapped around the saddle horn jerked enough to convince him he should follow.

The dogs came scrambling from the barnyard, barking and growling at the stranger. Jake saw a man come out of the barn, looking in his direction to see who might be riding into his headquarters. Jake waved a friendly greeting and approached the man, reining the sorrel to a stop when he was ten yards away.

"Howdy," Jake said. "I'm just riding along the river and spotted your headquarters."

"Carl Garrison. Get down, and I'll get some coffee made."

"Thanks. I'm Jake Dunn. Coffee would be just right."

"Put your horse and mule in the corral if you like. There ought to be hay in the feed trough."

"They'd like that. The desert where we camped last night was pretty shy of any feed."

Jake led the sorrel and the mule into the corral while Garrison went to the house. Once inside the enclosure he unbridled the sorrel, and turned the animals loose at the feed trough containing hay. He shut the gate behind him, and ambled toward the house. Garrison came to the door, and invited him in.

"The coffee should be hot in a bit. Come on in and sit."

"Don't mind if I do," Jake said, and followed Garrison to the kitchen.

"What brings you out here?" Garrison asked offhandedly.

"I'm looking for a man dressed as a priest."

"He ain't here, but he damn sure was. Caused me a bunch of misery."

"How so?" Jake asked, trying to be nonchalant.

"I had taken some cattle to Yuma to sell. When I got back I found that my wife had given my Sharps carbine to a man dressed as a priest. He's her old fiancé, Ben Hammond. The way she talked, I could tell there was more to it."

"Did she tell you the rest of the story?"

"She told me all right. Afterward I got rough with her. Then she got mad as hell 'cause I slapped her around. She told me that the bastard spent the night before movin' on."

"Did she say where he was heading?"

"She didn't say, but I'll bet it was Tucson, 'cause she packed her stuff and I took her to the stage.

She said she was goin' home to Tucson. I reckon I shouldn't have been so rough on her."

Jake thought to himself that Garrison's wife must be smarter than her husband. A lot of women would stick around and take abuse. Although he had never met Garrison's wife, he admired her for leaving. Jake never respected a man who would beat up on a woman, no matter what the reason.

Garrison went to the stove, poured two cups of coffee, and brought them to the table.

"What's your wife's name, and where is she staying in Tucson?"

"Why do you want to know all that?" Garrison asked defensively.

"She might be able to help me find the man I am looking for."

"Her name's Martha. She probably went to her father's house on Sixth Avenue. His name was Redmond. Why are you lookin' for the guy?"

"He escaped from the Hell Hole a couple of weeks ago."

"I'll be damned. I wondered why he was on the loose. You a marshal or deputy sheriff?"

"No, I just travel here and there trying to make a living."

"You'll probably find him before that no account sheriff does."

"Well, I reckon I'd better get back on that hombre's trail. Thanks for the coffee."

Again riding along the north bank of the river, Jake didn't bother looking for mule tracks. He kept the sorrel at a fast walk. He continued the relentless pace every day, stopping only to water the horse and mule, and to eat.

He was a day's ride from the point where the Gila bent north in a wide arch, gradually easing its way eastward again. Further upriver south of Phoenix, the Río Santa Cruz spilled into it. From past travels, Jake was acquainted with most of the Gila and its tributaries. He knew that the point where the river began its bend north would give Hammond the choice of staying along the river, or heading straight across the desert, through Papago country, to Tucson.

With the first early morning light beginning to ease its way into the desert, Jake had broken camp, saddled the sorrel and packed the mule. He'd been watching the huge, white cumulus clouds for four days wondering when a summer storm would cool him. There wasn't a wisp of a cloud on this early morning, but by midday the sky was filled with the thunderheads that looked like giant bolls of cotton and heads of cauliflower. They were lower to the ground than the day before, and drifting at a much slower pace.

Jake rode down an arroyo from the trail to the river to let the sorrel and the mule drink. The stream flow appeared cloudier, and seemed to have raised somewhat. He contemplated crossing to be on the south side in case the rains had begun in earnest in the mountains, engorging the streams and arroyos that would fill the Gila's flow from bank to bank. He had seen rivers in flood too perilous to cross. But, he needed to check for tracks at the bend to determine which route Hammond had taken to Tucson. There was always the possibility that the fugitive had headed north to Prescott.

The clouds began to darken after he had continued along the north side of the river for nearly an hour. Jake kept his eyes skyward, watching the clouds blacken, and begin billowing and boiling. He reined in the sorrel and dismounted. After untying the saddle strings holding his rain slicker behind the cantle, he unrolled it and put it on. The first streak of lightning lit up the desert landscape as he swung back into the saddle. The sudden appearance of the lightning bolt scared the sorrel, forcing Jake to grab the saddle horn until he had his right boot firmly in the stirrup. "Hey, old man, you've seen plenty of lightning. Quit all that nonsense," he muttered.

A monster brown cloud of wildly blowing dust formed in front of the storm as it pushed its way toward Jake. He saw its approaching fury, and turned into a grove of cottonwoods next to the river, stopping with the rumps of the animals facing the storm. The force of the wind increased just as the brown wall of dust screamed through the branches of the trees. With one hand holding the reins and the other grabbing the brim of his beaver felt hat, Jake closed his eyes when the storm hit.

The dust storm was momentary, followed by

large raindrops that would be flying at him almost horizontally had he not been in the partial shelter of the cottonwoods. Booming, crackling thunder-claps came simultaneously with the bolts of light-ning. Jake spurred the sorrel to get away from under the trees in case the lightning struck them. When they left the shelter of the large trunks and branches, the wind-driven rain smashed against them like a wall of water. Once back in the desert, Jake reined the sorrel around so that his rump again faced the wind. There was little else to do but wait out the storm.

Jake thought about the bend in the river where Hammond would have had the choice of routes to Tucson. The storm had, most likely, obliterated any tracks Hammond's mule might have left. The chances of the man dressed in the priest's robe going to Prescott were slim. Perhaps, during Hammond's so-journ at the Garrison ranch, he and Martha had planned on meeting in Tucson. His years as a bounty hunter had taught Jake that tracking fugitives was far more complicated than looking for horse or mule tracks on the ground.

The storm turned from blinding, wind-driven sheets of rain to a steady downpour. The lightning still danced around, and thunder boomed and echoed, but the danger for Jake and his animals was over. He rode east, looking for a good place to ford the Gila. Jake decided to cross where the chan-nel widened.

As he spurred the sorrel into the water, he noticed

the river had clouded even more, and the current had become swifter. He was glad he hadn't waited any longer to make his crossing. In another hour the river could rise a foot or even two.

Finally the rain stopped, and desert shrub sent the pungent smell of creosote to Jake's nostrils. The small leaves on the greasewood bushes dripped droplets of rainwater onto the desert floor that sparkled in the late afternoon sun that had appeared after the short, but violent storm. The force of the rain hitting the ground had brought a thin layer of silt to the surface that glistened in the sunlight as Jake headed straight east toward Tucson to find Martha Garrison.

From Garrison's directions, Jake found the Redmond house on Sixth Avenue, just north of the railroad track. Through the wooden picket gate and up the four stairs to the wide, overhanging porch, he reached the large front door and lifted the shiny brass knocker three times. He watched as a hand brushed the curtain aside and a young woman's face appeared through the etched glass window. He smiled. The door opened partway.

"May I help you?" the woman asked.

"I'm looking for Martha Garrison."

"I am Martha Garrison. What do you want?"

"My name is Jake Dunn, Mrs. Garrison. Your husband told me you might be able to give me information about Ben Hammond."

"Please come in, Mr. Dunn. I am not sure if I can help you or not."

Martha ushered Jake into the front sitting room, and invited him to sit down. "Would you care for coffee?"

"No thanks, I just came from breakfast."

"What kind of information are you looking for, Mr. Dunn?"

"Your husband told me that Ben Hammond passed through your ranch on the Gila. I am trying to find him."

"Ben did come to the ranch. When my husband found out, he beat me. That is the reason I am here. I do not intend to go back. I have already retained an attorney, Mr. Dunn. You cannot force me to return to my husband."

"You have the wrong idea about me, Mrs. Garrison. I am not here to force you to go back to your husband. I am only interested in Ben Hammond. In fact, from what your husband told me, I don't blame you for leaving him."

"What did my husband tell you?"

"He said when he found out about Ben Hammond spending the night at the ranch, he got rough with you."

"I could show you bruises that have not faded yet."

"No need of that, Mrs. Garrison. But I must say that I have no respect for a man who beats up on a woman."

"Ben was railroaded after he was involved in a scuffle with Kevin Randolph in which Randolph killed himself with his own gun. The judge in the case was very friendly with Kevin's father, a prominent

Tucson banker. The trial was a farce. Ben was sent to the Yuma Territorial Prison."

This banker Randolph is the same skinflint who gave me only fifty dollars for retrieving his eight thousand from that robbery years ago. Small world.

"I don't know the particulars of the trial. I only know that Ben Hammond escaped from Yuma, and was headed this way," Jake said.

"The judge who presided over Ben's case retired. My father was friendly with the new county attorney. I asked my father to see what could be done about reversing Ben's conviction, but my father passed away a year ago."

"Does Ben know about this?" Jake asked, trying to discover if Ben had been in Tucson to visit Martha.

"I haven't seen Ben since he rode away from the ranch on his mule. Why are you looking for Ben, Mr. Dunn?"

"There is a reward out for his capture."

"Why then, for heaven's sake, do you think I would tell you where he is, even if I knew?"

"I just try to find out as much as I can from anyone. It saves time. However, Mrs. Garrison, if your father was pursuing the matter of a reversal, it might be best for Ben if he gave himself up. His chances of exoneration would be greatly reduced if he remains a fugitive."

"I doubt if Ben has any faith left in the justice of Arizona Territory."

"It sounds to me as if he may have a good chance. At least from what you have told me."

"You may have a point, Mr. Dunn. But, I have no idea where Ben is. He told me about some map he had that would lead him to some Jesuit treasure. I suspect he's out somewhere digging."

"Did he say where this treasure was?"

"I don't think Ben would appreciate me telling you. I love Ben Hammond. I don't want him back in the Yuma prison. I want him with me."

"I can understand your feelings, Mrs. Garrison, believe me. But, if he were ever to be free again, it would be to his advantage to give himself up. If I can find him, I might have the opportunity to explain all this to him."

Martha hesitated. She wanted to believe what Jake Dunn had said. On the other hand, she wasn't sure if what he said was just to get information from her.

"Mr. Dunn, I think I have said enough. If you should find Ben, please tell him I am waiting for him. I will not make the same mistake I made once before. Good day, Mr. Dunn."

Jake rose from the chair. "Mrs. Garrison, Ben Hammond is a lucky man. I'll do my best to find him. When I do, I will give him your message."

The temptation to remain in Tucson for another night made Jake go to the Lucky Dollar for a glass of beer. As he stood at the bar, he thought over what Martha Garrison had told him about the Jesuit treasure. Recalling the various tales of treasure from the Mine With The Iron Door to the gold that was supposed to have been buried by the Jesuit priests of the Tumacacori mission, Jake decided to ride south along the Santa Cruz River. He had read about the fables and knew that in 1767, when the Jesuits were forced to leave their missions in New Spain, there would not have been enough time for them to bury anything, much less a bunch of heavy gold and silver. There had been many a disappointed treasure hunter in the Tumacacoris as well as in the Catalinas. Jake wondered where Hammond had found the map. Then it hit him. Henry Waters was probably posing as a priest to try to sell the map of the treasure of Tumacacori to some unsuspecting soul from the East.

The trail over Smuggler's Notch, between two peaks of the Tumacacori Mountains, was easy for Ben Hammond to follow. Smugglers had used it to bring cattle and other contraband out of Mexico since the Gadsden Purchase. He stopped the mule when they reached the highest point where the trail began its downward grade into the Santa Cruz Valley. The view of the pine-topped Santa Rita Mountains to the east was magnificent. Below his position, he saw the small mud adobe dwellings of Tubac. Looking south, he could just see the old Tumacacori mission church dome just on the west side of the river. Farmlands made patches of green between *bosques* of mesquite and the ribbon of lofty cottonwoods marking the river. Arriving at the mission he consulted his map, stopped in the store for a few supplies and a shovel.

The map told him to ride south to Tinaja Canyon. After branching off the stage route to a trail leading up the canyon, he rode for a mile before finding the cave made by tons of water rushing down the canyon to spill into the Santa Cruz River. After hobbling the mule up on the surrounding grass-filled mesa, he spotted a yearling buck mule deer and shot it. After gutting the carcass he hung it on a strong branch of a large mesquite tree that grew in a protected bend in the canyon within sight of the cave opening.

Once in the cave Ben reclined and using his saddle for a pillow, fell asleep.

Jake followed the clear tracks left by Ben Hammond's mule in the sandy arroyo of Tinaja Canyon. When he saw the hobbled mule nibbling at the grasses growing on the mesa above the canyon, he reined in the sorrel. Ben's mule raised his head, moved his long ears forward, and stared in the direction of the stranger.

Ben had awakened early, made his coffee, and eaten some of the deer heart after grilling it on the fire. With the treasure map spread open on the floor of the cave, he began to examine it in the early morning light. According to the map he would have to travel up *Cañon de las Tinajas* until he reached a point somewhere near the base of the mountains.

Then he noticed for the first time that the measurements of distances on the map were written in *varas* and leagues, not miles, yards and feet. "Hell, I don't know how far a league is," he said aloud to himself. "I'll never find this treasure until I find out how far a league is and what a *vara* is. I should have done this before I rode in. Maybe, the Mexican at the store knows."

Ben was getting ready to leave to bring the deer carcass up into the cave and out of the hot summer sun when he heard his mule bray. He grabbed the Sharps, cocked it, and crept to the mouth of the cave. As he peeked around the corner into the canyon, his eyes caught a man's figure under the mesquite tree where he had hung the deer carcass. Then his eyes picked out movement at the top of the canyon. He looked up as a cougar began its spring from the edge of the cliff. Quickly, he brought the carbine to his shoulder and fired at the plummeting feline. Before the cougar hit the mesquite, Ben saw a red splotch on its side.

The cougar fell on top of the man and knocked him down. Ben cocked the carbine again, but didn't aim at the man who was rising to his feet.

"Who are you, and what do you want?" Ben yelled.

"Looks like I owe you one," the man said. "I didn't see that cat. It must have been after your venison."

The man started walking toward the cave. Ben saw blood on the man's sleeve.

"It looks like the devil sunk its claws in you," Ben said.

"Better its claws than its teeth. Mind if I come up there?"

"You have to climb the ledge. Is your arm all right?"

"I think it's just a scratch."

When the man was in the cave, Ben leaned the Sharps against the wall and looked at the arm. "I've got some salt pork that might do to put on that wound," Ben suggested.

"I'd appreciate it. My name's Jake Dunn."

"Howdy," Ben said, not offering his name to the stranger.

He handed Jake a piece of salt pork after he sliced it from the chunk he had bought the day before.

"Thanks," Jake said as he rubbed the salty pork fat on the claw wound. "That sure does sting."

"How about some coffee?" Ben asked. "There's some left."

"Coffee will be fine. After that experience I might like some mescal better."

"I can't help you there."

As Ben put the pot back on the coals, Jake stepped over in front of the carbine where it leaned against the wall of the cave. *This man is no killer,* he thought. *Otherwise, that rifle would still be in his hands.*

"What are you doing afoot in this country?" Ben asked.

"My saddle horse and pack mule are down the arroyo. I'm just having a look-see. What are you doing up here living in this cave?"

"Just prospecting."

Ben rinsed the tin cup with water from his canteen, and filled it with coffee.

"I've only got the one cup, but you're welcome to it," he said, handing it to Jake.

"Like I said down there, I owe you one," Jake said.

"That's all right. I'm glad I had the carbine ready. I wouldn't have if that mule hadn't brayed."

"I'm going to level with you, Ben Hammond. I've been following you clear from Yuma."

Ben felt his stomach tighten. "Are you a lawman?"

"No, just a bounty hunter. Remember, I owe you one."

"So what does that mean now that you've found me?"

"I do not have to take you in, and, as a matter of fact, I do not intend to. But, I am going to give you some advice."

"I reckon I need all the advice I can get at this point."

"There are efforts being made on your behalf in Tucson. You have friends who are trying to get your life sentence pardoned because they believe you were railroaded. I may be wrong, but my advice is to turn yourself in. You'll have a better chance with the new judge."

"Jake, I was railroaded once. I didn't kill Kevin Randolph, he killed himself. He was drunker than seven hundred dollars."

"I heard the entire story. I can't say as I blame you for being gun-shy of territorial justice."

"You sound like an honest sort, Jake. And now, I've got another problem. I found this map on a dead priest near the Colorado River."

The two men continued their conversation. Ben told Jake all about his escape and entire adventure. Mostly Jake listened.

"Now, I'm here where the map says I should be, and can't figure it out because the measurements are in leagues and *varas*. I don't have any idea how long a league or *vara* is, do you?" Ben asked.

"I reckon that was not part of what little education I have."

"If you can find all that out, we could be partners on this treasure hunt."

"That sounds like you are not figuring to turn yourself in, Ben. You got that map off the body of Henry Waters, who never made an honest dollar in his life. I'll bet a year's worth of bounties that he was going to try to sell that map to some unsuspecting Easterner as he went around in the robes of a priest."

"Are you telling me that I am looking for a treasure that doesn't exist?"

"That's exactly what I'm telling you, Ben. Now, will you turn yourself in?"

"I don't know about that yet. It's going to take a heap of thinking before I take a chance on going back to that hell hole in Yuma."

"I'll be in Tucson for a while. I figure I'll put in a good word for you at the courthouse. Before I leave, I'll give you a hand getting that venison up here in the shade of the cave."

The two men climbed down the ledge, and went over to the mesquite tree.

"That's a beautiful cougar. I might just skin it and tan the hide."

"It would make a nice rug," Jake said.

They carried the deer carcass up the arroyo, and between the two of them got it into the cave. Jake turned to leave.

"I sure thank you for everything, Jake. I hope we meet up again."

"Well, Ben, you're free to do as you please as far as I'm concerned. But, I want to tell you one more thing. There's a real beautiful woman waiting for you in Tucson. She wanted me to tell you that she loves you. If I were in your boots, I'd forget about your map. Your real treasure is a woman named Martha."

The Wanted Man

Rita Cleary

"I'm a wanted man." He coughed it out to his high-stepping mule whose smooth, racking gait ate the miles like a wind-whipped fire on the prairie. He sat with shoulders hunched, toes pointed to the earth, lock-kneed legs stretched forward in long stirrups that swung to the rhythm of the shuffling animal. His seat never left the saddle but riding wasn't comfortable. His ailments were getting worse and he was losing weight. But he was going to see his daughter if it was the last thing he did before he died.

"Was a time I would've used you to pull freight, mule. You're big enough an' powerful strong." In fact the mule had been part of a team whose other half had died. The man continued, "But a wagon's too obvious for this trip and I got to be careful. Marshal Biedler knows me too well." And he knew Biedler. They bore the same first names, Francis Xavier, taken the vigilante oath and ridden along together when they took down the Plummer gang and hung twenty-two men in almost as many days. They called Francis Xavier Biedler *X*. But they called him *Zave*.

Zave McGowan was riding home. He had to skirt Biedler's law if he was to see the only child he'd ever fathered. He was a raw-boned ox of a man, well over six feet tall with the bulging muscles of a blacksmith. He'd worked as a blacksmith in his distant youth, then went to freighting when he married Mazie who craved the finer things like piano music, bone china, and lace curtains. Thoughts of Mazie evoked a pang and the memory of a four-room, clapboard house on the high side of town, a fire on the hearth, a parlor with cushioned chairs, a cupboard full of Mazie's gleaming white china, and the wide four-poster bed. A tear seeped from the corner of his eye as he envisioned Mazie with her flaming red hair tossed brazenly askew, pregnant, padding barefoot across the carpet.

Zave McGowan hadn't been home when Lucas Fites shot Mazie in the foot. Fites was a jealous man, not of Mazie but of the thriving freighting business Zave had established. McGowan Transport had driven Fites and Company into bankruptcy and Fites decided to even the score. He'd only meant to scare Mazie and drive Zave and his company out of the territory but Fites was a dreadful shot. He probably never aimed at Mazie.

Randy Nivens had brought Zave the news and Zave had rushed home. When he arrived, Eve

Jordan, who was helping Mazie clean and cook until the baby arrived, had wrapped the wound and seated Mazie in the rocker by the hearth with her foot raised on a milking stool. Eve explained, "A flesh wound, Mr. McGowan. It don't look threatening. I washed it and wrapped it good." Zave sent for the doctor all the same. One look at the doctor's red-streaked eyes and pasty leer and Zave knew he'd been drinking again. The doc had a lusty eye for Mazie.

With a wave of her hand, Mazie dismissed the old sawbones but she went into labor two days later, weeks before the babe was due. "Baby's comin' early, Zave. Eve's seen some midwifin'. She'll do me right. Promise me you won't call that lecher doctor."

Zave did as he was told. He waited in the parlor, wringing his hands, punching at the feather cushions of the chairs, pacing the pile carpet while Mazie delivered a baby girl in the wide four-poster bed.

He heard the baby cry. Eve Jordan came through the doorway holding the fussy infant a few minutes later. "I bathed her and tied off the cord."

He touched the single golden red curl on the baby's head and exclaimed, "Red like her mother's and so soft." He looked to Eve. "But she's so tiny. Are they all so?"

Eve nodded. "Yessir, when they come early." She jostled the tiny bundle. Immediately, the baby began to wail. "You want to hold her?"

A sense of awe bordering on fear came over Zave McGowan as he stammered, "Not yet. Not now. Take her to her mother. I'll hold her later when she stops cryin'." Except for Mazie, females had always been a fathomless mystery and he had a business to run.

"Then I'll get Mrs. McGowan ready to see you. She can soothe the babe." There was an edge to her voice as she continued, "Babes need cuddling. Daughter needs a father. The birthing was easy. It's Mrs. McGowan's foot that's paining her. I propped it on a pillow to let it drain. Give me a minute, then you come."

Mazie was smiling when he entered and sat beside her on the edge of the mattress. The baby lay quietly in the crook of her arm and seemed engulfed by clumps of quilt and pillow. Mazie's foot was covered with a clean white sheet. Together they named the baby Daisy. Mazie chose the name because daisies bloomed faithfully by their front door every year in the early summer.

A few days later, Mazie's milk gave out. Eve found a wet nurse and stayed to help care for Daisy because Zave had gone back to his thriving business. When finally Eve unwrapped the rags that bound Mazie's foot, Zave gasped in shock. He summoned the doctor, who wanted to cut off the foot and complained, "Fool woman wouldn't let me treat her when I could do any good."

Mazie would have none of him. She pressed a

hand into Zave's arm and begged, "Send him away. You stay with me, Zave."

Zave put Randy Nivens in charge of the McGowan teams and wagons while he wrapped and rewrapped her foot with hot compresses, packed the wound with a paste of astringent leaves as his old grandmother had taught him and stayed constantly at her bedside, but it was too late. Mazie's fever rose while poison invaded her body. Her words rang in his brain. "Careful, Zave. I see the red glow at the back of your eyes. You're angry an' it's buildin'. You're fixin' for a fight."

"I'm not angry, just losin' sleep." He never told her how he cried rivers when her back was turned. Red eyes were the only evidence he could not disguise. But crying was for cowards. He would never show a tear, especially to Eve and the wet nurse, who always reminded him, "You'vc a girl child to consider, Mr. McGowan."

He would nod and blunder. "My wife's the sick one who needs my care. You been hired to tend the baby." Mazie was dying. What did they expect? He'd blink his red-veined eyes at the suckling infant and turn to his ailing wife.

One day, Mazie dug her fingers into the soft flesh of his arm, closed her eyes, drew back her lips as if to stifle a scream and mumbled, "Zave, bring Daisy up right." Her voice was a soft tremulo, hardly more than a whisper. "Zave, you're a good man. I thank you." She smiled faintly then and lapsed into a merciful coma.

He sat by her bed all night long, watching fever burn through her body and beads of sweat drip from her brow while a thin stream of moonlight pierced the lonely windowpane until the gray light of dawn crept into the corners of the room. He was still sitting there when Mazie stopped breathing and the sun's thin rays stabbed the eerie dimness. Eve Jordan found him there, staring, gripping his wife's cold hand.

Eve called the undertaker, wrapped Mazie's corpse in clean linen and quieted Daisy during her mother's funeral. Zave McGowan paid for a hardwood coffin and a solid, stone marker. Preacher Bryan organized a solemn procession, hired a caisson pulled by a shiny black horse, and prayed over Mazie's grave. Finally, he walked Zave McGowan back to his home. "Think you can forgive him, Zave?" He meant Fites. He laid a hand on Zave's stooped shoulder. "Fites had no business maiming a woman. Marshal Biedler's come back. He's asking questions. You should talk to him, file charges."

Zave stared back and gritted his teeth to contain his anguish. "Why should I? Would that bring my Mazie back?"

"Might earn you some solace, Zave, ease the pain that breeds anger. Go on in. Go home."

Eve Jordan was waiting for him in the parlor, standing like a pillar, holding Daisy. Now she forced him to look long and hard at his sleeping daughter. "She's a simpleton, Mr. McGowan. You've a business to run. I can care for her better than you. You must let me take her."

He looked at her without seeing. The words twisted like a knife in his heart but the woman was right. She had no children of her own, lived in a clean, whitewashed bungalow with her carpenter husband and attended church weekly.

Daisy was so tiny and looked so fragile that Zave was sure the premature birth had caused the moon-like flatness of her face. He rubbed his weary eyes, nodded and replied, "Yes, do. That would be best. You'll make a good mother." Preacher Bryan would approve and so would all thc matrons in the city who knew how much Eve Jordan wanted a child.

An hour later, Zave strapped on his Colt, marched out the door, and down the boardwalk. Fites was in his office, in his swivel chair behind his wide oak desk, when Zave barged through the door. The skinny miser spent most of his days there calculating profits and losses and depended on hirelings to manage the crusty teamsters, heavy wagons, teams of horses, and yokes of oxen that moved his freight. He worried constantly about gangs of holdup men and petty thieves who'd been ravaging his shipments. The latest was a load of whiskey. Thieves had grabbed the wagon and its precious liquid out from under the careless noses of the driver and guard and left them standing at the side of the trail pleasantly drunk with four empty bottles between them. Next morning, a cowboy had found them sleeping it off. The four-horse hitch and its wagon had showed up parked behind Otis's Feed Store. Fites had accused Zave McGowan and filed charges with Marshal Biedler who hauled Zave before Judge Driscoll. But Driscoll had laughed them all out of his chambers. Humiliated, Fites had marched down the boardwalk to Zave's house and shot Mazie.

Now Zave McGowan stood in Fites's office as Fites swung his chair around to face him. Looking up from under a thick cornice of brow, he challenged, "What you want, McGowan?" The husky voice couldn't mask his antipathy.

"I come for an apology, Lucas. You owe me."

"I don't apologize to thieves, McGowan. Get out."

Zave stood fast. "Your own men are the thieves, Lucas, and your own hardheaded stupidity's the cause of your loss, not me. You should ride along with your boys sometimes, see what they endure, worry less about countin' your profits and pay 'em a decent wage."

Fites gave a cynical snort. "I should pay 'em more when they report for work drunk, so's they can't see past the wheeler horse." He laughed. "They slosh an' gamble away every cent I pay 'em. You ain't no angel, McGowan. You rob me, then pay your men too high with what you took from me. Give 'em grand ideas. Make 'em think they're God almighty but you're the thief an' cheat an' the devil's own deceiver, McGowan."

"I'm a fair man, Lucas. Thieves and cheats don't shoot women. What's that make you, Lucas? My wife's dead. That what you wanted? You too big a coward to come for me so you come for my wife?" Zave was breathing hard. The red spots glistened brightly at the back of his eyes.

"She died birthin' her brat, McGowan. You ride off with your damn wagons, you ain't even here. How'd you even know the kid is yours? Can't blame me for a fornicatin' woman. Can't blame me for what the devil had planned."

Rage pounded in Zave McGowan's breast. "Swallow those words, Lucas. My Mazie was a good and faithful woman."

"Ain't no such thing." Fites snickered and swiveled back to face his desk.

Zave felt his hand reach for the grip of the Colt at his hip. He raised the gun and shouted, "You're the thief and the murderer, Lucas. Tell that to the devil." His right forefinger squeezed the trigger. The bullet struck Lucas Fites in the back between the shoulder blades as Fites lunged to reach for a hidden gun in the top drawer of his desk. The drawer stuck. Fites wasn't holding a gun when he fell gagging over his desk, and George Otis had just stepped through the door into the office.

Zave shoved Otis aside and charged out as Otis shouted, "Gracious God, Zave, what'd you do? Call the doctor. Call the marshal."

Otis's screams and the clatter of running feet rang in his ears as Zave McGowan ran down the boardwalk. He didn't wait to hear if Fites died or if Marshal Biedler had summoned a posse for the chase. He fled that very day. He took his riding horse, packed his strongest freight horse, rode in the shallow wash of river water to hide his tracks and headed into the mountains. He never looked back.

Weeks later, grizzled and bearded, he emerged on the eastern slopes and sold his horses and tack. The money didn't last long. With a new name, he found work in the hard rock mines. Underground he became invisible. His whiskers grew thick and matted and his tanned complexion paled to pasty white while to all who knew him, he'd disappeared.

His fellow miners left the grim, silent man alone. In the dusty caverns of the honeycombed mountain, he swung pick and mallet, shoveled out ore, and wondered about the daughter he'd left behind. The coughing started a few years later and soon his hacking heaved up gobs of bloody phlegm. His sides ached with every swing of the mallet.

One day, the pain wrenched so hard he let go of the mallet in mid-swing. It sailed across the dark tunnel like a deadly flail and struck old Ike Thwaites behind the knees.

The mine foreman herded him topside and droned, "You could've killed that man. Pack up. Collect your pay."

Zave scraped together his belongings. He'd

hoarded enough money to buy an outfit and the racking red mule he rode and headed back home.

"Carry me back, mule. Carry me smooth. I'm dyin', mule and I got to see my little girl. Don't matter, mule, if she's flat-faced and dumb. Don't matter if she's dwarfed." Breathlessly, he spoke to the mule like he'd never spoken to his fellow man. "Climb that mountain, mule. Climb it fast. Carry me over the divide to the other side." And he imagined Daisy. "Baby Daisy, how old are you now? Do you look like your mother? I remember red hair but that's all I know. I'm sorry, girl."

The trail wound along the river then climbed the rocky mountain slopes and finally topped out over the divide. It was spring, the warming season when the winter's snow was melting, the mud was deep, and the mule's hooves skidded along the trail that wound down from the heights along the creek to the western slope. After the hot, choking air of the mines, the fresh, cold mountain air eased his aching lungs.

Without so much as a heaving breath, the red mule clattered on, then came to a stop on a bench overlooking Virginia City. "We're here, mule. Look down. There's my home." He corrected himself. "There *was* my home."

On a flat crook of land between two creeks, he spied the city, a bright smudge of new lumber huddled in a gulch. It had spread since he'd last seen it, like a glob of soft dough kneaded and pressed out in a pan. Sensing an imminent meal of grain, the mule swished its tail and tugged at the bit. He let it move on out and inhaled. "Light air breathes in easy. All downhill from here."

A mile or so from town, he coughed again and his voice rasped when he spoke. "Trees are thinning. Time to leave the trail, mule. Marshal Biedler'd spot your shiny red hide miles away." He reined the animal off the trail, down a low embankment, and into the cottonwoods that grew by the creek.

"Biedler'll clap me in jail before I see my Daisy. I wonder if Biedler would recognize me"—the talking left him gulping for air but he caught his breath and continued—"if he's still alive, an' somehow I think he is. Biedler's a good lawman but I ran faster and he let me get away. Had no more love for Fites than me. You listenin' mule?" He closed his eyes, paused again to catch his breath and shook his weary head. "Biedler couldn't catch me and I shot Fites, mule. I shot and killed him for Mazie and I'm glad for it."

A smile creased Zave McGowan's face as he steered the mule down from the heights onto the road into town. It was early afternoon and the sun splashed the new buildings with sparkling light. They dotted the roadside at first sparsely, then thickly. Shops, stables, a brewery, and saloons stood where stands of cottonwoods once thrived. A new bridge spanned the river where the ford used to be. Railroad tracks paralleled the opposite side of the river. A new cemetery reminded him of Mazie. A wagon passed with a load of lumber and an inscription painted on the side. It read NIVENS SHIPPING AND FREIGHT. Zave rubbed his eyes. "That was mine, mule." He nodded and moved the mule aside to let the wagon pass. Then he rode on, searching all the while for old landmarks he knew.

"There she is, the old house." He almost passed it by. The house where he'd lived, where Mazie had died and Daisy had been born, had sprouted a new wing. The porch had been painted and swept clean. The door was ajar and the yard was neatly fenced. Zave McGowan felt his heart heave and coughed deeply. The breathless coughing continued.

The mule stopped instinctively while Zave heaved mucus from his chest, began to dismount, then thought better of it. Who lived there now? Would sight of those rooms only bring him pain? Better to find Daisy, Eve Jordan, her carpenter husband, and their modest carpenter's home. He was about to turn the mule away when a woman peered out the door. "You sick, mister? I hear you coughin' loud. You need help? That's a fine-lookin' mule."

Zave shook his head. "Help yes, to find Mrs. Jordan. She has a child. She was friendly with the family who used to live here."

"Jordan." The woman repeated and narrowed her glance. "I believe she's lives up Pine two blocks. Turn right at the next corner, up the hill with the rich folks."

Zave tipped his hat and cleared his throat. "Thank you, ma'am." He turned the mule up Pine. He hardly tried to steer. His lungs were full and his heart pounded in his aching chest. Then he spotted Eve Jordan walking in front of him along the road, heading toward home with a sack over her arm. She was a dumpy, pear-shaped woman who walked with stiff knees, and she hadn't changed. He reined the mule alongside and inquired, "Mrs. Jordan, Eve Jordan?"

The woman shied back from the mule's hot breath, set down her sack, and looked up askance. "Take your hat off when you speak to a lady," she snapped, then stared openmouthed, scrutinizing the careworn lines of his face. Finally she found words. "Mr. McGowan, Francis Xavier McGowan?"

"It's me, Eve, the same. I'd like to see my Daisy."

"But Mr. McGowan, she's at school." Then she added, "You look like a ghost. She doesn't know you. Thinks my Jacob's her father. You'll frighten the poor child. We built a new larger house on the hill." She pointed. "And my Jacob works for Nivens now."

Zave sensed the anxiety in her voice and forced a smile. "No need to worry. I've traveled far. Where can I find a bath and a shave and a reliable livery for my mule?"

"Jacob built a barn behind the house. The feed bin's full and we've a loft of good hay. The mule can stay with us. Come back about four after school's out."

Zave McGowan began to cough, deep wrenching

hacks that shook his wide shoulders and caved in his chest. Alarmed, Eve McGowan shuddered and exclaimed, "You'd best tend to yourself. Barber Senks is good for the bath and the shave, down the hill just past the corner." She pointed and added defensively, "And the doctor's three entries farther on. You might pay him a call. Wouldn't want to sicken the child. I can take the mule with me now."

Reluctantly, Zave slid from the saddle and handed her the reins. "He's a good mule. Been good to me. Be good to him."

She took up her sack, watched him walk down the hill, then led the mule away.

Clean-shaven and bathed, Zave McGowan felt better. Inhaling the steam off the surface of the hot bath water had helped ease his breathing. He dressed and inquired of the barber where he could find the school. Then he trod slowly back up the hill to the new schoolhouse. It was a one-room, shingled building painted stark white and looked more like a church with a pointed belfry, huge bell, and a scrawny fir tree planted in the corner of the yard. He stationed himself by the tree until the bell clanged dismissal and a dozen children streamed out past the teacher who stood on the steps and watched them go.

Panic struck Zave McGowan. Which was his Daisy? There were three girls about the right age, all with pigtails but only one with red, curly hair that refused to confine itself in braids. None looked flat-faced and none seemed simpleminded as the Jordan woman had described his daughter but the redhead had the same curve to her nose and the same laughing blue eyes as Mazie. He stood glaring and the little girl, conscious of the staring stranger, frowned and ran after her friends.

The teacher, a man in his early twenties, approached him suspiciously. "You frighten the children for no reason, sir. Who are you?"

Zave took off his hat, wiped his brow and choked on the words. "A father, once a father, now . . ." He could not say *a murderer, a fugitive, an invalid, a haunted man who abandoned his child.* He said, "I mean no harm. Tell me, is her name Daisy McGowan?"

"Daisy Jordan. She's a pert little thing, intelligent beyond her years," the teacher replied. "Why?"

Zave McGowan tried to breathe. Daisy was a lively, cheerful child, not impaired as Eve had told him. He sucked gulps of air, then exhaled them in violent coughs and wiped the moisture from his lips with the back of his hand. He said, "I knew her father once." He clapped his hat on his head and turned away.

Zave McGowan did not return to the new Jordan house on Pine. Instead he crept shamefully back to the center of the old city, to Marshal Biedler's office, one of the few buildings that was still the same as he remembered.

An older, grayer man but the same X, Biedler

looked up from his desk when Zave entered and stood hat in hand in the middle of the room.

"Have you been lookin' for me, X?"

Biedler's jaw gaped. "Sounds like Zave McGowan." He glanced up at a poster tacked to the wall over his desk and back at the skin and bones hulk standing before him. "Is that you? Was a time I scoured these hills looking for you."

"It's me. I presume Fites died."

"He did. But in the end, we thought you were dead, the way you left your business, an' your daughter an' all, never left a flower on your wife's grave and never tried to contest a murder accusation. Nivens is a rich man, inherited your house an' your business. You come to take it back? But you're just a shade of your former self." Biedler pulled out a chair and mumbled, "Sit."

Zave shrugged and fell into the chair. "You should've arrested me. A jury would have convicted me. I wanted Fites dead and I wanted to hang for it."

"But Fites had a gun hidden in his drawer. He was reaching for it when you fired. You could've claimed self-defense."

"I didn't know that. I was angry. My bullet took him in the back." Coughing fits interrupted his speech as he continued. "Eve Jordan told me my Daisy was slow, that she might not survive. I thought . . ."

"That why you left?" Biedler shook his head. "Eve Jordan was a barren woman and wanted a child more than she wanted the truth. She lied.

She seized the opportunity is all. But she's done right by your child, raised a happy, healthy girl."

Zave blinked and held his aching sides as the coughing resumed and refused to quit. Biedler helped him drink, then lay him on a cot in the nearest cell at the back and went for the doctor.

Zave McGowan was sleeping when the doctor, a young man from Philiadelphia, arrived. Zave awakened and smiled as the doctor took his pulse and frowned. "Best you rest, mister. You're lucky you're alive. You have friends in town?"

Zave looked to Biedler as he replied, "I have my mule in Jordan's barn."

The doctor left but Marshal Biedler didn't fetch the mule. "Sleep the night here, Zave. Get a good rest, a hearty meal under your belt. Tomorrow or the next day's soon enough."

For two days, Francis Xavier McGowan slept soundly and ate good food. He and Biedler spoke frankly. "Maybe a jury would've blamed you, Zave, you confessin' the way you did. Maybe you would've hung. Maybe I should lock you in this cell right now. I got a poster up there with your face on it, but that's not the face you're wearin' now. There's folks here might still want you but I don't want a dyin' man. Don't make much difference now."

On the third day, Marshal X. Biedler helped Zave onto his high-stepping mule. Fed and rested, his coughing had subsided and the red mule was eager to go but Zave held it back. He said, "My daughter doesn't know my name. Will Daisy know who her mother is?"

"I can't answer that, Zave." He hesitated, then added, "Mrs. Nivens goes and tends Mazie's grave."

"Someday, when she's grown, X, you be sure an' tell her." Biedler nodded as Zave mumbled, "But don't tell her that her father was a wanted man."

Biedler held out his hand. "I'll do it, Zave. I promise, if I'm alive." Zave shook the hand and turned the mule down the road.

Dead Man Riding to Tombstone

Andrew J. Fenady

October 24

"I s'pose you're goin' to Tombstone for the big do-in's," said the old man who had been hitchhiking.

"No," the young man answered, "I'm going there to die."

"How's that?" the old man took the unlit cigar stub from between his false teeth and looked at the young man driving the van. "What was that you said?"

"I said I'm going to die in Tombstone. Actually I'm already dead. It's just a matter of making it official and getting buried. Looks like it's going to rain."

"Nah, it's not gonna rain. Them's just puff clouds. Are you sick, boy? You don't look sick."

"No, I'm not sick."

"Then what makes you think you're gonna die—and in Tombstone?"

"I don't think. I know."

"How do you know?"

"Because it happened before. It's going to happen again."

"Wait a minute, son, let me get this straight. You say you died there before?"

"Just over a hundred years ago."

"And you're gonna die there again?"

"Yes."

"Then why go there? Turn off and go somewheres else."

"I can't."

"Why not?"

"You ever read about the man who had an appointment in Sammara?"

"Can't say I have."

"He couldn't help it. He had an appointment. So have I."

"In Tombstone?"

"Yes," the young man nodded. "At the O.K. Corral."

William Cummins believed he was on his way to Tombstone to die on October 26 just as Billy Clanton died there over a hundred years ago on October 26, 1881.

Billy Clanton was the young, sensitive, sensible member of the Clanton Clan who went to the rescue of his hotheaded older brother and died of bullets to the wrist, chest, and stomach fired by the Earps and Doc Holliday at the O.K. Corral.

More than a century later William Cummins was inexorably drawn to the same scene where the town of Tombstone would celebrate the annual reenactment of the infamous gunfight.

But for William Cummins it would be no celebration. It would be a crucible.

Cummins believed he was the reincarnation of Billy Clanton somehow destined to die once again on the dusty streets of Tombstone.

There would be parades, songs, dances, and demonstrations—and of course a re-creation of the world famous gunfight. People by the thousands from all points of the compass would swarm into Tombstone, many of them dressed as the Earp brothers—Wyatt, Virgil and Morgan—and some as the wasted, tubercular killer Doc Holliday.

Still others would be wardrobed as the Clantons and the McLaurys—Earp's sworn enemies.

They'd all be carrying guns—just as a long time ago—but this time the guns would be loaded with blanks.

Or would they?

Cummins arrived in Tombstone a couple days before the reenactment. The festive carnival atmosphere had already arrived—a veritable western Mardi Gras. He visited those same structures on Fremont and Third Streets—Papago Cash Store, Bauer's Union Market, Fly's Photograph Studio, Harwood House—and of course the O. K. Corral.

As the hours passed, the periodic attacks of pain that had plagued Cummins' right wrist, his chest, and stomach occurred with greater frequency and effect.

He met the modern day marshal of Tombstone and one of his deputies—an old-timer who knew every detail of the events and conflicts that led to the outburst of gunfire and death on that cool October day. As the deputy narrated and choreographed the details of the gunfight, William Cummins reenacted the events in his mind's eye, seeing himself in the role of Billy Clanton. He relived the gunfight as it really happened—not as it has been portrayed in dozens of counterfeit movie and television reenactments.

Billy Clanton disarmed his drunken, hot-tempered brother Ike, as their friends Frank and Tom McLaury watched. Billy tried to prevent the showdown. But it was too late—destiny was already unreeling its drama.

In their black Stetsons and greatcoats, string ties dangling down their white shirt fronts, the Earps moved three abreast on Fremont Street. In their wake trailed Doc Holliday, wearing a long gray coat.

"Doc, this is our fight," Wyatt said over his shoulder. "No call for you to mix in."

"Hell of a thing to say to your best friend. I'm already mixed."

"Then I'm swearing you in as a deputy," said Virgil. "Whatever happens, it'll be legal."

They moved on as Doc nodded and patted the shotgun under his coat.

Sheriff Behan, a friend of the Clantons, ran toward them and the McLaurys.

"Ike, gimme your gun!"

"I don't have one." Ike looked at his brother Billy.

"But the Earps do and so does Holliday," said Billy. "And they mean to use them."

"I'll stop 'em," said Sheriff Behan. "Stay here."

He moved toward the Earps and confronted them under the awning of Bauer's Meat Market. "Earp for God's sake don't go down there!"

"We're goin'," said Wyatt.

"Stay back. I'm the sheriff of this county."

"And I'm the marshal," Virgil spoke softly. "They broke the law. We're taking their guns."

"They haven't got any guns," Behan snapped.

But even as he spoke they all heard the hammer click as Frank McLaury unholstered his six-shooter.

"No Frank!" yelled Billy Clanton.

"They haven't, huh?" Wyatt whipped out his pistol and fired at McLaury, whose shot had missed. Wyatt's didn't and Frank staggered as the deadly melee began.

Billy Clanton drew but Morgan Earp's pistol blazed, and Billy was hit in the right wrist. Another bullet smashed into Billy's chest and he fell back against a window of the Harwood House. Even as his body sagged and slid to the ground, Billy switched his pistol to his left hand, steadied the barrel across his arm, and fired.

Ike, sobering up fast, screamed, "I haven't got a gun! I haven't got a gun!" and ran between the photograph studio and Harwood House then disappeared unharmed between the stalls of the O.K. Corral.

Sheriff Behan had already leaped for cover—gun still holstered. It stayed that way.

Holliday let go the shotgun and ripped Tom McLaury's chest with pellets. McLaury managed to wobble a few steps down Fremont Street, then collapsed and died.

Billy Clanton's next shot tore into Virgil's calf and Virgil buckled.

Frank McLaury, though wounded in the stomach from Wyatt's shot, was not ready to cash in. Frank shot at Holliday, who returned fire along with Morgan Earp. McLaury crumpled when someone's bullet hit him below his ear. McLaury's last shot tore into Holliday's hip.

Billy Clanton, who never wanted the shootout, fired his last shot. It hit Morgan in the shoulder. Morgan stumbled and fired as he fell. Wyatt fired simultaneously. Both shots smashed into Billy's stomach. He slumped, squeezing the trigger of his empty gun, and groaned, "Give me some bullets."

Billy Clanton died.

The gunfight was over. But not for William Cummins.

* * *

Cummins stood on the street, rubbing his wrist and pressing his palm across his chest and stomach trying to soothe the searing sensation that burned his insides.

October 25

William Cummins was a stranger in Tombstone, but among all the others strangers he saw a familiar face. Her face. She had followed him from Los Angeles.

"How'd you know I'd be here?" he asked.

"Where else would you be? I went to your place. All those books and magazines. All about one thing."

"How'd you get here?"

"Bus," she shrugged. "Busses."

"Go back Laura."

"Together."

"I'll come back when it's over. If everything's—"

"Okay? If everything's okay? Is that what you were going to say? But you still think you're going to die—don't you?"

"Everybody dies. The difference is I know where and when. Get out of here."

"It's not that easy Billy, when you love somebody."

Cummins realized people on the street wearing

cowboy outfits were listening. "Too many people." He started to walk away.

"Billy, where are you going?"

He was going to Boot Hill, one-half mile west of the O.K. Corral.

William Cummins stood at the foot of the grave staring at the inscription on the headstone of Billy Clanton. He turned as Laura approached. "Laura I told you—"

"It was the accident, Billy. The accident and that old movie we saw that night about the gunfight at the—"

"No. Even before I smashed that car and my head I always knew I was different—no mother, father."

"Everybody's got a mother and father . . . even orphans."

"The name they gave me. Same initials—same number of letters." He pointed to the tombstone. "That's me buried there."

"Even if there is such a thing as reincarnation—the same things don't happen again."

"They will to me. I can see it coming. Feel it happening."

"Billy, it's that writer's imagination of yours."

"Some writer. I've sold zip."

"It'll happen."

"Yeah," said Cummins, looking at the grave. "It'll happen."

* * *

Tires screeched and the flasher blazed on the Arizona State Highway patrol car.

An enclosed van the color of the desert sand raced up ahead on the highway. Inside the van a Johnny Cash tape blared from the stereo. Johnny was singing about guns and women—women and guns. The driver, a string bean of a fellow named Reuben (Ruby) Jones, was swigging from a pint of Jack Daniel's and driving erratically. There were three other men in the van—the Bundy brothers. Mase and Dill were awake and the leader Wingate had been asleep on the sofa but he bolted up as Mase topped Johnny Cash, hollering "Dammit, the cops!"

"Pull over Ruby, you idiot," said Wingate, as he made his way to the driver's seat. He jerked Ruby from the chair, slapped him hard across the face, grabbed the pint, and handed it to Dill. "Ditch it!"

When the patrolman approached, Wingate sat at the driver's seat with a good ol' boy smile on his handsome face.

"Lemme see your driver's license."

Wingate handed it over.

"Guess I was speeding a little."

"And then some," said the officer. "Plus driving erratically. You been drinking?"—he looked at the license—"Wingate?"

"No sir. Just got carried away by Johnny Cash on the stereo. Sober as a judge."

"You boys going to Tombstone?"

"Yes, sir. Staying over for the celebration."

"Well we don't want any cheap funerals. Take it easy or you'll be staying permanent."

"Yes sir, sorry sir. Appreciate the advice."

The patrolman handed back the license and walked toward his car.

"You sure lullabyed him, Win," smiled Dill.

"I'll roll 'er in," said Wingate.

"Don't ever slap me again." The words came hard through Ruby's rat-thin lips.

"Slap you?" said Wingate. "Ruby, you screw up this deal—and I'll *kill* you."

Tombstone is bordered on three sides by mountains—the Dragoons to the north, the Chiricahuas to the east, and the Mule Mountains to the south. It is flanked on the west by the San Pedro River.

Ordinarily Tombstone's population is calculated at 1,795. But for the next two days it would at least double—and maybe triple.

In the meantime Cummins and the Bundys saw and participated in the celebration that featured songs, dances, and even a good old-fashioned fist-fight at the Crystal Palace Saloon. There was a personal appearance by Eddie Rabbit. Cummins and Laura walked past the *Tombstone Epitaph*, which would soon carry a story explosive as the one more than a hundred years ago—as would hundreds of other papers across the country—even the world.

During the reenactment of the gunfight, while thousands, including William Cummins, would be watching—the Bundy brothers along with Reuben Jones planned on visiting another attraction in Tombstone.

The Bank of Arizona on Allen Street—just south of the O.K. Corral.

They'd be dressed as the Earp brothers and Doc Holliday right down to their six-shooters and shotgun filled with live ammunition.

Wingate Bundy had planned the caper in a fashion that would do credit to Jesse and his brother Frank—including the escape route to Mexico where the loot would buy a cache of cocaine that would be converted into millions of dollars on the streets of Los Angeles and San Francisco.

But tonight Tombstone was festive and even William Cummins found himself caught up in the festivities. Maybe he *could* defy destiny—hurl away the fates. He laughed and danced and later beneath the full white harvest moon he and Laura made love in their room.

His fears seemed dispelled until he woke trembling, with his insides screaming in pain. Laura kissed him and did her best to allay his obsession. But William Cummins was more than ever convinced this was his last night on earth. The town of

Tombstone might be too tough to die, but William Cummins knew that he was not.

During the night, the Bundys and Reuben Jones went over the plan step by step and moment by moment, once again.

Later, Reuben, more drunk than sober, sneaked out for another bottle of Daniel's—and whatever else he could find.

Cummins, unable to sleep, left the beautiful slumbering girl at his side and walked the moon-blanched streets of Tombstone. Drawn as if by an unseen desert tide toward the O.K. Corral, he literally bumped into the drunken, belligerent Reuben Jones, who had picked up an obliging blonde. Cummins apologized and did his best to avoid a confrontation but Reuben was spoiling for a fight and to show off in front of his newfound lady friend. The fight began when Reuben swung wildly at Cummins.

It was broken up by the arrival of the Bundy brothers who got to the O.K. Corral just ahead of Laura.

As Wingate made an apology for his friend a strange, almost mystical look was exchanged between him and Cummins.

Later in their room, Cummins told Laura that he had the feeling he'd seen that man before. She placed a cold washcloth on Cummins' bruised face and he finally fell into a fitful sleep.

October 26

The day dawned bright and clear with a slight wind from the west—a chilly wind. Hungry and hungover pilgrims flocked into The Lucky Cuss Restaurant and Bar, Top-O-Hill Restaurant, Wagon Wheel Restaurant and the Corner Snack Bar for everything from steak and eggs to burgers and Bloody Marys.

Streamers were strung, banners fluttered, balloons bounced from their strings, and bands blared country and western music. From the shops and loudspeakers came the familiar lamenting voice: Merle Haggard wailed, "I turned twenty-one in prison doin' life without parole." Johnny Cash serenaded the Ghost Riders in the Sky, Kenny Rogers told the tale of The Gambler. The ladies were heard too. Dolly Parton, Loretta Lynn, and Barbara Mandrell.

William Cummins took a cold shower and thought of how cold it would be in the earth. Cold and dark.

The Bundy brothers and Reuben Jones dressed in their black coats and string ties like the Earps and Doc Holliday. Wingate Bundy pasted on his Wyatt Earp moustache and they all checked the chambers of their guns.

The Bank of Arizona opened for business—but it would not be business as usual. The business would be blood and death.

The streets were stacked with spectators as hired actors portraying the roles of the Earps and Doc Holliday began the reenactment. They started their march north on Fourth Street while men, women and children clapped and cheered them on. "Wyatt," "Virgil" and "Morgan" turned west on Fremont Street three abreast, trailed by "Doc Holliday."

"Doc, this is our fight," Wyatt said over his shoulder. "No call for you to mix in."

Near the corner of Third and Fremont, as hundreds watched, the imitation "Clantons" and "McLaurys" waited for the showdown—and so did William Cummins—rubbing his wrist and pressing his palm across his chest and stomach. Laura Young stood at his side.

At that moment the Bundy brothers and Reuben Jones, dressed as the Earps and Doc Holliday, entered the nearly empty Bank of Arizona and drew their guns. Reuben Jones leveled his shotgun.

"This is a holdup," Wingate announced.

At first it seemed like a bad joke. Some of the tellers started to laugh but the laughter stopped suddenly when Reuben crashed the shotgun barrel across a teller's temple and the man dropped, bleeding and senseless.

On Fremont Street "Sheriff Behan" confronted the "Earps" under the awning of Bauer's Meat Market.

"Earp for God's sake don't go down there."

"We're goin'," said Wyatt.

"Let's get goin'," Wingate commanded the men in the bank.

Reuben spotted the manager pressing a silent

alarm and the silence was shattered by the shotgun's blast. The manager fell dead as a lady teller screamed.

Outside there were more shots. The Gunfight at the O.K. Corral had begun.

The lady teller still screamed hysterically until Mase slugged her unconscious while the others scooped up the money and headed for the door.

"Don't anybody move or you'll die," yelled Reuben.

Outside there were more gunshots from the Corral. As the bandits poured out of the bank door, guns leveled, they ran into two deputies. Reuben let go another barrel and one of the deputies dropped. The other fired, wounding Dill, but Wingate creased the deputy.

The meticulously planned robbery turned a shambles—just like Jesse and Frank at Northfield.

The desperados dashed west on Allen Street then north on Third—without realizing they were heading toward the O.K. Corral—with the wounded deputy firing in pursuit.

The crowd and William Cummins watched the tail end of the gunfight as "Billy Clanton" took two shots in the stomach from the guns of "Wyatt" and "Morgan Earp."

"Give me some bullets," groaned Billy and "died" as the Bundys and Reuben Jones ran toward the crowd with the bleeding deputy firing at them and calling for help.

At first the people thought this too was part of the act.

But Reuben fired into the crowd and a woman

screamed and fell gripping her blood-smeared shoulder.

The deputy yelled that they'd robbed the bank and the marshal stepped out of the crowd, aimed at Dill, and dropped him. A couple other deputies joined in the gunfight as the spectators screamed and scattered.

All but William Cummins, who stood paralyzed. Wingate fired and the marshal crumpled at Cummins' feet.

As if by instinct or reflex Cummins reached for the marshal's gun on the ground as a bullet kicked at the dirt. A strange, mystical look gleamed from Cummins' eyes. Once again he was Billy Clanton. Once again the inexorable machinery of fate had set him on the same spot where he fought and died just over one hundred years ago.

Once again Billy Clanton's sworn enemies, the Earps and Doc Holliday were trying to kill him.

Would it end the same again?

Cummins knew he should drop the gun and run. But the hand that held the gun was no longer Cummins'. It was Billy Clanton who fired at Wyatt Earp.

A bullet tore into Billy's right wrist—another grazed his chest. He fell back against a window of Harwood House. But even as his body sagged and slid to the ground Billy switched his pistol to his left hand, steadied the barrel across his arm and kept firing.

He seemed prepared to accept his destiny but this time fate dealt a different hand.

Billy's next shot dropped Mase. As Reuben was about to fire into Billy, the ol' time deputy unloaded both barrels of a ten gauge into Reuben's midsection.

And Billy's last shot found its mark as Wingate stumbled and fell.

It was all over. The curtain had dropped on a different ending. Billy Clanton had beaten Doc Holliday and the Earps.

Laura ran to Billy who was propped on one elbow—a curious, quizzical look of disbelief on his face. And no pain. Absolutely no pain.

October 31, Halloween Day

William Cummins' picture appeared on the front page of the *Tombstone Epitaph* and in dozens of other newspapers throughout the country. His slight wounds had been tended and the Bank of Arizona saw fit to bestow upon him a suitable reward. And the annual celebration was over. The streamers, the banners, and the balloons were gone.

Once again the population of Tombstone was calculated at 1,795 as Cummins and Laura drove his van northwest on Highway 80 parallel to the ridgeline of the Dragoon Mountains.

On the van radio Johnny Cash was singing the song about "poor Billy Clanton who lies cold in his grave."

"Poor Billy Clanton," said Laura.

"And rich Billy Cummins," smiled Cummins.

"I knew you'd be okay."

"Yeah, looks like somebody else had that appointment in Sammara."

"What did you say, Billy?"

"I said, I never felt better in my life."

That's when the semi hit the van head on at Deadman's Curve.

Moments later the police and ambulance were on the scene.

Laura stood dazed and bleeding as they carried Billy Cummins on a stretcher toward the ambulance. "He's going to be okay, isn't he?" Laura asked one of the attendants.

The attendant just shrugged.

"He's going to be okay," she assured herself. "If he can beat the Earps, he can beat this."

"Sure he can, sister," said the attendant.

From a nearby car came the voice of Johnny Cash singing the song about "poor Billy Clanton who lies cold in his grave."

Hap

John D. Nesbitt

A lone rider turned off the trail and onto the hard-packed dirt in front of the way station, the slow hoofbeats sounding hollow until they came to a stop. The dark horse snuffled, and when the man swung down from the saddle, the animal gave a rolling shake that rattled the stirrups. The horse was mid-sized and husky, with black mane, tail, and legs, while the shoulders and haunches shaded to a dark brown. His long winter hair bristled on his jaws and neck, and he had a worn, steady look to him as if he had been on the trail for a while. The bedroll and rifle scabbard appeared to be snugged on for the long ride as well.

The man wore a drab, low-brimmed hat, a double-caped gray wool coat that reached halfway from his waist to his knees, and a pair of charcoal-gray wool pants. Worn leather gloves, slick on the palm side and weathered across the knuckles, matched the scuffed boots and dull straps on his spurs. As the man loosened the cinch, he glanced in the direction of the board sign tacked to the wall on the right side of the station door. STONEMAN'S BLUFF. The man turned and looked across the road, where a sandstone bluff rose out of the grass and sagebrush a quarter of a mile away. The late-morning sun cast pockets of shadow where the elements had chiseled features on the face of the bluff.

The door of the roadhouse opened with a scraping sound, and a man's voice sang out. "Hullo, there. Anything we can do for ya?"

The traveler turned toward the doorway. "What's the chance of gettin' a bite to eat?"

"Pretty good. Tie up your horse and come on in."

The interior was dim as well as chilly. The stationkeeper, wearing a dark knitted cap and a canvas coat, bustled about as he threw a couple of chunks of firewood into the cast-iron stove. He turned to his guest, showing a pair of watery blue eyes and a week's worth of gray stubble.

"I hope bacon and spuds agree with you, 'cause that's what I've got."

"Then that's what I like to eat."

"Good." As the older man went about slicing a few withered potatoes, he kept up a string of chatter. "Been cold, lots of wind, not much snow. Stage used to come through but doesn't any more. More ranches than there used to be, though, and would-be dirt-farmers that come out with not much more than the shirt on their back. Nesters. Eat everyone else's beef, come and beg bacon grease. Cowpunchers are a different story. A lot of them boys go back home and feed hogs through the winter. Coal, now, there's work in that, and in the winter time, too."

He set the skillet on the stovetop, cut half a dozen slices from a slab of bacon, and laid them in. Turning to look at his patron, he said, "You a puncher, too?"

"Sometimes."

"Well, don't mind me. It's just somethin' to talk about."

"Sure."

The old man poked at the strips of bacon with his knife. "Didn't notice which way you came in from."

"Travelin' north."

"That's what I thought. Goin' to the Black Hills?"

"Don't know. Depends on where my trail takes me."

"It's been an open winter, and travel's not too bad. Fella the other day said he come down from Miles City, on his way to Denver. Now that's a long ride, this time of year."

"I'd say."

"You wanna go east, now that's different. You can take a train a good part of the way. You like salt?"

"A little bit."

"These spuds can use it." He pointed with his knife at the raw slices on the cutting board. Then he laid the knife down and said, "I'd better get some coffee going."

By the time he put the coffeepot on the stove top, the bacon was sputtering. He flipped the pieces, let them cook for a minute more, and lifted them out onto a tin plate. Then he slid the potato slices into the skillet. "This'll stick to your ribs." After a pause he added, "You say you're not goin' to Deadwood, then."

"It's not my intention."

"Just as good. There's men there that'll cut your throat for the price of a bottle of whiskey."

"If you let 'em."

Silence hung until the man in gray spoke again. "Been a bit of traffic, then?"

"Some, but you don't see 'em all."

"I imagine."

"There's one fella they think came through here, but they're not sure."

"Oh."

With his thumb and two fingers, the old man lifted a pinch of salt out of a little wooden box and scattered the grains across the top of the cooking potatoes. "Bad sort, name of Perkins. They say he stopped at a ranch house down by Shawnee, where a man and his wife were livin' by themselves. This Perkins, as the story goes, tied the husband up, cut off all the woman's hair, and then had his way with her, with the man havin' to sit there and not be able to do anythin' about it. Then he shoots the man, burns down their house, and makes off with the woman. Next day he stops at a homesteader's place, kills him, takes the woman into that cabin and does who-knows-what, and burns all her clothes. Leaves her there wrapped in a blanket, with snow on the ground outside, and goes on his way. They're lookin' for him."

"The woman lived through it, then."

"Not in very good shape, but she was able to tell what happened and describe him. That's how they know it's Perkins."

"Sounds like a bad one. What's he look like, anyway?"

"They say he's about average height, kind of stocky. Got a walleye, and no pointer finger on his right hand, though I've heard you wouldn't know it from the way he handles a gun."

"So everyone's on the lookout for him."

"Like I said, the word's out. And there's a reward." The old man's glance took in the guest, who sat with his coat unbuttoned and his six-gun in view. The proprietor narrowed his eyes. "You're not after him, are you?"

The man in gray shook his head. "No."

"Too bad. The more the better, for that son of a bitch." His eyebrows went up. "But you're lookin' for someone, huh?"

The traveler didn't answer.

"You're not sayin'. Well, that's all right, too. Like I said, it's all just a way of makin' conversation while the grub cooks." The old man put his hands out to take in the heat of the stove. "Warmin' up in here all right. By the way, my name's Dean. Harry Dean."

"Mine's Cooper."

"Good to meet you, Cooper. Here, why don't you eat the bacon before it gets cold, and I'll have these spuds ready in a few minutes."

The man in gray opened a jackknife and tipped it to one side as the host set the plate on the table.

The features on Stoneman's Bluff had darkened when the traveler came out of the roadhouse. He put a bundle in the near saddlebag, untied the horse, and led him out a few steps.

The way station man called from the doorway. "You come back this way, stop in."

The gray hat brim lifted, and the man looked across his saddle as he snugged the cinch. "I'll do that."

By late afternoon the sky had gone overcast and the sunlight had weakened. The dark horse kept a steady pace as the trail ran parallel to a dry water-course. Up ahead on the right, a fire blazed in front of a canvas-topped wagon. Farther back from the campsite, two sorrel horses grazed on picket ropes. A bearded man crouched by the fire, while another stood at the tailgate of the wagon.

The man in gray reined his horse about a hundred feet out from the wagon and called, "Hello the camp."

The man by the fire stood up and said, "Come on in."

The rider swung down and led the horse into the camp as the man from the back of the wagon came into view. Both he and his partner looked over the newcomer's outfit.

"Long trail," said the man by the fire, who was the shorter of the two.

"Sure is. You're the first two fellas I've seen since I left Stoneman's Bluff."

"You stop there?"

"That I did. Had a hot meal with the old man who runs the place."

"He likes company."

The traveler smiled. "Seems to."

The taller man, who had a knife in his hand, spoke up. "You're probably about ready to eat again."

"The thought would occur."

"Well, you're welcome to eat with us. We've got plenty. I'm just now cuttin' it up."

"Oh, I don't know . . ."

"We've got plenty," the man said again. "We're hunters. No fine wines or tropical fruit, but you won't find us livin' on cold flapjacks, either. We got good deer meat."

"I'd hate to be the kind to turn it down."

As the steaks sizzled in the skillet, the two men gave an account of themselves. The taller one was named White, and his partner was O'Neill. They'd been trapping and hunting all winter and had just sold their pelts and hides. O'Neill made a point of saying they had put the money in the bank. Now they were meat hunting, and picking up a few more hides, until the ranch work started.

White stabbed a piece of meat and flipped it over. "How 'bout yourself?"

"Lookin' for work."

"What kind?"

"Ranch work, if I can get it."

O'Neill spoke up. "It's a little early for that. About the only work we've seen, and not up close, is out-of-the-way work. Cinch-ring artists, runnin'-iron men. We stay away from them."

"That's the best."

"You bet. And you know how the big outfits are. If they do it, it's all fair. But if someone else does, he's a rustler."

"Has there been a little bit of it, then?"

"It's hard to say. The way they set up a howl, you'd think there were legions out there. And they brought in a stock detective."

The man in gray lifted his head. "Is that right?"

White took his turn at speaking. "Fella by the name of Stook Wilson."

"Do you know him?" O'Neill asked.

"I think I might have heard the name."

"He's not hard to pick out," O'Neill went on. "He rides a dark horse, darker'n yours, and he dresses in black. Wears a dark overcoat and carries a black slicker. They say it's for night work, and I believe it. He works for three or four of the big outfits, moves around from one to another. Drops in on people's camps at any time of the day or night."

"Around here?"

"He works this whole country from the Cheyenne River down to the Niobrara."

"How long has he been here?"

O'Neill looked at White. "What, about three months?"

"Something like that. Long enough to pick off a few."

"No one does anything?"

O'Neill shook his head. "No proof. A man steps out of his cabin door in the morning, and that's it. Wilson disappears for a little while, someone sees him up in Deadwood on a three-day drunk. They say he passes out in a whore's room, where he gets his money's worth about half the time."

"Is he there now?"

"No, he's been back for a couple of weeks. They've seen him around in the past few days."

"Around here?"

O'Neill motioned with his head. "Over west and a little north of here. Near Corrigan Dome."

"What's that like?"

"Oh, kinda ugly country. Oil seeps, alkali flats. Right by the Dome there's a spring, where sulfur-smellin' water comes out all year round. Warm water. I wouldn't drink it, but it's good for any other purposes—you know, clean up, wash clothes. Anyway, there's a cabin there, and they say Wilson hangs out there when he's in between jobs."

"West of here, you say, and a little north."

O'Neill gave a close glance. "Are you lookin' for someone?"

"I'm lookin' for work. But if there's someone like that out there, I don't mind knowin' where he is. Stay out of his way and go about my own business."

White spoke again. "Be glad to help if we could. What's your name, anyway?"

"Cooper. Jim Cooper."

"It'll be a while till anyone's puttin' on more men, but we'll remember your name."

"Appreciate it. Never know when it might help."

"You bet," said White. "Meanwhile, don't be shy. You can roll your bed out here tonight, have some good hot coffee before you hit the trail in the mornin'."

"That's mighty good of you boys. I'll remember you for it."

The flat country sloping away from Corrigan Dome looked bleak in the pale light of an overcast afternoon. Outside the cabin, two horses were picketed on sparse grass. A wisp of smoke rose from the stovepipe, and a small cloud of mist showed where the warm water came out of the spring.

The man in gray pushed himself up onto his feet and sidestepped down the hill to his horse. He put the field glasses in the saddlebag, checked to see that his six-gun was in place, and swung aboard.

He rode half a mile across the flat, slow hoofbeats thudding as he approached the cabin. When he had come within thirty yards he stopped and called out a greeting.

The cabin door opened, and a dark, lean figure in a tall-crowned hat appeared, rifle in hand. "What do you want?" he called.

"Wonderin' if I could put up for the night. I think I lost my road."

"Where is it that you think you're goin'?"

"They said there was a way to get to the Powder River country."

"There's more than one way, but you're a good twenty miles from the closest one."

The traveler let out a long sigh. "I've been ridin' since sunup. I could camp outside if it's all right with you."

"Naw, hell." The man in the doorway turned and said something, then looked outward again. "Come on in."

The two horses on picket, one dark and one sorrel, watched as the man rode a little farther, then dismounted and led the saddled horse.

"There's a lean-to in back," said the man with the rifle, not so loud now. "You can leave your gear there and put your horse out near the others."

"Good enough."

Inside the lean-to, a small pile of firewood, none of the pieces bigger around than a man's wrist, sat by the back door. Against the far wall, one saddle sat on a rack while another rested off-center on a battered box. The man in gray laid his saddle and all its gear on the floor against the side wall. Then he set the horse out to graze on the meager grass with the other two.

He stood still for a long moment. The sun was slipping in the west, and the evening chill was setting in. The sulfur smell from the hot spring hung in the air, and the world was quiet except for the shifting of horses' hooves.

The front door of the cabin was ajar, so he knocked on the doorframe and pushed the door open. Two men sat at a table in the middle of the room. The man in the tall black hat was facing the entry, while the other, not so lean and not so tense, sat at a right angle from him and also watched the door. To the right of the table, a small sheet-iron stove showed a glow through the half-open hatch.

"Come on in," said the man in the black hat. "Pull up a chair."

The second man, who wore a brown hat and leather vest, pointed at a cane-bottom chair next to the stove. It had a woolen undershirt draped across the back, as if it had been set out to dry. "Just gimme the shirt," he said.

The man in gray picked up the chair, tilted it to the stocky man who had just spoken, and held the pose for a few seconds. As the other man took the shirt, his walleye came into view. He laid the garment in his lap and turned back to the table, where a whiskey bottle stood between two glasses.

The newcomer took a seat about three feet from

the table and perpendicular to it, so that his back was not to the door either.

"What's yer name?" asked the man with the walleye.

"Bell. Tom Bell."

"Huh. Seems I've heard that before."

"It's a common name. And yours?"

"Just call me Ace."

"Pleased to." He turned to the man in the black hat. "And yourself?"

"Wilson." The man had green eyes, the shade of bottle glass, and his hair was the color of autumn corn stalks. "Where you comin' from?"

"I come in from the east, by way of Harrison."

"What news along the way?"

"Don't know. I didn't talk to anyone very much. Just enough to get off on the wrong trail, I guess."

"You sleep out?"

"Last night I camped with a couple of hunters, but I didn't talk to them very much. My piles were botherin' me, and I turned in early." He paused. "At least I ate good."

Ace shifted in his chair. "We were just startin' to think about grub ourselves. That time of day."

"I'll tell you what. I bought a hunk of bacon a couple days ago, and I'd be glad to contribute it."

"That would be all right." Ace wrapped three fingers around his whiskey glass, just as natural as if he had all four.

Wilson and Ace paid no attention as the visitor got up and went to the back door. In the dusk of the lean-to he rummaged for the piece of bacon. Before straightening up, he laid his hand on the stock of the rifle, gave the gun a tug, and eased it back into the scabbard.

Both men's eyes were on him as he stepped inside. He set the bundle on the table and unwrapped the coarse paper. Then he opened his jackknife and began cutting slices.

"Guess I'll chunk up the fire," said Ace. He let out a long breath through his nose, then turned toward the stove. As he did, his holster and pistol rode up into view.

Wilson spoke in a sharp tone. "No news, then, huh?"

"Didn't ask for any."

"You say you came in from Harrison?"

"Through therc."

"And what have you got in mind for the Powder River country?"

"Lookin' for work."

"It's a little early for that. Anyone who's out on the range right now is likely to be up to no good. These outfits won't even bring in their horses for another three or four weeks."

The newcomer did not answer.

Ace settled into his earlier pose with his fingers curled around his whiskey glass. "We've got time for at least one more snow before the range work starts up."

"Maybe," said Wilson, who then made a sucking

sound, as if he was cleaning out a molar with his tongue.

Ace took a sip of whiskey. "I know a couple outfits, they go to Cheyenne and hire a full crew of men, and then walk 'em all the way back to this country. Like prisoners. Then they bring in the horses, and each man gentles his own string."

Wilson sniffed. "Not everyone does it the same. Outfits that've been around for a while, they have a lot of the same men come back every year."

The man in gray laid half a dozen strips of bacon in a crusty skillet, then crossed in back of Ace to put the pan on the stove. Wilson's eyes followed him as he returned to the table and resumed slicing.

"Thing is," continued Ace, "a lot of these fellas are no better'n hoboes. Got nothin' more'n the clothes they're wearin'. Takes the first month for 'em to get rid of the shakes."

"Some are that way," said Wilson, who was working his left side with a toothpick. "Not all."

"I didn't say all. I just said 'a lot.' They don't have their own saddle, and some of 'em have to learn to ride a horse. They get a real edgi-cation."

"You seem to know a great deal." Wilson hiked his right foot up onto the other knee and sat up straight. His boots were black, scuffed on the toes from going in and out of stirrups, and he wasn't wearing spurs. Quiet.

Ace tipped his head up and smiled. "This ain't my first time out in the country."

The man in gray folded his knife and put it away.

He passed in back of Ace, crossed to the other side of the stove, took out his knife and opened it, and began poking the bacon slices. The skillet had heated enough that the fat was starting to melt.

Wilson's voice came up again. "What outfits do you know of, over in the Powder River country?"

The man at the stove shrugged. "None yet."

"There's the Hoe outfit," said Ace. "They're a big one. And the Six Pines. I've heard of it."

"There's a bunch," said Wilson, clipping the last word. "I was just askin' if he knows of any." Then, raising his chin and lightening his tone, he said, "Damn, I've forgotten your name already. What did you say it was?"

"Tom Bell."

"Sure. That's right."

"I'm certain I've heard that name," said Ace. "Seems to me it was someone who got into a jackpot."

"I don't doubt it," said the man at the skillet. "Like I said before, it's a common name."

Wilson leveled his gaze now, the pale green eyes looking like a cat's. "Have you got any heel-flies after you, Bell?"

"Not that I know of. I haven't done anything."

Ace gave a coarse, short laugh. "Nobody ever does." After a couple of seconds of silence he went on, as if to rectify what he just said. "Like that back-shootin' Frank Canton. Now there's someone to know in the Powder River country."

Wilson's voice came up sharp again. "Why do you call him that?"

Ace shrugged. "Why not? That's what he is."

Wilson's face drew hard and tight. "People shouldn't say things they don't have proof of."

"People are afraid to talk. That's why they haven't been able to prove anything against him."

"I'll tell you this," said Wilson, his voice tense. "People are afraid to say it to his face, that's what. But they say it behind his back."

"Well, there's people right there in the Powder River country that know where he came from, what his name was then, and why he left."

"Talk's cheap. That's why there's so much of it."

Silence took over for a little while. The bacon fat sputtered, and the man with the knife flipped the pieces.

"Is there anything else to go along with this?" he asked.

"There's some biscuits," said Ace. "They're a day old, but they're all right." He pointed with his three fingers toward the back wall, where a heap of kitchen objects sat on a wooden crate. "Over there on a tin plate, covered with that cloth."

The man in gray fetched the biscuits and two additional tin plates. He set the cloth on the table and the biscuits on top of it, then laid out the three plates. Using a glove to hold the skillet handle, he lifted the fried bacon pieces with his knife and set them three in one plate and three in another.

"Go ahead," he said. "I'll eat from the second batch." He put the skillet on the stove and laid the remaining six slices in the hot grease. The pan crackled.

Ace pushed a plate toward Wilson and drew the

other to himself. Then he reached for two biscuits. "Good grub," he said. "Never pass up a hot meal, for you never know when the next one'll be." He lifted a piece of bacon with his right hand, the big finger serving as first finger, and bit off a chunk. "Damn good," he said, smacking his lips.

The white strips were swimming in grease, and a thin black smoke rose from the pan.

The smacking sound came again as Ace took another bite. His finger and thumb were greasy, and the top of his chin had taken on a shine as well. "Three things to enjoy in this life, whenever you can. There's good grub, good drink, and good snatch. Don't you think so, Tom?"

"I suppose." The man who called himself Tom Bell flipped a slice of bacon.

"'Course, you know what they say. It's all good, just some of it's better. Speakin' of snatch, of course."

Wilson unbuttoned his coat and scooted his chair up to the table, showing no hurry to start eating.

Ace waved a stub of bacon in the air as he held forth. "Thing is, you can make it better. Last one I had, she was slobberin' and beggin'. Now that's when it's good, when you've got her broken like a whipped dog."

Wilson tilted his head and gave a narrow, sideways glance. "You know, you've got a low-class way about you."

"Call it that if you want." Ace took a drink of whiskey. "But maybe you don't know how much the old devil rises up in a man and makes him throb till he thinks he's gonna split."

"You talk too much."

"Aw, hell," he said, with a backward wave of his free hand. "Maybe all you've ever done is pay for it. But if you just take it, get that woman broken, the whole pleasure runs a lot deeper."

"Ah, shut up."

"No, I mean it. When you get 'em whipped so—"

His words were cut off by a blast of gunfire, piercing loud in the close space of the cabin. Ace fell back, the chair skidding out from under him as he glanced off the corner of the stove and sprawled on the floor with the woolen undershirt still in his lap.

The man in gray jumped. Reaching for the skillet to get it centered on the stove again he turned to look at Wilson. His gun was still pointed at the man on the floor.

"No need to get shook up," said the gunman. "There's a reward for this fella, so he was gonna get it sooner or later. Just came sooner, from not knowin' when to shut up." Wilson had his eyebrows lifted as he surveyed the dead man. "Let's get that gun out of his holster—no, I'll do it. Just stand by for a minute." He stood up from his chair, slipped his dark-handled six-gun into his holster, and bent forward to reach for the ivory grip on Ace Perkins's pistol.

In that instant, with a backhand swing of his left hand, the man at the stove swung the skillet and flung the hot grease and bacon pieces in Wilson's face. As the gunman rose, took a staggering step backward, and clawed for his gun, the man in gray drew his own pistol and shot Wilson twice in the chest.

The tall-crowned black hat went flying, and the man's arms flailed as he spilled over backward.

With his pistol still drawn, the man in gray walked around the other side of the table, avoiding the knocked-over chairs and sprawled bodies. He stood above Wilson, whose fresh-blistered face, framed by the shock of hair the color of corn stalks, was motionless. His thin lips pressed together with a seam of blood.

"Stook Wilson," said the man holding the gun. "I don't know if you can hear this, but it does me good to say it. My name isn't what I said it was. It's actually Hapgood. Maybe that name rings a bell with you."

The man in the double-caped coat stood in silhouette, holding the reins of his saddled horse as the flames from the cabin lit up the night. When the first section of the roof fell in, he moved to each of the other two horses, which had pulled back to the ends of their pickets, and he untied them. Their hoofbeats died away as they headed for the open range. A soft thud sounded from the cabin as another rafter fell in, sending a shower of sparks upward. The man turned his horse so that the saddle leather shone in the firelight. He put his foot in the stirrup, swung aboard, and rode away.

Stoneman's Bluff frowned in the shadows of early afternoon as the man in gray turned off the trail and rode up to the hitching rail in front of the way station.

Old Harry Dean appeared in the doorway, again in his dark knitted cap and canvas coat. "Oh, it's you," he called out.

"It sure is." The rider swung down and tied his horse.

"What did you find out?"

"Not much. It's too early to get work."

"That's all you were lookin' for, huh?"

"Look for more, you look for trouble."

"Isn't that the truth? But I was hopin' you were lookin' for Ace Perkins. Too bad you didn't come back with him tied across a saddle." The old man shook his head. "Someone ought to take him down, and there's a good reward for the man that does it."

"Well, maybe so, but not me. I wouldn't kill for money, and I'm glad I'm not in that line of work."

"You gotta be good at it." The old man doubled his fist and gave it a quick shake at chest height, and his watery blue eyes flashed.

"Yeah, and even men who think they're good at it get tripped up. Maybe some of 'em live to an old age and die in their bed, but I'd guess even they have to be lookin' over their shoulder. As for the others, they might do well to remember that the more men they kill, the better the chance is that one of 'em's got a brother or some other kin that might come callin' some day. Nah, I'm glad I'm not in the business."

"Can't argue with you on that." The old man motioned with his head. "I've got some coffee goin'. Come on in and chin for a little while, Cooper."

"I guess I can. By the way, you can just call me Hap."

Gunfighter's Lament

Ellen Recknor

My name is Southgate, Annie Southgate, and I admit that as the aforementioned Annie Southgate, I have killed sixteen men that I know of. Some say it was because my daddy beat me with a razor strap. Some say it was because my mama coddled me too much, or whupped me too much, or didn't pay enough attention.

But none of that was what set me on a life of crime. What is true was that my folks both died—it was Apache what done it—when I was a little girl. They got Daddy when he was out working his traps line, and they got Mama a year after, when she was out front hangin' clothes on the wash line.

I guess to Apache, winter brings the fun of killing.

Anyhow, my folks didn't have nothing to do with the way I turned out. If a person was looking to lay blame, maybe they could blame it on the Apache, who came into the house after they killed my Ma and raped my big sister, Kelly. Most all of them. And then they killed her. I was hiding in the closet under the floorboards at Kelly's orders, and they left without finding me. I was only seven, so I was pretty little and hard to find, but also pretty little to be the one to bury my mama and my only sister, too.

It was more than a year before anybody found me. I was outside, weeding the daisies growing on Mama and Kelly's graves, when the Reverend Ezra Whittle came riding up on that chestnut Walking Horse he'd brought all the way from Tennessee. He nigh on had himself a fit because I was so ragged and grimy—until I got chance to get a word or three in edgewise, and told him he was standing on Mama's legs and that Kelly lay beneath the ground right beside her.

Then he hopped off the grave and he listened, all right. He listened good. Then he had me go through the house and pick out what few things mattered most to me while he got our family Bible and Mama's treasure box and some things that had belonged to Daddy, and said a few words over the graves.

I had kept our horse Fiddler alive (although I had killed and eaten every chicken on the place) and when I showed up on the front porch again, flour sack packed full in my arms, Fiddler was saddled and ready to go.

I was impressed that the Reverend was so tall. I had not been able to reach Fiddler's saddle on the rack, let alone get it down, nor brush him much higher that his elbows without standing on a bucket. That was something that Daddy was death on—brushing your horse and keeping him groomed real good. When Daddy said something, I always paid attention.

"I will see to his hooves when I get you back home, Annie," Reverend Whittle said as he boosted me up into the saddle. "They are a holy terror."

And that was that.

I guess I made up my mind to run off from the Reverend Whittle—and his wife and his thirteen kids—when I was about ten. I didn't have a chance till I was close to fourteen, though. That was when a wagon train came through town on its way to Arizona. I had heard nice things about Arizona—except for the Apache part, that is—but I figured to be able to evade them. I'd done it once before, hadn't I?

The night before the wagon train was to set on its way again, I snuck out of the Reverend's house at about three in the morning, crawled up under a wagon, roped myself and my meager possessions to the underside, and waited. I must have fallen asleep, because when I woke, we were far out of town and on our way west.

Now, whoever their wagonmaster was, he was sure not a good one, because he had chosen the old Ox-Bow route to travel over. About an hour or so after I figured we had crossed the New Mexico-Arizona border, the Apache attacked us. They circled the wagons while I hung on for dear life on the underside of mine. After a long while of shooting and arrows flying and spears splitting boards—and a few skulls, I bet—those wagon people had cut the Apache numbers down to what must have been a perilous point, because they retreated. The Apache, I mean. What was left of them rode off to the south.

Those pioneers did the smart thing. They gathered up their dead and loaded them into their wagons and took off for the west lickety-split, and didn't stop until nightfall.

I was getting awful hungry, so while they buried their dead, I helped myself to somebody's food stores and thieved some jerked beef and part of an old loaf of bread. It didn't taste like much, but it was filling. I also helped myself to somebody's old Navy pistol, which I concealed in my clothing before I roped myself back up into place. I guess that was what started me on a life of crime—stealing that food and that Colt Navy—but some things just happen.

A few more days of stealing food and hiding and trying to sleep under that damned wagon—and no more Indian attacks, praise the Lord (like The Reverend used to say every five minutes)—we pulled into Tucson. The first chance I got, I was free of that wagon undercarriage and on the streets. Well, what passed for streets in Tucson. It was a dirty town any way you looked at it. There were dead animals left to rot in the roads and left-to-melt adobe walls and buildings, and painted-up saloon girls and tame Indians by the score.

I had swiped a twenty-dollar gold piece one night during a thieving soiree, and checked myself into the Cactus Wren, which was a newer hotel farther into town. They looked at me funny, being only a girl of not-quite fourteen, not yet five feet tall, all by my lonesome, and with a twenty dollar gold piece to pay for my bill. But I guess the money spoke louder than my age and they gave me a room. I have to say that they had awful nice beds there, and I must've slept about sixteen hours straight.

I do not recommend the underside of a Conestoga as a good place to sleep unless you are desperate, like I was.

I will spare you the travel up north and the arranging of it, but rest assured that I found myself transport and ended up just south of Phoenix in a little town that had just got the name of Tempe. It was chock-full of Mexicans, and had been called Santa Rosa before some fool—who I later found out was that English meddler, Lord Darrell Duppa—changed its moniker during a drunken fit of poetics.

I lived there for the next few years—until I was seventeen, anyhow—until the killing of Xavier Tortuga sort of forced me into moving. Xavier was a bad man, who had raped at least three of the Mexican ladies there in town, but whom the law could never get enough evidence to take to trial. Me, I think it was because the ladies were Mexican and the law was white, but I don't want to pass any judgments.

Anyhow, I was seventeen, like I said. It was January, and I was on my way to work. I had a pretty nice singing voice even back then, and I had got myself a job singing at one of the saloons in town—the only one that didn't expect me to do anything except sing, that was. I was just crossing Main Street and had got onto the sidewalk, when somebody grabbed me and jerked me into an alley.

That somebody was Xavier Tortuga.

I knew what he was up to right then, because he started right into ripping at my skirts. But he didn't know—most folks didn't—that I had got into the practice of carrying my gun. I had traded the Colt Navy and some cash for a Peacemaker somewhere along the line. It was in the waistband of my skirt, hidden by the short jackets I wore in wintertime.

I pulled that gun without thinking twice and shot him right up close, in the heart. He stood there, hanging on to me, for maybe two seconds before the life went out of his eyes and he dropped like a stone.

I jumped back. I didn't know what to do. He was the first man I had ever killed, and it scared me to death no matter how much he deserved it.

I must have stood there over the body for maybe

five minutes, until I realized that there was no one on the street, and that the gun, being so close between us when it went off, had been muffled. Taking that for a sign from God, I shoved my Peacemaker back in my waistband, tugged my jacket closed over it, and went on my way like nothing had happened.

I sang my heart out that evening, and cried real tears whenever I had a chance, like during "Bury Me Next to My Mama" and "The Gunfighter's Lament." Believe it or not, I was still pretty teary by the time I returned home, but I had got over it by the next day. They had found Xavier's body by then, and were questioning folks right and left and calling it murder.

I decided it might be the time to leave town.

At the saloon the other night, I had heard some fellas talking about their coming trip up to Prescott, and how they wished one of them knew which side of a skillet to use. I took that to mean that they wanted somebody who could cook, so I took it upon myself to find one of those fellas and see if I filled the bill.

After two hours of looking, I found one—a tall, good lookin', salt and pepper haired, weather-beaten man who told me his name was Chic Peters. I'd be welcome to come with them if I made him some dinner and it passed his test.

The test cost me a chicken—which I bought from the bartender, but I cooked it and some canned butter beans and mashed a potato and baked up some biscuits in the saloon's little kitchen, and Chic

Peters said I'd do fine. They were leaving in the morning, so that didn't leave me much time for saying farewell to the boardinghouse and the saloon, and getting myself to the livery to buy a horse.

I never did find one as good as I remembered old Fiddler to be, but I did find a nice bay gelding I thought would do. He was called Pepper. I guess when he was a foal somebody thought he was going to gray out, but he didn't. He already knew his name, so I let it be.

We left the next morning real early, and Chic had all the supplies he promised, packed onto a mule. The mule was called Rastus, and he was pretty nice for a mule. Meaning that he didn't kick or bite me, or stop all of a sudden and jerk me off Pepper.

I had bought denim pants and a shirt and a holster the night before, and rode with my Peacemaker in the holster, not hid by anything, so everybody was real nice to me and did not try anything bad all the way to Prescott. They also liked my cooking a lot, and asked if I'd like to go with them when they went on up to Flagstaff, which they called Flag. I said to contact me when they were ready, as I might admire to, depending.

Two nights later I was ready to go. While I was singing on the stage at the Glory Hole Saloon on Whiskey Row, minding my own business even though they had an awful bad piano player, some stupid, drunk cowboy started taking potshots at me.

I stopped singing and hollered at him to stop,

but he just wouldn't listen. Some people are like that. So I pulled up the side of my skirt, and while the men were catcalling and whistling, I drew my Peacemaker and shot him dead, in the heart.

Some people have said that I was a bloodthirsty woman, always going for the heart, but to my mind if you want to stop a body the best place to aim for is smack in the middle. I can't help it if my gun shot just a tad to the one side, can I?

Anyhow, Chic came to see me the next day, by which I mean he came to the jail. Yes, they had thrown me in, and were going to take me to trial! I told Chic what had happened, and that very night he and his boys came and busted me out using a crowbar and some ropes tied to the pried-loose bars. Oh, it was quite the deal, all right!

We rode off into the night, and I later found that Chic had not only got my horse from the livery and all my things from the hotel, he had brought the pack mule, freshly supplied with a new load.

I guess it was in the next day or so that Chic told me what they really did. They robbed banks, sometimes people, if they were rich enough. If the people were rich, I mean, not Chic. And they had just robbed the bank in Prescott that evening, before they broke me out. They said I could keep riding with them as long as I liked. Boy, I made them a good supper that night!

* * *

Well, I rode with Chic for quite a while. First, they made me stay outside of the town they were hitting until they came thundering back, and I'd have to jump on Pepper, have Rastus all packed and ready to go, and light out in a hurry. But later, they let me start going with them. My job was to guard the horses while they were inside. I never shot anybody else until they hit the First Bank of Strawberry—which was the only bank in Strawberry. Somehow, they knew we were coming, and three men with rifles started coming toward me and ordered me to throw down my arms and give up! Well, I couldn't do that, could I?

I pulled my Peacemaker and shot all three of them dead about the same time that Chic and the others came running from the bank, all of them firing in all directions. I hopped up on Pepper real fast, as you can well imagine, and set the spurs into him. I fired again on my way out of town and my target fell down, although I don't count him in my total. One of Chic's men was shooting at him, too, and he may have hit home.

So that brought my total up to five.

All in all, during the time I was with Chic, I shot and killed fifteen men—adding in the first one in Tempe, but not counting that one fella at Strawberry. I figured the Reverend Whittle would say I was hell-bound for certain-sure, although I have to say it was partly his fault, on account of him teaching me how to use a gun. I suppose he meant it to be protection from Indians or rattlesnakes or something. But all those cans I shot up while I was with him taught me the skills to kill.

Do I hear an Amen?

I have said that I killed sixteen men during my career as Annie Southgate—two of them Indians—and now I will tell you about the last one, the one that led to my downfall.

Tired of killing and robbing, I left Chic. We parted on good terms, and his men—what were left of them—were sad to see me go. Three of them said they would never again have such a fine cook, and two of them cried.

It was real touching.

But I settled in Promise, Arizona Territory, anyhow. I bought a little house on the edge of town that had an acre of pasture and a little barn for Pepper, and settled in to live on my share of the ill-gotten gains. It was nice for a while. Nice to not always be patching up wounds, not to hear the screams of men or the gunfire that went along with it.

I got to be good friends with my closest neighbors, the Bests, and especially with their kids, Becky and Bobbie. They showed me how good it was to have parents your whole life. Well, as much of it as they'd lived so far, anyhow. Becky used to come see me after school and we'd talk and talk, and Bobbie used to take care of Pepper for me, grooming him and turning him in and out and such.

They were good kids.

I ended up telling Becky some about my past,

although not all of it. But then, kids being kids, she told Bobbie. He put two and two together and figured me out to be Annie Southgate, not Anne Gately, like I had been using in town. He never said a word to me, though, until his daddy, who was President of the First Bank of Promise, had been taken hostage by the Tomkins gang.

They had promised to kill him, then the wife, and then the kids, if he didn't agree to hand over the big shipment of gold that had just come in from the mines, on its way to Denver. Oh, and whatever other cash they had on hand, too.

They had delivered a note to that effect to the Best family, and let me tell you, they were scared as scared could be. Becky brought it over for me to read and it spooked me, too, though mainly that Tibor Tomkins couldn't spell worth spit. I was kinda mad that they were trying to hit the bank that had my money in it, too, to tell the truth.

I was sitting on my front swing, listening to Becky Best cry over her poor Daddy and ask me over and over again what were they gonna do. Well, hell, I didn't know. I had never met Tibor Tomkins, only knew him by reputation. But nobody had ever mentioned that he was a crack shot, not once—which kind of gave me hope.

I asked Becky, "Who is Tibor Tomkins runnin' with these days? Anybody I would've heard tell of?"

She rattled off three names I didn't know, although that didn't mean much. Back then, some men—even drifters on the up and up—changed names like they changed underwear. For all I knew, he could have been riding with the James gang, if Jesse hadn't gone and got himself killed by that coward, Bob Ford.

But Jesse was deader than a swamp log, so I was stuck with just knowing it was Tibor Tomkins and three others.

A while after Becky left, her brother came knocking at my door. Right out, he said, "Miss Gately, I know you are Annie Southgate."

"Congratulations, Bobbie," I said. "Would you care to step in for some lemonade?" Once he got in and got sat, I told him his sister had been to see me not two hours before and told me the situation. "What can I do, Bobbie?" I asked, throwing up my hands. "I thought about riding in there like Banker Jones, like I was delivering the money, but Banker Jones is more than six feet tall and I am five-foot-one. They would know me for a ringer before I even got fifty feet from them."

Bobbie stared at the floor for a minute. "You're right. And you couldn't go in as a woman. They'd know that Jones would never send a woman to do a man's job." He sighed, and there was more pain in that heave of air than in any I'd ever heard. And I've heard quite a few.

Suddenly he brightened. "Wilmer Fordham, the teller, is short. Mama said once that she'd bet her buttons he didn't make five-foot-one!"

And just like that, I was in it again. Not that I didn't want to help the Best family, mind you. They were real good neighbors, and Roberta, Becky and Bobbie's mama, always pressed fresh produce on me in season, saying she had grown too many beans or ears of sweet corn or cabbages or such. Richard Best, their daddy, was always real polite to me. Tipped his hat on the street and everything. When half my fence fell down after that bad dust storm we had last summer, he and Bobbie came over without being asked and fixed it up for me.

I owed them. I don't know that I owed them my life—which I figured that Tibor would most likely take the same way as another man would swipe an apple from the front of the grocer's—but I owed them something. And well, I was pushing thirty at the time and figured my life, the good part, anyway, was just about done with and over.

So without further thought, I said, "All right, Bobbie. I'll meet with Banker Jones and Wilmer Fordham. Don't worry your head anymore, and tell your mama and Becky that everything's going to be all right." I hoped I sounded more sure than I felt.

I must have, because a giant smile spread across Bobbie's face, and he fairly leaped out of his chair and hugged me tight. And then he was off, running for home. To tell his mama the soothing news, I guess.

Me, I clapped my bonnet on my head, closed the door behind me, and headed for the bank.

* * *

Much to my frazzlement, both Banker Jones and Teller Fordham were in, and they met with me in Banker Jones's office. It was real embarrassing, 'fessing up to them that I was the infamous Annie Southgate, but even harder getting them to believe it. I finally had to sever three do-bobs off the Banker's crystal desk lamp—from across the room—before they finally accepted me for who I really was. Of course, then came the promising that they wouldn't tell the sheriff—or anybody else for that matter—the facts of the situation. That was even harder, but I think I got them convinced.

Anyway, this was the deal: I (pretending to be Wilmer) was to ride out to the old Laughlin place with a sack full of money. I was to stop in front of the cabin, get off my horse, ground-tie him, and wait for somebody to come out. Three other men would be waiting in the cabin, along with Banker Best, to shoot me if I tried anything funny. I thought about doing a soft-shoe, but decided against telling anybody. Banker Jones already looked scared enough to stick his head in his desk drawer and slam it shut, anyhow. Wilmer mostly looked relieved.

When the day came. I borrowed one of Wilmer's suits and stuffed out my belly with feather pillows. I took a big sack stuffed mostly with newspaper with a little real currency on top, to fool a quick look, and I started out for the Laughlin place, riding his horse in case the thieves knew which one was his.

Nobody had lived there for at least ten years or so, so the place was kind of beat up. The sun takes its toll down here in Arizona. But I did as I was directed, and rode up in front of that cabin, got off my horse, and just stood there with the sack.

I had been thinking over the past few days what a clod old Tibor must be, if he couldn't hold up a piddlin' little bank with three men and the element of surprise on his side. Been thinking on that a lot.

I'd also been thinking about where to hide my firearm. Make that firearm*s*. I couldn't count on him to do anything a certain way, or even to act like he had a brain in his head, that's how impressed I was with Mr. Tibor Tomkins.

So anyhow, there I was, standing outside, but nobody came out. Making my voice as low and heavy as I could, I called, "Tomkins! You in there? It's Wilmer Fordham!"

No answer.

Of all the things I had been expecting, this hadn't been one of them. I was just plain stumped. I stood there a minute longer, and then I decided to try the lean-to over by the falling-down horse barn.

Nothing there, either.

I looked in the horse barn, just in case, but there weren't any people there. Just tracks and prints where horses had been tethered. And tracks going out the back door. There were none fresher coming in, so I figured Tibor Tomkins and his boys had skedaddled. But why would they leave before getting their ransom? Had Banker Best killed himself, or been murdered?

Figuring that Tibor Tomkins wasn't the type of man to actually dig a grave, I walked back to the cabin, hollering every once in a while for somebody to answer me. When I got there, all the curtains were pulled tight. I slid a hand into my pants pocket, where I'd hid a derringer, and tapped at the door. Then I knocked. Then I pounded. And I finally shoved open the door, which wasn't much effort since the leather hinges had long since rotted.

There sat Banker Best, bound, gagged, and tied to a kitchen chair. Across the room from him sat Tibor Tomkins, in exactly the same position and circumstance, except that somebody had knocked him out cold.

It was a head-scratcher, let me tell you.

Since Banker Best was trying to say something through his gag and squirming like a cat in a sack, I decided to untie him first.

The first thing he said, once I got the gag off, was, "Why, you're not Wilmer!" Then he squinted at me and said, "Is that Anne Gately under that dirty face?"

"It's meant to look like chin stubble, not dirt," I remarked as I freed his hands, then his feet. He rubbed his wrists, then his ankles.

I went over to start untying Tibor Tomkins, but Banker Best said, "Wait, Anne. Let me think this over."

I let him think for about five whole minutes

before he asked, "Is anyone with you, or did you come alone?"

When I said I was alone, he asked if I'd brought an extra horse. I said no.

He asked if I'd brought the money, and I smiled and said, "'Course not."

I thought that would make him happy, but he swore under his breath! All of a sudden, something went *click* in me. He was up to no good! My steadfast, hat-tipping neighbor had gone bad, badder even than I was, because he was robbing his friends and neighbors and those folks that respected and trusted him, while I had just stolen from complete strangers. Well, that's how I saw it, anyway.

Plus which, he had just reached behind him to the tabletop, and brought out a big Smith and Wesson pistol.

Before I got the gag off Tibor, Banker Best said, "Stop right there." I did, and tried to make a quick play for my derringer, but he'd seen me shove it in my pocket and told me to hold, and take it out real slow. I pushed it across the floor to him and he laughed.

"Who do you think you are, coming out here with such a dinky little pistol? Calamity Jane? Belle Starr? Annie Southgate?" And he laughed even bigger than before.

He was really beginning to piss me off.

I climbed up to my feet and demanded, "And just who the hell do you think *you* are? What were you plannin' on doin' with that bank money, anyway? Move your family back east, buy a big house, and send Bobby to Harvard? I doubt it."

He kept smiling. "You're correct to doubt my motives, Anne. Not that you have any business thinking about them at all. Especially for one who has such a short time to live."

I must have furrowed my brow or something, because he went on, "Why'd Jones and Wilmer pick you to come out here, anyway? What makes you so special?"

I said, "Your kids came cryin' to me. I volunteered."

"My kids? Why would my kids come to *you*?"

"I don't know," I said, my hand inching toward my jacket pocket. "They just did, you old warthog." I leaned in toward him, and his eyes got kind of big around at the warthog thing. "Furthermore, I think it's a lousy kind of pa what wants to cheat his own kids out of what he thieves!"

And BLAM! I fired my Peacemaker right through the pocket of Wilmer's suit and shot Richard Best in the heart. Like usual.

And he died. Also like usual.

Did I feel bad? No, sir, and no, ma'am. I felt kind of . . . justified.

Anyhow, it was a real pain getting them both back to town—Best, tied over my saddle, and me leading Tibor on the end of a rope—but I did it without once thinking about what Tibor knew. When we were standing in front of the jail, and Tibor got this kind of nasty grin on his face, I said quick and low, "You got any ideas 'bout springin' a little surprise on the sheriff 'bout me or anything else, your days are numbered. And they don't get up onto the double digits, either. Remember that."

He blinked and swallowed, and I knew I had him buffaloed.

I told you this story for a reason. The part about when I was a kid wasn't needed, but I figure that authors get to grandstand a little, right? And I thought it was interesting. But what I wanted you to know was that you should never do nobody a favor. Not ever.

Right after I dropped Tibor and the money sack at the jail, and Banker Best at the undertakers, I went on to the Best's house to tell them about their husband and daddy's untimely demise. Mrs. Best (who I had spoke to last, and at length, so she could chose when and if—and what—to tell the kids) then marched her fanny down to the jail and turned me in for being Annie Southgate, and blabbed her husband's whole bank caper plan out to the sheriff.

Talk about stupid—both her and me!

I made it out of town about two steps ahead of the posse—me and Pepper and a bundle of clothes and food. After around three or four weeks, I found Chic Peters again, and started riding with him once more. Me and Chic got married and had three kids, two boys and a girl, with the boys as bookends and little Annie smack dab in the center.

We kept up robbin' until it got too complicated, and then we went straight. I ain't gonna tell you where we live, that'd be too much like Mrs. Best, but I'll say that Chic has done real good in business, the kids are almost all the way through school, and I haven't picked up a handgun for near ten years. Don't ever want to pick one up again, either.

And don't ask me about body counts for Annie Peters. Some things, a lady doesn't tell.

Shootout at White Pass

John Jakes

He came suddenly, wrenchingly out of the dream. *Oh God it's cold.*

His bare feet stuck from under the comforter, which had pulled out while he slept. Two woolen blankets on top of the comforter, and his nightshirt on top of his union suit with its whiff of mothballs, and he still woke with rattling teeth and shivering shanks. *God God it's cold.* But then it was always cold in White Pass, except in high summer.

Why do I stay here?

Because he was sheriff. Because he didn't have any other place to go.

No, wrong. There was a place. But not, somehow, the energy to reach it. He always blamed it on his age. He'd be forty-six, next birthday.

He put his bare feet on the old crocheted rug beside the bed. His tin-plated clock showed half past six. He shuddered going to the window, where he lifted the blind and gazed with despair on the frozen mud and dirty snow piles along the main street. Above the false fronts and shoddy cottages of the town, the Sierra ramparts looked down, heartless as gravestones, and just as cold.

Downstairs, he heard loud, excited voices. An ore wagon creaked past in the street, traces jingling in the frosty air. It had snowed night before last. A howler of a storm, a foot or more dumped on the trails and high passes. He stood scratching his paunch, which had lately grown till it was impossible to ignore, and wondered about the hurrah below. Sure didn't sound like the normal conversation of the snatch-and-grab breakfast table.

The drab furnished room depressed him unbearably. He sat on the edge of the bed, arms crossed, hands tucked in his armpits, and hung his head. He'd been having a dream, all about home.

In the dream, the sky was cloudless and hot. The sea grape and palmetto stirred gently in the noon breeze. Little nervous sandpipers scurried up and down the sand, and hungry gray pelicans soared and dove for prey, splashing the bright smooth water of the Gulf into the air like flung sapphires. Sitting here, growing old in White Pass, he could feel the blessed heat of the Florida sun.

He thought about his boyhood and young manhood as he pulled on his worn pants and plaid shirt. He thought of picking up great clattery handfuls of shells on the beaches, and putting them in jars just because they were pretty. He thought of crabbing from an old skiff in Red Fish Pass, between two of the long narrow coastal keys. He'd had a decent enough business, clerking in the mercantile with the prospect of buying it when the owner gave it up. Why had he left? Why had he left the sunshine and slogged all the way out here to this?

With a curious look of contempt on his face, he touched the reason. A clipping from an Atlanta newspaper, years old, crackly and yellow. It was part of an article about Mr. Horace Greeley of the *New York Tribune.* He had underlined the famous charge of the journalist. *Go west, young man, and grow up with the country.*

He was over thirty when he married. He'd courted Marthe Schiller, the teacher at a one-room schoolhouse in Hillsborough County, south of Tampa. Marthe was a sturdy, square-jawed woman of German descent, with eyes as blue as the Florida heavens; they relieved the severity of her face. He first admired Marthe because of her book-learning; he was poorly educated, leaving school eagerly at age ten. When love came, it came quickly, completely, generously: he wanted to find a much better existence for them. Although Florida was home, life there was a hardscrabble existence, in a beautiful but poor place to which man had added exactly nothing except towns that seemed to consist mostly of windowless shanties, impoverished farms populated by scrawny red cows, and the sad-eyed black folks who seemed all but abandoned by the world in the hovels you found at the end of nearly every sandy track into the scrub; abandoned, that is, until there was a need for bending the back in the pitiless sun doing work even the dirtiest, most ignorant white cracker wouldn't touch. That was the real Florida if you looked at it with clear vision.

Greeley's charge inspired him. It was inspiring a lot of Americans, single and married. He and his wife of one year set out for California. Eleven months later, marooned in White Pass by another snowstorm, Marthe died of influenza. That was nine years ago. He was still here. Longing for Florida and somehow incapable of going back.

Maybe it was the responsibility. The job. Which he cared for as little as he cared for the town. He picked up the yellow metal star with the word Sheriff stamped in, and pinned it on his plaid shirt with a little puff of his lips, as though he' d just tasted something bad.

He walked downstairs and turned into the dining room, where the Widow Thome's three other boarders of the moment were already ravaging the plates of eggs, thick tough sowbelly slabs, fresh baking powder biscuits.

"Morning, Lou," said Bill Toombs, the recent widower who ran the hardware.

"Morning, Sheriff," said a man who stopped for a night every month or so; a drummer with a handlebar mustache and showy Burnside whiskers.

Lou Hand greeted both of them, then the thirteen-year-old boy, Will Pertwee, who sat at the end of the table, watching him with a peculiar intensity.

"Sheriff, did you hear?" Will asked. He was a shock-haired kid; an orphan. Jesse gave him room and board in exchange for his work around the place.

The door to the kitchen opened. Jesse Thome looked in, rosy-faced in the heat rolling out in blessed waves from the unseen stove. "More coffee here? Why, good morning, Lou. Sleep well?"

"No, I nearly froze. I'm getting old, Jesse. Blood's too thin."

"If you got thin blood, a place at this altitude ain't no good," announced the drummer.

Lou shot him a look as if to say, Tell me something I've not heard before.

Will Pertwee was practically jumping out of his chair. "Sheriff, did you hear, or didn't you?"

"Hear what?"

"About the gent who came to town last night. Walked in 'cause he had to shoot his horse up at Five Mile Wash. It's Bob Siringo."

Bill Toombs was watching him, resting his fork in the gooey yellow residue of his eggs. The widow Thome looked stricken, noticeably pale; even women knew the name of the notorious gunman who had been through trials for murder at least four times, had done a stretch in Nevada Territorial

Prison, and was said to have done away with up to a dozen enemies.

"How do you know it's Bob Siringo?" Lou Hand said with a deadly heaviness filling his belly, where only a moment before there had been the first pleasurable and diffused warmth produced by Jesse's strong coffee.

"Well, I don't," Will said with a grin, as if he knew very well what the whole conversation implied for Lou. "But he sure looks like Bob Siringo. I mean, he's a ringer for that drawing on the dodger hanging in your office."

Lou swallowed. "And where is the man?"

"Staying at the Congress Hotel." Will Pertwee leaned so far forward, his chin nearly upset his glass of buttermilk. "Guess you'll have to look him up and see he behaves, huh?"

"Not necessarily," Lou said. "Not if he is behaving." It came to him that, in his customary fashion, he'd left his .44-40 Frontier Model Colt and gunbelt hanging on the bedpost, where he always kept them. That was his morning routine, to walk downstairs for breakfast without the gun. Other times, it was of no importance. This morning the absence of the familiar pressure against his thigh seemed of keen, even dangerous significance.

Jesse Thome gave him a long, quizzical look. She was a heavy, handsome woman, ten years younger, with red-gold hair and large slightly tilted gray eyes. She had a soft, billowy breast; Lou had always fancied the buxom kind.

Jesse was self-educated, and religious in a quiet way. She read the Bible every evening before she retired, but he hadn't learned this until they'd been acquainted for over a year. She wasn't prudish, though. She loved to dance, and play cards, and mix up a rum toddy on cold nights. She didn't belong to a regular church, no doubt because they'd have scorned her, and her habits, as unchristian.

Lou and Jesse often shared cups of hot tea of an evening, when White Pass was quiet—as it usually was—and they enjoyed playing hands of rummy once or twice a week. In the all too short season of warmth, they walked in the high meadows and occasionally had a picnic supper on a Sunday evening. Now Jesse gave him that long, level look full of anxious concern. "Lou, could I see you privately a moment?"

With a nervous, unconscious brush at the lock of oiled hair carefully curled over his forehead in the fashionable mode, Lou exchanged the table for the hot haven of the kitchen. There he was warm, actually warm, for the first time since arising. The kitchen, old but spacious, smelled of flour, and skillet grease, and all the good odors of the best part of a home.

"Do you think it's really Bob Siringo?"

"I don't know, Jesse."

"If it is, will he cause trouble?"

"Don't see why he should. Maybe he's simply passing through."

"Won't you have to find out? Talk to him?"

"Not unless he causes a ruckus. The morning will tell, I imagine."

"Well, I just wanted to say"—she cleared her throat while avoiding his eye—"you're my dear friend, and a good sheriff. I wouldn't want anything to happen to you."

"Oh, I don't think it will." It was a hope, not a certainty. He was frightened. After Marthe died, his ambition for heading on down to California had died too, and in those first dull-headed, glaze-eyed weeks after his wife's burial, he'd accepted the offer of old Sheriff Jeffords, who needed a deputy because his previous one, Neddy Wattle, had died. In bed. Of old age.

"Little or no crime in White Pass. Never has been," old Jeffords assured him. Truthfully. After Jeffords died of a stroke three years ago, Lou Hand didn't think very long about the town council's offer of a promotion.

Over and above his experience, one work-related incident of heroism made Lou Hand the logical candidate. While Lou was a deputy, a jobless man named Jocko Brust had held up the now-defunct Merchants and Miners Bank of White Pass. Chancing to walk by at the precise moment, Lou Hand heard screams inside, then saw the culprit come backing out the door wearing a bandanna up to the bridge of his nose, as if that would possibly conceal his identity from anyone who knew him.

It was a sunny spring day, full of hope and the gurgle of melting snow; the time of year when some men left their wives or hung themselves. Lou was in fine spirits, however, and he jumped Jocko without thought. Jocko shot him, a grazing shoulder wound. The bank manager ran out with a heavy cuspidor and nearly beat out Jocko's brains, leaving him bleeding and washed with tobacco-colored water.

People hailed Deputy Hand as a hero. Pastor Humphreys lauded him from the pulpit of the Methodist chapel (he was told). Lou Hand had nightmares for months after, realizing what could have happened if the bullet had traveled a little more to thc lcft.

Still, he didn't deliberate long before he accepted the council's offer and put on the sheriff's star. The incident of Jocko Brust (he went to prison) was unusual, not to say unique, for White Pass. Never once in all his years as deputy had Lou Hand fired his pistol in anger, and he'd only drawn it half a dozen times, to cow noisy but harmless Saturday-night drunks. The same proved the case during his tenure as sheriff.

But now someone purporting to be the notorious Bob Siringo was staying at the Congress.

"You'll be careful," Jesse said. "I wouldn't want to lose my boarder and card-playing companion . . ."

The words trailed off, and Jesse impulsively touched his sleeve. Lou rested his hand on hers and gazed into her eyes, realizing again how much he cared for her. That affection had grown almost unconsciously over the months and years he'd lived under her roof. He wanted to say something to her . . . something meaningful and important. The desire had come on him several times before, usually in the evening, by lamplight. But he was a shy man. Told himself there was always another time. Plenty of time . . .

The kitchen door banged open and Will Pertwee jumped through. "Say, that drummer's hollering for more flapjack syrup, Mrs. Thome."

"All right, tell him to keep his britches on." She reached for the crockery pitcher while Will danced past her, fairly jigging on the old linoleum in front of Lou Hand.

"You going after Bob Siringo, Sheriff?"

"Not unless he gives me cause."

"But outlaws, gunfighters, they always do, don't they? That's why they're outlaws."

He couldn't refute Will's bloodthirsty logic. It angered him. He grabbed Will's shoulder and shoved him aside so hard, the boy exclaimed, "Ow!" Jesse gave him a startled, alarmed look as she prepared to take the full pitcher of syrup to the dining room.

Lou tramped through the dining room and up the stairs, strange leaden pains deviling his belly all of a sudden. Though fully dressed, he was freezing. On the stair landing he paused by the lace-curtained window and stared at the vista of the Sierras with the sun above their icy peaks. The sun was a pale yellow-white disk, clearly visible in blowing misty clouds. *Wish I could shoot down that sun,* he thought. *Shoot it down here for some warmth.*

Or go back to Florida. Why didn't I have the gumption? There were so many mornings I could have turned in the star and said, "That's it, I resign." Any morning up till this one . . .

He trudged on up the stairs. He hauled his gun-belt off the bedpost and cinched it around his expanding middle. He resettled the Frontier Colt in the holster, and as he did so his eye grazed the yellowed news clip with the admonition from Mr. Greeley. Lou Hand made a face. "You damn fool," he said.

He walked past the Congress Hotel, but on the opposite side of Sierra Street. He saw nothing more alarming than Regis, the colored porter, emptying last night's slopjars in the street.

White Pass smelled of woodsmoke this morning, and horse turds in the street, and the cold-metal stink of deep winter through your half-stuffed nose. Lou Hand shivered and stuck his gloved hands deep in the pockets of his sheep-lined coat. Under the slanted brim of his flat hat, he saw the main drag of White Pass for what it was: a pitiful excuse for a town. It was a way-station on the California stage route—one through coach a day, each way, when the passes were open—but the mines in the neighborhood didn't produce much ore any more. The White Pass Reduction Mill filled the morning with a slow *chump-chunk* that had a lugubrious rhythm of failure about it.

Reaching his one-story office on the corner opposite Levering's Apothecary (CLOSED PERMANENTLY said the crude paper sign in the window), Lou Hand drew the door key from his pocket. When he put it in the lock, the door swung in. Lou felt his heartbeat skip.

"Come on in, it's me," said a voice he recognized. Then Lou Hand smelled the vile stink of his caller's green-wrapped nickel cigars. The visitor was installed behind Lou Hand's desk, his tooled boots resting up on the blotter. "I let myself in with the council's key."

"Perfectly all right, Mr. Mayor," Lou Hand said, shutting the door and shucking out of coat and hat.

Marshall Marsden ran the livery, one of the few businesses in White Pass that wasn't failing or up for sale. He was a slight, bald man with eight children, all of whom were named Marshall Junior or Marcella or Marceline or some other M-variant of his own, apparently-revered name. The mayor loved off-color stories. This morning, however, there was no trace of humor in his small brown eyes.

"Did you hear about Bob Siringo?"

Lou Hand pulled the dodger off its tack on the bulletin board. The illustration was one of those pen-and-ink sketches of infinite vagueness: the bland features, staring eyes, and mandarin mustache of the desperado could have belonged to any number of innocent-looking young men.

"I heard about some guest at the hotel who looks like Bob Siringo."

Marsden jerked his boots off the desk and landed them on the floor with a bang. "Well, it's him, he's making no secret of it."

"Is that right?" Lou Hand had dreaded some such confirmation. He began tossing kindling into the stove. His hand wasn't steady as he lit the match.

"That's right," Marsden said, and Lou Hand noticed a glint of perspiration on his brow despite the chill of the tiny office. "And what I've got to say to you, Sheriff, is short and sweet. Get him out of town."

Lou Hand lit a third match and finally got the kindling started. The warmth was small, of no use against the mortal chill that had invaded his heart and soul after he woke from the frequently repeated dream.

"Why?" Lou Hand said to the mayor.

"We don't want his ilk here. He was down at the livery first thing this morning, talking to Marcy. Trying to find a new horse. She said he made—lewd suggestions."

Lou frowned. "Is she positive he meant—?"

"You calling my own daughter a liar? I want him out, Lou. As elected mayor of White Pass, I'm officially telling you to get him out of town."

"I surely hate to push something like that if there's no—"

"I'm *ordering* you to push it, in the name of the town council. Why do you think we pay you? Hell, this is the first time you've ever faced something this serious."

And the last? he thought, with a strained, almost wistful look at the dodger tossed onto the desk.

"Time you earned your wages," Mayor Marsden exclaimed as he grabbed his derby and put it on with a snap of his wrist.

"If he hasn't got a horse—" Lou began.

"No, and Marcy refused to sell him one. She was scared to death, but she stood up to the little slug. If a woman can do that—"

"I hear you," Lou Hand interrupted, beet-faced and furious all of a sudden. "But you hear me for a minute. If it's Bob Siringo, and he doesn't have a horse, he can't get out of here until six o'clock earliest, when the Sacramento stage comes through." The eastbound presumably had cleared the way station at half past five, while Lou Hand was still enmeshed in his dreams of Red Fish Pass at high noon. The place he never should have left.

Mayor Marsden sneered. "It's a convenient excuse for stalling all day. But all right, six o'clock is your limit. See that he's gone."

Marsden slammed the door and Lou Hand listened

to his boots tap-tap quickly away on the plank sidewalk. The sheriff felt heavy and old and doomed as he walked to the potbelly stove, yanked the door open and swore. For the kindling had gone out, and what wafted against his upraised palms from the black ashy interior was cold; just more cold; a brush of air that seemed, to his worried imagination, cold as the breath from a grave.

Lou Hand fooled around the office all morning. It was his custom to stroll back to Jesse Thome's for his big meal at noon, and he started in that direction but gave up the idea after walking one block. His stomach hurt, too severely for him to eat so much as a mouthful of Jesse's usual: pot roast with horseradish on the side; boiled or mashed potatoes and a gravy boat almost big enough to float a Vanderbilt yacht.

He leaned his hip against a hitchrack and squinted over the swayed back of an old gray looking half dead from the weight of its saddle. Diagonally in the middle of the next block, opposite, Lou Hand had a fine view of the portico of the Congress Hotel. As he studied the hotel and chewed on his lower lip, a recognizable figure walked out jauntily, almost colliding with an old woman in a bonnet and faded cloth coat.

Lou dodged back, into the shadows of the entrance alcove of Weinbaum's Hardware, boarded up and plastered with TO LET notices. The man outside the hotel wore a stained tan duster and boots with very high heels. When he bumped the old woman, knocking a parcel out of the crook of her arm, he immediately snatched it from the dirty snowbank into which it fell, presented it to her, then swept off his tall loaf-crowned hat with a deep bow. In a sorry place like White Pass, that kind of bow should have brought a snicker, but somehow, the man made it look not only graceful but proper.

Mollified, the old woman patted the man's stained sleeve and went on. The man watched her go, then started walking, cutting left into an alley beside the hotel and there disappearing.

But not before Lou Hand had a clear look at the pale cheeks and mandarin mustache under the tall hat. No mistaking the features from the dodger. It was Bob Siringo, or his twin.

Where was he going? In search of a horse? He wouldn't find any but plugs in White Pass. That was probably the problem, Lou thought. He glanced at the icy disk of the sun, still mist-shrouded, and noticed his own faint shadow fading in and out as he walked slowly back to his office. There he shut the door and sat bundled in his coat in the chill silence, wondering—asking himself—how long he could wait before he carried out Mayor Marsden's charge.

* * *

The sun vanished behind threatening clouds of dark gray that rolled over the mountains from the northwest about four o'clock. Hungry and bone-chilled, Lou Hand stared at the ticking wall clock and realized he couldn't procrastinate any longer—principally because he could no longer bear the nervous pain torturing his gut. He checked his Colt once again, and set out on what he fancied might be his last walk anywhere.

Sid Thalheimer, the hotel clerk, was scratching a pen across some old bills at the counter of the Congress.

Lou pushed back his hat. "Sid, I hear you had a Mr. Bob Siringo registered. Is he still here?"

Sid caught the hopeful note and gave Lou Hand a sad, even pitying look. "He was upstairs taking a nap. Came down ten minutes ago. He's in there." Sid's thumb hooked at the connecting door to the hotel's saloon bar.

"Say anything about checking out today, did he?"

"No, he's staying one more night."

Lou swallowed back a large lump in his throat. "No he isn't. You can have the room."

Without waiting for a reaction, Lou Hand pivoted on the scuffed heel of his boot and walked across the old oriental carpet to the batwings in the archway, and the incredible pregnant silence that seemed to be waiting in the dim room beyond. Lou's boots sounded loud as the trampling of a mastodon; at least they sounded that way in his inner ear.

He unbuttoned his coat before he pushed the doors open. Clarence, the day barkeep, flashed him a look from behind the long mahogany counter, then quickly found some glassware to polish at the far end. The Congress saloon bar held but one customer, standing up in front of an almost untouched schooner of beer that had lost its head. Like everything else in White Pass, the saloon bar looked dark; grimy; cold.

"Bob Siringo?" Lou Hand said from the entrance, hoping his wild inner tension didn't show.

"I am, sir," said the young man, taking off his loaf-crown hat and smoothing his thinning oiled dark hair with his palm. The desperado's smile was polite but wary.

"I'm the sheriff."

"Yes, sir, so I figured," Bob Siringo said, in a tone that revealed nothing.

"Lou Hand's my name."

"Pleased to meet you. May I invite you for a drink?" Lou Hand's cold nose itched. Was this some trap? He took three steps forward, between the flimsy stained tables, and paused by the upright piano whose keyboard resembled a mouth of yellow teeth with several missing. From there he had a better look at Siringo's eyes. Pale and keen in their awareness not only of the sheriff but all the surroundings of the room—even, somehow, the barkeep behind Siringo's back, furiously polishing glassware near the hall leading to the rear door. "Yes, that'd be all right."

"Over there?" Bob Siringo said, picking up his schooner and gesturing. He didn't leave any room for Lou to answer one way or another. He'd chosen the round table in the corner at the front of the bar.

He dropped a coin, *ka-plink,* on the mahogany, and said to Clarence, "Give Mr. Hand anything he wants, please." Then Siringo walked quickly to the table and slid around to the corner chair, dropping his hat in front of him. Where he sat, his back was fully protected, and he could observe not only the room but, on his immediate right, a good portion of Sierra Street beyond the streaked and dirty front window.

Lou Hand picked up his shot of whiskey with a short nod to Clarence, who was still staying out of range. He sat down opposite Bob Siringo, who had a pleasant, watchful expression on his face. The sheriff sipped from the shot of redeye, wanting the Dutch courage, every last drop of it. But he held back because he was fearful of losing whatever advantage a clear head might give him.

Noting again the alertness of Bob Siringo's pale eyes, he realized that was exactly none.

"Mr. Siringo"—Lou Hand cleared his throat—"what are you doing hanging around this town?"

"Well, sir, I didn't know a man had to explain himself that way in the free United States . . ."

"A man like you always has to explain himself."

Siringo didn't like that. He started to reply, then

checked as a shabby man Lou Hand didn't recognize rubbed some dirt from the outside of the window and peered in at the drinkers.

The man's jaw dropped; he knew who was sitting there in the corner. He rushed away. The winter twilight was closing fast on the sad, nearly deserted street. A few snowflakes flurried suddenly, and Lou Hand wished he were lying buck naked and frying on a sandy beach back home.

Bob Siringo sighed. "Day before yesterday, up the trail a piece, when the snowstorm hit, my mount foundered and snapped a leg in a drift. I had to shoot Rex. Then I had to come the rest of the way on foot. That was a pisser of a storm, Sheriff. For a long time I didn't know whether I'd find a town. Whether I'd make it. I did, and here I am, resting up." He smiled and lifted one shoulder in a shrug, then drank a good swallow of beer.

Lou Hand helped himself to another sip of courage. "Well, I'm not on the prod, Mr. Siringo, because you haven't caused any trouble. But the town fathers want you to leave White Pass."

"Shit," Bob Siringo said, losing his smile and thumping his stein on the table so hard some of the golden beer slopped out. The smell was strong; sweet; melancholy, somehow.

"It's that girl, I'll bet. The one at the livery—?"

"You're a quick study, Mr. Siringo. Yes, exactly right. You see—ah—unfortunately, she's the daughter of the mayor."

"Just my Goddamn luck," Bob Siringo said with

another sigh. "I've got two bad, bad weaknesses, Sheriff. One is for young females with a lot of stuff up here." He patted the bosom of his duster. Now, instead of smiling, he smirked.

"Every man's got a weakness, Sheriff. What's yours?"

Mine? I hate this place. This job. I don't want to die here . . . for the sake of a godforsaken, frozen, no-account town full of people with no hope left.

"Never mind. May I ask you to move on, Mr. Siringo?"

"Well, you can ask. But I can't find myself a decent horse. I've looked."

"There's a coach through here at six p.m. every evening. Going the way you want to go—down toward Sacramento."

"Oh, no, I don't take that kind of transportation," Bob Siringo said. "Too many strangers. Too many windows for people to get at you."

Lou Hand swallowed again. "I'm afraid you haven't got any say in it. I'm ordering you."

Bob Siringo's pale eyes showed a moment's murderous malice. Then he covered it by leaning back, relaxing, letting the tension visibly leave his shoulders.

"Oh, come on. You do that, Sheriff, you'll probably draw to back it up—I'll kill you—what's accomplished? I came to this burg by accident. I'll leave when I can."

"No, not good enough—"

"I'm not getting on any fucking stage, do you understand?"

Lou Hand just stared at him, terrified.

Bob Siringo turned in his chair. "Barkeep? What's the time?"

"Quarter past five, sir," Clarence sang out.

Bob Siringo put on another smile, though Lou Hand thought this one was false, intended to lull him. "Then we've got at least forty-five minutes to be friendly. Don't go wild when I unbutton my duster and reach, Sheriff. I'm going to put my hogleg on the table as a gesture of my goodwill. You can take hold of yours if you want, just in case. But don't shoot me by mistake, all right?"

"All right," Lou Hand whispered.

He lowered his hand down to his Colt while Bob Siringo pulled his. It was a .45-caliber Colt, U.S. Army model, with the intimidating 7.5 inch barrel. A real show-off piece. Well cared for, too. It gleamed faintly with oil, showing not a spot of rust, as Clarence illuminated the room by lighting three of the kerosene chimney lamps in the fixture hanging from the ceiling.

"There," Bob Siringo said. That's my one and only weapon. So relax." He rubbed his upper arms. "Jesus, it's cold in here."

"It's always cold in White Pass." Outside, Lou Hand saw someone dart along the far side of the street, pointing toward the window. A second dimly-glimpsed figure rushed away. Youngsters, he realized as he watched the first one tie a muffler tighter under his chin and over his ears. Will Pertwee.

"Sheriff," Bob Siringo said with apparent sincerity, "I want to show you I don't have any bad intentions. Barkeep? Bring us a bottle. A good bottle. On my tab." Clarence delivered a bottle of expensive Kentucky whiskey. Siringo uncorked it and sniffed. "Very fine. Put a good tip down for yourself, barkeep." Clarence swallowed his answer and hurried away. Siringo shoved his stein to one side and gestured for Lou Hand to finish his shot, which he did. Then Siringo poured.

"Have a good drink, Sheriff. Warm up. Think it over. Do you really want to push this issue of my leaving town?"

Lou sipped the smooth warming whiskey. "No, but it's my job."

"Wouldn't you rather be doing something else?" Siringo asked, and Lou Hand had the feeling that the young gunman was mocking him somehow, but he was not clever enough to figure out how he could be sure. Siringo leaned back and smoothed his long shiny pointed mustache with his index fingers. "Wouldn't you rather be sleeping, or reading a fine novel, or eating a plate of stew, instead of sitting here wondering if, and how soon, I'm going to blow you to kingdom come because I can't take your orders?"

Just a little fuzzy from the whiskey, and knowing he was probably in even more desperate trouble because of it, Lou Hand answered. "You're right, I'd rather be doing something else. Rather be sitting in the sunshine in a rowboat in the middle of Red Fish Pass."

"Where's that?"

"Back home. West coast of Florida."

"Why'd you leave?"

"Why did everybody leave the East? To start over. To make a fortune. I listened to Mr. Greeley."

"Who?"

"Horace Greeley. 'Go west, young man, and grow up with the country.'"

"Oh, him." It was clear Bob Siringo didn't know who the devil Mr. Greeley might be.

"Tell me about Florida," the younger man said affably. "I've never been down there. I'm from Hoopeston, Illinois, originally."

"Well," Lou Hand said as the darkness settled faster outside the dirty window, "first thing is, it's warm there. Warm, and bright. The light's almost unbearable when the noon sun hits the sand and the water on a hot day. A man could go blind, and fry his hide red as a lobster, too. But it isn't a bad way to d . . ."

He cut it off, realizing what he'd almost said. All of a sudden his mouth was dry as sand above the tide line. The liquid he'd drunk was exerting a ferocious pressure in his bladder. He wanted to run. Jump up, and run. He just sat there.

"Why don't you go back to Florida?"

"I don't know. I've sure thought about it. Maybe

one day I will. Meantime"—he stared—"I'm responsible for doing this job the best I can."

Bob Siringo stared right back for what seemed forever.

Then he said, "Barkeep? What time is it now?"

"Twenty-five to six."

Lou Hand coughed. "The coach is almost never late. We've got to get back to the main discussion."

In a flat, mean voice, Siringo said, "Subject's closed, Sheriff."

"No. You're going."

"That's it?"

Hoping he wasn't shaking, Lou Hand looked him in the eye and said, "That's it."

"Well, shit." Flurried motion outside the window caught his eye; whipped him around in his chair. "Get away. Get away, you little fuckers," he shouted, gesturing at the shadows lurking on the other side of the steamed-up glass. Two of the boys ran. The other, Will Pertwee, simply darted back to the edge of the walk and hovered there, captured by the spectacle of the adversaries facing each other across the table.

Slowly, carefully, Lou Hand pushed aside his coat. Freed the butt of his gun. His heart pounded like surf in his ear.

Bob Siringo eyed his Army Colt gleaming there, then suddenly wriggled in his chair. "Damn, some kind of vermin in this place. Bit me."

Angry, he reached under the table.

Alarms rang in Lou Hand's head. "Siringo, keep

your hand up where . . ." Then, the small popping shot. Lou Hand felt the bullet hit his foot and stiffened with a cry. He tried to draw, but there was sudden pain, and a feeling of warm blood in his boot, to distract him. Before he could act, Bob Siringo had a small two-barrel hideout pistol above the table, aimed right at Lou Hand's brain.

"You draw on me, Sheriff, you're guaranteed dead. Hands flat on the table. Flat!"

Lou Hand obeyed. He was sweating despite the cold. Cringing behind the bar, Clarence looked embalmed; he gestured wildly toward the lobby door, where, apparently, the clerk had rushed. "Stay out, Sid, stay out!"

Bob Siringo blew a whiff of smoke off his little pistol. Then he managed a tense smile.

"One of my bad faults is a weakness for big-busted females, but the other one is lying, Sheriff. I lie right, left, and Sundays. I lied about my hogleg. This is true, though. If I placed that bullet right, your left foot won't be much good any more. A gimpy sheriff, a sheriff who isn't agile, who can't run, that kind of sheriff's not much use to anybody. I'd say it's time for you to go back home."

He jumped up suddenly, overturning his chair, sweeping his hat onto his head, then switching the hideout pistol to his left hand and snatching up the fearsome long Army Colt with his right.

"You bastard, you really fucked things up for me," he said, spitting it like a little boy robbed of his candy and the privacy to enjoy it. "By God, I'm not too sure why I didn't kill you, so you damn well better speak some good about Bob Siringo after this. Don't say he never did anything but bad to folks."

And he ran, straight back past the bar, brandishing his weapons and screaming venomously at Clarence, "What are you looking at, shit-face?"

Clarence dropped to his knees, out of sight.

Bob Siringo ran through the penumbra of lamplight, down the hall, out into the wintry dark with a slam of the back door, and was never seen again.

Still seated, with his boot full of blood, Lou Hand was gripping the table's edge while trying to keep from fainting.

He failed.

Four mornings later, Jesse Thome called on Lou Hand in his room at eleven o'clock. She brought him a mug of hot beef broth, which she'd been doing ever since the shootout at the Congress saloon bar.

"Here's the weekly," she said, showing him the four-page single-sheet tabloid paper. "The editorial calls you the town's hero."

"Oh, yes, sure," he said, turning his face away, toward the lace curtain and the familiar sad spectacle of Sierra Street all churny with mud and dirty water from the snow-melt. And no sunshine; just winter gray.

"Well, it was very heroic . . ."

"Just to sit there? I don't think so."

"You're wrong. Maybe it wasn't dime-novel heroics, but it was brave. You knew he was a killer. But we won't argue," she said, coming closer. "Time for you to drink this nice hot . . ." Through the steam from the mug, she sniffed something. "Lou Hand, have you been imbibing?"

"Definitely. Bottle in the drawer over there."

"Why?" she said, with mystification and some outrage.

"To work up courage."

"For what?"

Almost as terrified as he had been at the Congress Hotel, he couldn't reply for a minute. Inside the heavy bandage on his left foot, which was resting on an old footstool, he hurt, badly. Doc Floyd had confirmed that the vanished Bob Siringo was an artful shot, or at least a lucky one, because Lou might indeed be permanently crippled, since some muscle or other had been severed.

"For what, Lou?"

"For asking—Jesse—would you consent to become my wife?"

When she got over the surprise, he asked her politely whether she would bring from the bureau the little news clipping from the Atlanta paper. She knew what it was; she saw it when she cleaned the rooms of her boarders once a week. He uttered a soft thank-you and immediately tore the clipping in half, then in quarters, which he dropped on his lap robe.

"Why on earth did you do that?"

"Because, Jesse, I realized the last day or so that the same dream won't work for everybody. And it's nobody's fault that it doesn't." He clasped her big, work-rough hand. "I've got my own dream, Jess. Come with me back east. We'll make out somehow. Let me show you Florida while there's still time. Sitting there with Siringo, I realized there isn't as much as I always pretended. Will you go?"

She crouched down beside him, eyes tear-filled, which was something quite unusual for a woman of her independence and strength. "Of course I will, Lou. I've always wondered why you couldn't work up nerve to ask."

She smiled and put her right arm around the shoulder of his nightshirt. He was, as usual, dreadfully, resentfully cold.

But that wouldn't be the case much longer.

The Long High Noon

Loren D. Estleman

No one but Randy Locke and Frank Farmer knew what it was that had blackened the blood between them, but it didn't lose its kick with time. If either of them remembered the original cause, it rode drag behind the immediate need to annihilate the other man whenever they wandered onto the same plot of real property. I really think they got so they could smell each other across a slaughteryard.

Most likely whatever set them on the prod happened when both men were working for the old Slash Y in south Texas three years after the Rebellion, potting and being potted at by Don Alvarado's vaqueros across the border over cattle of unclear claim. Randy and Frank were a close match with pistols, although Frank had the edge with a carbine after so much experience sniping Confederates from trees. It became a point of honor with him not to use that advantage over Randy, because he didn't want it to take the shine off doing a jig on top of his enemy's grave.

The first time they turned their pistols away from Mexicans and on each other was in the Bluebottle Saloon in El Paso, from either end of the fifty-foot bar the Bluebottle touted as the longest to be found west of St. Louis. Both missed, being of an alcoholic temperament at the time, but Randy corrected that the next morning when he rousted Frank out of a tub of bath water in the Cathay Gardens on Mesa Street and broke one of his short ribs with a .44 slug when Frank lunged for his Colt in its holster hanging on the back of a chair.

Frank recovered, of course, or the story would end there, and went looking for Randy, who'd been turned out of the outfit for shorthanding it just before the drive to Kansas. He caught up with him in a stiff Wyoming winter in the middle of wolfing season and shot his horse out from under him due to windage, which is easier to miscalculate when you're using a short gun at a distance. The horse rolled over on Randy and shattered his leg.

That more than evened the account, by just a little. While Frank's wound had healed, leaving him with nothing worse than a throbbing misery when it snowed or rained, Randy's injury left him with a limp and not much prospect of ranch employment unless he put in for cook. And prolonged exposure to greasy fumes gave him the Tucson Two-Step.

The situation was one more charge against Frank's side of the ledger.

As it happened, Randy's fortunes improved. The buffalo harvest was coming to its peak. The Industrial Revolution was in need of leather to make the straps to drive the gears of the manufactories in the East, warm lap robes were in fashion among the carriage trade in Chicago, and the army was offering to redeem spent shells for cash in order to encourage the starvation of the pesky Indian. Randy traded his range gear for a Sharps Big Fifty and a wagon, and made more money selling hides his first season than he had roping and branding semi-tame beeves the previous three years. But don't think this meant he was grateful to Frank Farmer. He knew that game leg was not the result of an altruistic act. Over open fires he chewed on buffalo tongue, pretending it was Frank's liver, and whenever he rode into a town to market his wares he circulated a description of the man he hated among all the locals.

They weren't much help, being locals and not inclined to travel and gather news in those brief few years when railroad construction was progressing at a crawl against natural obstructions and hostile tribes were determined to eject the white man from their ancestral hunting grounds. A year went by with no response to his queries beyond blank faces and shrugs.

This was irony; for if he'd had but access to one

of those hot-air balloons that were the subject of so much interest in New York and Paris, Randy Locke could look down upon the prairie and learn that he and Frank Farmer had been separated by fewer than a hundred miles for many months.

Frank was working for the Kansas Pacific Railroad, grading track and keeping his Winchester handy to pick off Sioux raiding parties through that same buffalo country. It's possible that he and Randy spied each other at a distance without realizing it; since the big shaggies had grown too wary of man to venture within a thousand yards of a rowdy construction gang, the man who hunted them altered his course wide upon spotting one at work. And so once again their reunion depended upon fate.

When the spur reached Dodge City, Frank put in for provisions and was emerging from the mercantile with a double armload of bacon and coffee when Randy called him out from across Front Street. Randy was smoking a cigar he'd just purchased from the profit of his latest delivery of hides and left it burning in the corner of his mouth when Frank dropped his packages and went for his hardware. Both men drew simultaneously; their reports sounded as one. Frank's slug grazed Randy's collarbone, missing the big artery on the side of his neck, and exiting out the back, taking along a measure of flesh and muscle. Randy's aim was higher still in his haste and sliced off the top of Frank's left ear.

Both men required medical attention, but because Randy's condition was more serious he was still recovering on a cot in the room behind the doctor's office when he opened his eyes to see what appeared to be a two-headed demon coming through the door with a pistol. (Using a rod of bandage to wrap a severed ear was a typical precaution then against infection.) Devil or mortal enemy, the intruder was cause for swift action, and the patient rolled off the edge of the cot an instant before his pillow exploded. With the air filled with feathers and the stink of spent powder, he managed to grasp the edge of his bedpan and skim it in the general direction of his assailant. He was lucky in the trajectory. Frank yelped.

The cry woke the doctor, a laudanum addict who had passed out in his desk chair from the effects of self-treatment, who rushed in and manhandled Frank out of the room. This and the action of disarming him took place somewhat more easily than it might have under most circumstances, because the bedpan had struck Frank's injured ear as surely as if it had been aimed, distracting him with the fiery pain. A summons to the law deposited Frank in jail, where the doctor was forced to amputate the rest of the ear.

Frank was vain of his appearance. When the flesh healed, he ordered a prosthesis made of pink gutta-percha from a medical supply firm in San Francisco. This necessity, together with the inconvenience of a daily application of sealing wax to fix it in place, put Randy's account deep in the red, to Frank's estimation.

Payment was delayed, because by the time Frank was released, Randy had returned to the buffalo hunt, conscious of the fact that his shooting arm needed time to recover before he took on anyone more challenging than a dumb brute. Frank's fine for disturbing the public peace emptied his poke, so he rode back to the railhead to shoot Indians and grade track. The first gandy dancer who kidded him about getting his ear bit off by a Dodge City whore got shot in the foot for his joke; the foreman who bound the wound, a former medical orderly with the Army of the Potomac, told him he was fortunate that Frank was saving his homicidal impulses for Randy Locke. Their relationship was by this time entering the country of frontier legend.

The bottom didn't fall out of the buffalo market so much as it fell out from under the buffalo. Where the great herds had darkened the plains only a few years before, little remained but scattered bones, and soon even they were gone, scoured by pickers to sell by the ton for the refinement of sugar and the manufacture of china. Randy drank up the last of his profits and took his meals and shelter serving time in various jails for drunk and disorderly.

Then God opened a window.

Its population swollen by the easy life of gorging

upon millions of skinned carcasses left to rot, the Great Plains wolf crunched down the last overlooked bone and turned its attention to cattle. The wolfing trade prospered. Randy, who was no stranger to it, exchanged the pelts for bounty, which in the case of some white-muzzled veterans shrewd enough to avoid traps and poison frequently matched the rewards placed on the heads of human desperadoes. Soon he could afford to dine in the best Denver restaurants and sleep in the finest hotels in Virginia City, but the improvement in his finances did not extend to the habits he'd formed as a piteous drunk. Waiters served him only at back doors, where the stink of old guts on his rags wouldn't offend fellow diners, and hotel clerks refused him accommodation entirely. He slept in stables and out in the weather and practiced his draw for hours, wearing down the scar-tissue that slowed his right arm. In his impatience he shifted back and forth, until he could clear leather and hit his mark with either hand as well as most men did with the one they favored.

After Custer fell, the Indian situation changed drastically, and with it Frank Farmer's fortunes. Wisely anticipating reprisal, the Sioux and Cheyenne swarmed north to Canada, and the subsequent army crackdown on the stragglers brought respite to the track gangs who'd sought to stitch up the prairie with rails and ties while peering anxiously over their shoulders for arrows. Frank's talents with a carbine were no longer required.

When he was offered work as a full-time grader—at reduced pay—he demanded his time and rode to the nearest poker game. There he shot and killed a man over one pat hand too many and barely escaped a lynch mob when the deputy who'd arrested him, a naive New Hampshire native lured West by dime novels, changed clothes with him and took his place in the cell while Frank left by a back door. (The mob, which had come there to lynch *someone,* strung up the deputy.)

Frank's period in custody had not been wasted. A drunk in the next cell had mentioned that he'd had his skull laid open a month earlier by a wolfer with a bottle named Locke in Salt Lake City, over some difference of opinion the drunk couldn't remember. Once free, Frank stole a horse and lit a shuck for Utah Territory. Mormons weren't supposed to partake of hard liquor, but he spent several nights lifting flat-brimmed black hats off men sleeping in alleys until an apothecary he bribed with a double eagle told him he sold two bottles of snakebite medicine nightly to a tramp who answered Randy's description. Frank gave the man another double eagle, his last, for two bottles and the loan of his apron and waited inside the alley door for an hour that night for the knock that would avenge his ear and bring him release from ten years of fear and hatred.

When it came, he shifted the decoy bottles to his other arm and drew the Colt from under his apron, only to put it away in haste when he opened the door on a young woman in a red wrap with feathers in her hair. His unfamiliar face didn't seem to faze her as she thrust a fistful of coins at him and reached for the medicine. Nonplussed and broke, Frank stuck out his free hand to accept the money. The woman's painted face dropped from sight, revealing the leering, filth-smeared visage of Randy Locke, who was crouched behind her with his .44 in his fist.

The impact of the shot flung Frank on his back.

Miraculously, the bottles were spared, rolling harmlessly across the floor to a stop at the base of a crate filled with headache powders, where the apothecary rescued them and placed them back in inventory, snakebite apparently being very common on the shore of the Great Salt Lake and the source of a large percentage of his income.

The doctor, a respected elder in the Church of All Saints, despaired several times of his patient's recovery. The slug lay close to the heart, too deep to reach from the chest, and had to be extracted through the back with a sure and steady hand. This required hours of surgery, as nerves and fatigue led to tremors and many breaks for rest were necessary. Much blood was lost. When at great length the bullet was free with no damage to the heart or spine, infection set in. Frank took fever and raged deliriously for days until the series of poultices took effect and his temperature dropped to normal. During his long recuperation, the patient learned that Randy had caught wind of the stranger's search, anticipated the trap he'd lain, and bought the services of a woman of dubious occupation to confuse Frank and slow his hand. He'd ridden out of town directly, his mission was accomplished, long before a citizens' commission could be appointed to pursue him.

Upon regaining his strength, Frank worked off his debt to the doctor by sweeping his office and scrubbing his medical instruments. By the time his obligation was dismissed, Randy's trail had grown cold. Frank struck out in search of employment and a place to bide his time until news surfaced of the whereabouts of his ancient antagonist.

Seasons passed before Randy discovered that he'd failed to lift the burden of Frank Farmer from the world. In Carson City, he celebrated his victory with a long, blistering soak in a bathhouse, got a shave and haircut, bought himself a complete new wardrobe and a valise to pack it in, and secured first-class passage in a Pullman to San Francisco. He'd saved enough by eating simple fare and staying out of hotels to keep his wolfing profits largely intact, and there was no better place to burn money than the Barbary Coast. He leaned back against the plush headrest and dreamt about his first holiday since Appomattox.

Unnoticed by the pair in their relentless determination to destroy each other, the West had begun to extract a deep fascination from the East. Custer's spectacular finish, gun battles in the gold camps and cattle towns, and the professionally promoted exploits of a saddle tramp who called himself Buffalo Bill had kindled a fire that demanded fresh fuel by the week. It was only a question of time before a running gunfight that had involved the same two men for more than a decade aroused journalistic interest.

Randy had made the rounds of San Francisco's saloons, music halls, opium dens, and bordellos for months. His capital was running low and he'd removed his baggage to a hotel far less lavish than he'd grown accustomed to when he bought a copy of the *Examiner* with the intention of finding work through the classified notices and came upon the following paragraph in the local section:

> It has come to our editors' attention that Mr. Randolph Locke, the notorious pistoleer, is visiting our fair city and at last word was stopping at the Eldorado Hotel. Readers familiar with our columns will recall that Mr. Locke and Mr. Frank Farmer have been taking target practice upon each other across the map of the frontier since the spring of 1868. Mr. Farmer was last reported in Salt Lake City, U.T., recovering from yet another mortal attack upon his person by Mr. Locke.

The maid assigned to Randy's room complained to the hotel manager that she had been forced to pick up hundreds of torn fragments of newspaper that had been flung about the premises before she could begin dusting.

Randy's chagrin upon learning that he had failed to finish the job at the apothecary shop was exacerbated by the army of newspaper reporters who tracked him to his current lodgings, each crying for an exclusive interview. He refused their shrill requests and directed the hotel detective to prevent any more such visits. He was greatly annoyed when within hours a fresh knock came to his door.

The small fellow who greeted him when he tore it open was dressed rather better than the grubby gentlemen of the press, in a printed waistcoat, striped trousers, velvet lapels, fine boots, and a pearl-gray bowler. He introduced himself as Mr. Abraham Cripplehorn, originally of New Jersey, and in lieu of a calling card presented him with a volume slightly larger than a banker's wallet, bound in crimson and yellow pasteboard, and titled *Brimstone Bob's Revenge, or Gun Justice in Abilene.*

Cripplehorn's proposition was simple, yet grand: He was uninterested in penning merely another dime novel commemorating a long-standing feud between dangerous men, but in producing an extravaganza that would pit the two bitter enemies against each other in mortal combat before a paying audience. Ticket prices would run as high as two dollars and he would divide the take equally between himself and the survivor—or his designated heirs should both combatants expire as a result of the contest. He provided extra incentive by holding up a thick sheaf of greenbacks and offering it as an advance against the final sum.

"The only obstacle," Cripplehorn added, "is the difficulty of locating Mr. Farmer at this time."

"If that piece in the *Examiner* went out on the wire, he'll come here under his own steam." Randy snatched the bills from the little man's hand and sealed the bargain with his own strong grip.

The promoter, however, preferred to leave nothing to chance. He placed prominent advertisements addressed to Frank Farmer in newspapers as far east as Milwaukee, stating his purpose and offering to reimburse traveling expenses on top of the same emolument he had given Randy Locke if Farmer agreed to his terms. The offer received free publicity in human interest columns across the country and drew mentions in both *Harper's Weekly* and *Frank Leslie's Illustrated Newspaper,* virtually eclipsing the U.S. presidential race between W.S. Hancock and J.A. Garfield.

Weeks went by, and an impulsive decision to return to the luxury of the Eldorado Hotel made serious inroads on Randy's windfall, before the news reached the prospective third member of the partnership. Frank Farmer was in Montana Territory, earning his keep as a regulator for the Stockmen's Association shooting down suspected rustlers. This engagement kept him far from civilization, sleeping in cold camps and remote line shacks, where current events traveled on pack animals led by rare visitors on their way from one lonely outpost to another. By the time he learned of the event it was no longer current. As luck had it, he read a wire account of the original notice of Mr. Randolph Locke's visit to San Francisco in a filler on a page of the *Billings Gazette.* The newspaper was wrapped around a pint of Old Gideon, brought by a barbed-wire drummer named Helfers who registered astonishment when the man he'd handed the bottle to in return for a plate of beans handed it back. The man gathered his possibles and struck out into the teeth of the worst blizzard in years.

An old acquaintance from his cowhand days recognized Frank on a railroad platform in Boise, and by the time his train crossed into California, reporters were gathering at every station clamoring for his comments. Their subject was more gregarious than his rival, answering most of their questions and posing with his head turned carefully to reduce the prominence of its false ear, for a photographer who set up his camera on a tripod.

Abraham Cripplehorn used his stick to pry his way through the jam of reporters in San Francisco and seize Frank's hand the moment he stepped down from his parlor car. The promoter was aggressive. Within the hour and with great effort he had dissuaded Randy from meeting the newcomer at trackside with his .44. By the time the pair were seated in the carriage Cripplehorn had waiting, he had Frank's mark on the contract in his pocket.

To avoid the disaster of an unexpected confrontation, Frank was registered at the Asiatic, with appointments equal to Randy's at the Eldorado but located many blocks away, while Cripplehorn attended to the arrangements for the spectacle. These were seriously incommoded by the intervention of the county sheriff, who served him with an injunction prohibiting the murderous exhibition from taking place within his jurisdiction. Appeals to all the other counties in California came to an abrupt halt when Sacramento banished the event from the state.

No sooner was this reported in the public journals than representatives of the neighboring states and territories of Oregon, Nevada, Arizona, and Utah declared that they would not host so callous a display of savagery. Others followed suit all the way to the Eastern seaboard. Under pressure from the Hayes administration in Washington, President Díaz announced that any attempt to hold such a contest in Mexico would be met with the arrest of all the principals. An official wire from Ottawa warned that the Northwest Mounted Police would turn Cripplehorn & Company back from the border of the Dominion of Canada should it attempt to cross.

Asked by reporters over liquor and liverwurst sandwiches in the promoter's suite at the Forty-Niner if this meant the end of his plans, Cripplehorn smiled and responded with two words: "The Strip."

He was referring to the Cherokee Strip, a rectangular portion of the panhandle of the Indian Nations (later the State of Oklahoma). Through an oversight when the territory was divided by Congress among the Five Civilized Tribes it had gone unassigned, and was therefore outside federal and local law. It presented a bolt-hole to every wanted fugitive in the West. Where better, Cripplehorn reasoned, to stage an outlaw entertainment?

The arena chosen was a farmer's field on the south bank of the Cimarron River, whose proprietor, a Choctaw who'd struggled for years to raise something better than a cry of despair from the rocky soil, pocketed the equivalent of a rich season's harvest in return for its use. A great tent with advertising stenciled on both sides of the canvas to defray expenses was erected to discourage freeloaders. Bleachers were built. Legal waivers were printed on the backs of tickets indemnifying the exhibitors against damages in the event of injury or death as the result of a stray bullet. Sales were brisk and the tent was filled to capacity when Randy Locke and Frank Farmer entered from opposite openings and faced each other for the first time in two years. They squared off, hands hovering above the grips of their pistols.

"Hold!" thundered a new voice. "I'll kill the first man who draws his weapon!"

The man who rose from the front row of spectators held a shotgun to his shoulder and wore a bright star on his blue tunic.

An Indian, with features the color of brick and seemingly as hard, he identified himself as an officer of the Cherokee Light Horse Police and declared his intention to prevent murder from occurring on ground entrusted to him.

Walter Red Hawk's reflexes were slower than his sense of probity, and were no match for Randy's relentless practice or Frank's experience in the field. He had both hammers eared back, but managed to discharge only one barrel before two pistol bullets struck him full in the chest, killing him instantly. Pellets from the shotgun pelted Randy and Frank both, but as he'd been aiming in the middle between them and the two men were separated by fifteen feet, the spread was too broad to injure either seriously.

The officer was known to many in attendance and popular. Before the contestants could recover themselves, they were seized and disarmed by members of the audience and held until reinforcements from the Light Horse Police took them into custody. Abraham Cripplehorn, it was reported, fled with the cash box before he, too, could be apprehended.

In Fort Smith, Arkansas, where Judge Isaac Parker exercised federal jurisdiction over the Nations, there was debate as to whether Walter Red Hawk had overstepped himself in attempting to arrest non-Indians, but the willful slaying of a tribal officer and a ward of the U.S. government was a federal offense. The prisoners were removed to the Fort Smith jail, convicted in court, and sentenced to hang.

But things had changed since the days when Hanging Judge Parker could depend upon suffering no interference from Washington. Seeing the advantage in publicity, the attorneys assigned to Randy and Frank pooled their gifts and petitioned for a new trial or commutation from the president. Further questioning of the coroner cast doubt upon whether Frank's smaller-bored Colt had helped deal the fatal wound; certainly the slug that had shattered the officer's heart was a .44, and the weapon that was confiscated from Randy was chambered for that caliber. Apprised of these details, and mindful of his legacy, Rutherford B. Hayes on his final day in office commuted Frank's sentence to life imprisonment but let stand the order of Randy's execution.

Ironically, a petition filed later by Randy's attorney resulted in a second trial. It ended in a hung jury, and when his case returned to court, he was acquitted on the grounds that Officer Red Hawk had lacked the authority to arrest the defendant and that Randy had acted in self-defense. He was free, while Frank was removed to the Detroit House of Corrections to serve out the rest of his days at hard labor.

Fifteen years passed, and it's difficult to say which man suffered more. Frank, because of the unremitting hardship and monotony of incarceration, or Randy, because the purpose of his existence—to end Frank's—had been stolen from him with the flick of a gavel. He attempted suicide, but owing to his drunken condition missed his temple and shot off the end of his nose, resulting in copious bleeding but not death. After the bandages came off he entered a period of low comedy by trying to have himself arrested and sent to Detroit, where any sort of makeshift weapon might save the nation the expense of boarding Frank Farmer for the remainder of his natural span, but he was constitutionally incapable of planning any murder apart from Frank's and the infractions he managed to commit drew him a total of six months and twenty-three days in the jail in Fort Smith, five hundred miles from his target. He drifted from job to job: loading bales of cotton and barrels of molasses aboard flatboats in New Orleans, shoveling horseshit from stables in Houston, cleaning cuspidors in saloons in Juarez. The Mexican government appeared to have lost interest in banishing him from the republic. He was a ghost, a figure of derision in rags with a short nose.

Judge Parker died in office after twenty years on the bench. The honest Indians of Oklahoma Territory mourned him, but years of simmering resentment against him in Congress led to a revolt against the monomaniacal authoritarianism he appeared to represent. His decisions were reviewed and in many cases reversed. Frank Farmer was granted a parole hearing. Satisfied of his contrition, the board released him after a decade and a half in custody.

The announcement was worthy of five lines in newspapers whose editors vaguely recalled the drama of Locke vs. Farmer. Randy, who was then tending bar in Bisbee, Arizona Territory, overheard the gossip among his patrons. His heart quickened, but he allowed as how Frank would require time to adjust to freedom and reacquaint himself with firearms. He knew they would face off again, whether he went looking for Frank or Frank came hunting for him; for they were of the same character, and while the flames of vengeance might burn low within them, they would never flicker out until one of them was in the ground.

Came a new century. Big mining interests had claimed the gold fields of California and Colorado from under the feet of individual prospectors, the silver mines had played out or flooded, and the ticking of horseless carriages was too faint as yet to excite much interest in the vast pools of oil slumbering beneath Texas and Pennsylvania. Then a new source of gold erupted in Alaska. Hordes of men armed with picks and pans swarmed north in search of a few months' hard labor followed by a life of ease. Randy went along out of boredom. Frank did, too, to escape poverty. These were the excuses they gave fellow excursionists; each knew from long instinct that the other could not resist the opportunity to gravitate to the same place.

They got as far as the Canadian Yukon. Like the *federales* in old Mexico, the Mounties had forgotten their differences with two aging gunmen, so their interest was impersonal. Entering the Dexter Saloon, a stuffy place hung with mooseheads and snowshoes smelling pungently of unwashed wool steaming in the heat of a wood stove, Frank shoved his way up to the crowded bar and gave the gaunt, moustachioed barkeep a cartwheel dollar for information leading to "a mangy piece of wolfbait named Randy Locke." Neither man had ever shied from leaving his true name lest he be accused of cowardice toward his sworn foe, and in all candor Frank's description of the one he sought wouldn't be of much use after nearly twenty years. The gaunt fellow nodded and said he believed that was the name of the party he'd conducted to his storeroom to sleep off a drunk and spare him from being waylaid for his goods. He offered to show Frank into the room.

The customer hesitated. That wasn't the first saloon he'd visited that day. His blood flowed sluggishly of late, a snort or two per stop got him through the icy blast from place to place. His defenses were muzzy. He gave the man another cartwheel and followed him through an elkhide flap into the blackness of a short unchinked passage to a door the barkeep opened and held. A lamp burned low with a dirty-orange flame within. He ducked his head to clear the frame, but failed to duck the hard object that struck him from behind.

When he came to, wrists and ankles bound and slung facedown across a pack saddle, he knew himself for a fool. The party of fur-clad Mounties who dumped him into a snowdrift on the American side of the border explained to him, each man taking a part, that he and his "friend" had both been gulled by Wyatt Earp, the Arizona gunsharp and proprietor of the Dexter Saloon, who only held with violence in his place of business when it was initiated by him. The officer who leaned over Frank to cut him free of his lashings added that if he cared to look around, he might find Randy Locke in a neighboring snowdrift.

Frank didn't care to look. The Randy he remembered was too wily to lie around freezing to death when a trek south might spare him to fight another day. And what had become of Frank's rubber ear?

The calendar shed leaves like buffalo hair, singly at first, then in clumps. Model T trucks took the place of buckboards, mercantiles filled orders placed by telephone, a Johnny Reb named D.W. Griffith had moved into the vacancy left by P.T. Barnum, a good Yankee. The only place you saw an Indian was on a billboard selling chewing tobacco. The top hands who used to ride the big spreads dreaming of the day when they'd set aside enough to buy outfits of their own hung out at the Watering Hole in downtown Los Angeles, doing rope tricks and waiting for a studio truck to come along and load them into the bed like cattle for a day's pay doing extra work in front of a crank camera. Hollywood was the last western boomtown. A man with range experience could stand on a corner for a couple of hours and see everyone he knew. Tom Mix and Will Rogers stopped by to bum smokes and swap lies.

Neither Randy nor Frank was interested in meeting featured players; *stars*, they were calling them now. The years since they'd been booted from the Yukon had not been kind to them. Randy had taken a wife, who'd left him because every conversation turned inevitably to Frank, and the woman Frank took up with had abandoned him not because he was missing an ear but because of the months she'd spent alone whenever Frank went chasing after some rumor of Randy. There had been spells when each had wondered if the other was dead, but the thought was impossible to bear. Anyway, their relationship had outlasted most marriages, and the death of either—no matter if they were separated by a thousand miles or a country block—would be known for certain to the survivor the instant the spirit was divided from the body, so deep was their bond of hatred.

They had, in fact, been separated by considerably more than a thousand miles, and by something less than a country block. For a time, Frank Farmer had joined one of the lesser Wild West exhibitions as a sharpshooter and toured with the troupe to England while Randy was driving a milk wagon in Bismarck. When Randy Locke lay near death from malaria in Panama City, contracted while digging the great canal, Frank, who'd been stranded abroad when the exhibition went broke, was working his way home by way of Nova Scotia, shoveling coal into the firebox of a tramp steamer. On another occasion, Randy's stake in an oil-drilling operation went up in a duster and he was forced to stow away in a freight car to escape his creditors while Frank was on his way there to try his luck. Their trains passed only yards apart, each feeling a chill on the instant.

The West was settled. Barbed wire made line riders unnecessary, a rail stop in every city had ended the era of trail drives, and all the subterranean wealth had been dug up and tapped into. There were no rip-roaring cowtowns, no sprawling mining camps where men gathered from every corner of the land to get rich on the strength of their backs or on their ability to palm an ace. They stayed where they stopped. Two men who sought nothing but each other could wander the great reachers for the rest of their lives and never make contact. Until Hollywood.

Randy got there first. His grizzled hair, comically stubbed nose, and pronounced limp typecast him immediately as a cantankerous ranch cook, a part he played in a dozen two-reelers produced by C.B. DeMille and Thomas Ince. The pay was better than punching cattle, and since the smoke in his kettle came from dried ice there was no burning grease to send him hobbling to an outhouse twenty times a day. He received no billing—his notoriety had yellowed and crumbled away along with the newspapers that had carried it—but for the first time since that oil fiasco he was confident that the increasing popularity of the western moving picture and the need for experienced frontiersmen to lend an authentic background to Eastern stage actors like William S. Hart would one day cast its loop around Frank Farmer and drag him to the slaughter.

It was 1918. The war was ending in Europe and prosperity was just around the corner. The feud between Randy Locke and Frank Farmer was approaching its fiftieth anniversary. Randy felt lucky.

The producer of *Fort Mescalero* was hosting a wrap party at the Watering Hole. The place was closed to the public for the evening and the first drink was free. Randy, still wearing the getup he'd been given from the wardrobe grab bag—sweat-stained Stetson with the brim turned up in front, shirt made of ticking, patched dungarees tucked into stovepipe boots with the heels ground down by dozens of pairs of feet—was sharing a bottle with a dago made up like an Indian when he spotted a pair of slumped shoulders he knew as well as his own at the end of the packed bar. He left the phony warrior in the middle of a drunken gripe and went over to tap one of those shoulders, loosening the working prop pistol in his holster, loaded with live ammunition he'd substituted for the blanks. Cooks in movies never shot anyone, so there'd been no danger of mustering out an actor, and Randy believed in always being prepared.

No tap was needed, however. Frank sensed his presence and turned quickly from the bar, resting his hand on the Colt on his hip—not the same one that had been confiscated from him in 1880, but a near relative. He was dressed like a tinhorn, in a plug hat and a claw hammer coat. His face was gaunter than Randy remembered, and it had never been much for flesh. It had deep gullies and his moustache had gone white and untrimmed. He had a new ear, a bright pink one fashioned from celluloid or some other modern material. It stuck out like a blossom in dead soil.

"How do, Frank?"

"Not so bad, Randy. Yourself?"

"Middling."

Both men looked embarrassed after this exchange. After so much time they had only the one thing in common.

They filled the gap with small talk. Frank had just finished shooting on his first day with Famous Players-Lasky. A fellow extra who'd finished his bit with Randy's crew the day before had invited him to the party. He said he'd been in town only twenty-four hours. It was like the old days when there were more ranches starting up than men to work them.

"Just like Fort Worth, only bigger," Randy said. "Where you want to do this?"

"It's still light out."

They went outside, Randy first on account of his game leg. He'd sooner expect a priest of the faith to backshoot him than Frank.

It was suppertime. Traffic was light. They waited for a streetcar to pass, then stepped out onto the asphalt and faced off. There was no need for talk or signals, no whenever-you're-readies or dropping of bandannas. When each man was satisfied the other was set, they went for their pistols.

Frank was at a disadvantage. Indolent by nature, he'd never been one for practice, and no gun work had come his way in many years. Randy's slug pierced his heart while he was still raising his muzzle. He fell spreadeagle on his back and didn't twitch.

Randy didn't bother to check for signs of life; he'd known the outcome the moment the pistol pulsed in his hand. He dropped it back into its holster and turned away.

A crowd formed around the dead man. A police officer came blasting his whistle to clear a path. No one paid any attention to the elderly bean-slinger hobbling in the opposite direction.

On the sidewalk, Randy whistled an old cattle lullaby, waiting for the next streetcar to come along. When it did, he stepped out in front of it.

The Two-bit Kill

C. Courtney Joyner

"I split his melon good with a piece of pine. You know the one, with the made-special curved handle."

Eli Greene nodded and made a sound in his throat that Clyde Crutcher took as agreement, as he always did. Light danced on the blade in Eli's hand as he brought it in close, skating the sandpaper on the back of Crutcher's neck, and gathering a row of gray wiry hair against the sharp edge.

Crutcher dropped his too-wide chin with, "The crazy sum'bitch had one eye and a pair o' Colts! I clubbed him, and them pistols went flyin'. Had him kissin' the floor before the bar knew a damn thing had happened. Hell, folks'll be buyin' me drinks for the next six months for savin' 'em."

Eli made a gesture toward the holster snug under Crutcher's arm, then wiped lather from the razor. "Why didn't you just use your gun?"

Crutcher coughed and his voice dropped, "Well, I thought better of it. You've gotta know when to pull a gun. And believe me, I know. There's even talk about takin' my picture and namin' me 'Stick Man of the Year.' So do a good job."

"I didn't know they had a 'Stick Man of the Year.' That's quite an honor."

"Well, you'll never get it."

Eli angled Crutcher's head with the two fingers that remained on his right hand, while making a sweeping motion with the razor in his left, "Probably not. But you best not tell a tale and get a shave at the same time. I might start laughing and that's how you lose an ear."

"You sayin' I'm lyin'?"

"Oh, no sir."

"Scarecrow like you ought to keep his thoughts to his self, 'cause I can always take my business across the street. And that's after I show ya what for. I've got a reputation."

"I heard that, "Eli said as he dropped the razor in a pan of hot water scented with rose oil and picked up a pair of shears. The words kept tumbling out of Crutcher's mouth but the barber wasn't there anymore. He was fourteen years old and running along the ragged edge of the Mississippi at midnight, praying to reach the Canal Street ferry landing.

Eli's matchstick legs were trying hard, and his chest was burning, when the bottle of Wolfe's Schnapps hit him between the shoulders. The glass heel split with a shriek, and the shards tore into his collarbone. Red bloomed across Eli's shirt as he tangled in an old shrimp net and fell face first into the muddy black sand. The impact was soft; a wet cushion that felt cool and soothing for the few heartbeats before the huge man with the knife caught up to him.

"You shouldn't have made me run like that, Jew-boy!"

Eli stayed perfectly still, his face half buried. He held his breath as a fleshy paw grabbed him by the scruff of his neck and rag-dolled him to his feet. The man held Eli just under the jaw, suspending him six inches off the ground using only one hand. In the other, he had a knife that was all blade—a sharpened spike with a small wrapping of leather on one end. Eli twisted, his feet kicking at nothing, as the man's fingers tightened on his windpipe.

The boy gasped and the man snorted. "Chokin'? Now you know how I feel every damn day."

The summer moon shadowed the man's face, but Eli could see his eyes. The pupils had swallowed the iris, and the lids seemed pinned open. All Eli had done was introduce himself to a stranger, but it was enough. The man said, "There's an order about Jews, and General Grant signed it! You're supposed to be gone! This was my ferry. I get fired for a couple of drinks and now your—papa—is runnin' it?"

The voice cradled Grant's name, and spit out "papa" like an obscenity. Eli knew about the General's infamous "Order 11" to expel "Israelites" from the agricultural states so they couldn't deal in cotton. There had been an editorial in the *New York Herald*, and with Eli's help, his father read it out loud twice, shaking his head at Grant's excuses and thanking Lincoln for repealing the "error in judgment." Mr. Greene tore the article from the paper and periodically he would show it to his son to remind him to "take care, and don't be obvious. That's how you get by in this world."

The massive hand squeezed tighter, and the boy could taste the corrupted air trapped in his lungs. Consciousness was just a hazy awareness for Eli, his eyes rolling back white and red, as the man whispered, "I've been dyin' for years. I've got no money, and your family's eating regular? Stinkin' bullshit."

Eli felt the hot breath of the words as his mind started to blank, and his body went limp. The man smiled and his grip relaxed. A roaring scream erupted from Eli as he jerked his knees up, and then pounded his foot into his attacker's chest with all of his strength, knocking him backwards. The sand bogged the drunk's feet and he tumbled, the homemade knife dropping from his hand.

Eli landed hard against a barnacled anchor chain that dug into his side. He couldn't catch his breath and spots floated before his eyes like red fireflies, but his body moved quickly. There was no thinking, just instinct. He grabbed the spike and spun around, letting it fly from his slender fingers in a natural and perfect motion as if the blade had been shot from a Navajo bow.

The weapon hit its target between the second

and third ribs on the left, and buried itself to the leather. The man struggled to one knee, then collapsed, blood gurgling around the wound. He shivered, whispered something, and then all rage was gone.

Eli froze, waiting for the thunder in his ears to stop. Slowly, he bent over the man and pulled out the blade. It fit naturally in his palm and felt good, as if it was a part of his body, but the rush of new feeling gut-scared him. He dunked the weapon in the water, washed away the blood, and then placed it next to the dead man's hand.

Eli looked from one end of the landing to the other, expecting an angry crowd or a blue-frocked Parrish Policeman coming for him. But the shore was empty, because screams along the New Orleans waterfront meant nothing. There was only the sound of the river, calm and running forever.

Eli's lungs filled again and he settled by a broken piling, the drunkard lying quietly at the river's edge, the water swirling pink around his face. Eli tried not to stare at his attacker, but he couldn't help it. This was the first dead man he had ever seen, and he was the one who had taken his life. The thought was too much; Eli didn't want to talk to his papa or God, Eli just wanted to ride to the end of the world.

The night broke apart and Eli hid behind the remains of an old pier that had been shattered by Union cannon fire. At first light, he watched his father walk a team of mules and a lumber cart onto the ferry while teamsters, sharing biscuits and coffee, boarded behind him and settled against a wooden railing. The teamsters were a strapping pair and Mr. Greene was stoop-shouldered, but he secured the load without their help then asked for their money as if he were apologizing. Mr. Greene called out over the morning din of Canal Street, "Son! We've got customers!"

Eli ducked down, waiting for the cast-off bell. Mr. Greene spotted his son's bay hitched by the fire station and shouted his name again, clanging the rusty signal three times. The ferry broke for the opposite landing, Mr. Greene pulling the guidelines, as Eli took a few fast steps from the pilings and stopped, his eyes fixed on the corpse. The man's threatening hands looked like shapeless bags, and purple blotches were surfacing under the skin turning his face into a clownish mask.

"You're dead," Eli finally said aloud so he'd believe it. "You're dead and I'm alive," he repeated as instinct took over again. He grabbed the knife, struggled to put on the man's wet jacket, and then ran like hell.

Mr. Greene wasn't looking back at Canal Street when Eli swung onto his bay, weighed down by a dead man's coat with a knife in the pocket. Eli didn't have a gun, canteen, or bedroll as he spurred his horse toward Faubourg Marigny. Behind him, he could hear the fading shouts of his father and the laughter of the others as they spotted a "dead 'un!" lying in the mud.

* * *

Crutcher sneezed, then locked back his lips with his thumbs, trying to force a smile from his crooked teeth. "I've got to look damn good. When folks come into the place, they're gonna wanna shake my hand."

Eli trimmed an eyebrow that was curling wild. "I wouldn't smile too much, Mr. Crutcher. You're a serious man and people want to know you mean business."

"You're a barber and you only got seven fingers! Who takes you serious?"

Eli steadied the tip of the scissors next to Crutcher's eye and snipped a few stragglers. "You've been coming in since I opened."

"I come in because you got the two-bit shave and haircut."

"There are other shops, but I'm a good barber. Just like you're very good at what you do."

Adding the compliment is something Papa would have done, Eli thought. He trimmed the back of Crutcher's neck and glimpsed himself in the long, gilt-edged mirror he had brought in from San Francisco. He'd inherited his father's widow's peak and adopted his moustache, but now he thought he saw a familiar servitude in his shoulders and manner. His expression darkened and his eyes knit together. The transformation wasn't sudden, but this was the moment it hit him. He stopped cutting.

Crutcher adjusted himself in the leather chair and gave his bib a snap, sending clumps of hair to the floor. "Yeah, I'm good. And I'm a real part of this town 'cause I was born right here in Prescott, not two blocks from the Palace Hotel. You'll always be an outsider. That's just the way it is."

"But you're a man of the world, too." Eli began snipping again.

"I've knocked around some. There's parts of the country where folks are afraid to say my name out loud."

"Because you were, well, a gunfighter."

Crutcher cranked his neck around, "That's right. I lived on the other side of the law and I built me a rep. That's how come I got the job keepin' the peace in the saloon, but I don't make it no secret. If folks are scared, then they behave. Nobody trifles with me."

"There was the gentleman with one eye."

"He made a damn mistake, didn't he?"

Eli nodded again. "Oh, I didn't mean any offense. And I know your deadly reputation because you told me all about it the first time you came in for the two-bit."

"So you'd know not to trifle with me! Why don't you tell me somethin' for a change? Hell, nobody knows nothin' about you."

Eli straightened Crutcher's tie with the thumb and index finger on his right hand. The stick man winced at the lump of congealed flesh that had grown over the open wound left by the missing three fingers. "I tried to get a job as a barber at the Palace, but the manager said my hand would make the guests a little squeamish."

"You just come out of nowhere, lookin' for work? You shoulda written a letter first."

"Except I'm right-handed. After my accident, I taught myself to cut hair with my left, but my handwriting's just chicken scratch."

Crutcher leaned back with his eyes closed, "You're doin' all right for a cripple."

Eli poured hot water on a towel, and rung it out, his mind full of the sweet time before he killed his second man.

Eli didn't know if he was wanted for murder, so he stayed off the main roads and stuck close to the river, following it into Arkansas. He thought he could lose himself in Helena with a new name, and make enough of a stake to get himself to Utah or Arizona. That was the plan as he sat by a low fire in the evenings, a dead man's coat around his shoulders, and practicing with his homemade knife.

The weapon was never out of his hands, flicking it from his hip or throwing it under-handed, depending on where he needed the blade to go. Bringing his arm down from the shoulder was the surest throw, and he hit his target dead-on every time so he could eat. When Eli rode into Helena, it was with empty pockets and a sack of rabbit pelts.

He got a job in a whorehouse as a bar wipe, and

he was washing glasses when a mule skinner, who couldn't afford any of the better girls, decided he didn't like Eli's "half-nigger" face. The old boy wrapped his arms around a five-dollar whore and started to pull her upstairs when the spike flew from Eli's hand and tore through his windpipe.

Eli didn't remember throwing the knife, and thought he'd woken from a deep sleep when he found himself in the back of a wagon, huddled under a canvas tarp, as the five-dollar girl snuck him out of town. A reporter wrote a no-fact version of the killing and dubbed Eli The Bayonet Kid, and that's what he was called from then on, no matter what his age. Loudmouths and nervous punks challenged him, and they found out that he was faster with a knife than they were with a gun.

Eli read about himself in the paper, and prayed his papa hadn't seen the articles and torn them out. Small, mail-hack jobs paid his way as he headed west, and he was wanted in two states when he rode into the foothills of the Colorado Rockies and met up with Fancy Jess Archer. Jess was the man who blew his hand to pieces.

"This ain't my day off." Crutcher's voice slapped Eli's ears as he pulled the towel off of his mashed-apple face. "I got things to do, even if you ain't."

Crutcher held his palms out and Eli slathered them with Bay Rum. Crutcher tapped his face lightly, rising on his toes as he did it.

Eli grinned, "Sorry, Mr. Crutcher. I didn't mean to talk you to death."

"Hell, you haven't said a damn word for ten minutes. You ain't much otherwise, but you do got a way with soap and razor."

Eli turned the strop over, and struck the razor against the linen side to heat the blade. Crutcher smothered his face with his hands, running his palms over his jowls, "What the hell are you doin'? I already got a shave and it feels fine. Not 'tip fine,' but good enough."

Crutcher started out of the chair and the razor was instantly at his throat, forcing him to sit back. Crutcher strangled the armrests as Eli leaned in close with a quiet, "Do you remember the time I told you your mouth would get you killed?"

"What . . . ? You never said nothin' like that to me."

"Look in the mirror—look! And think!"

Crutcher tried to focus on the mirror, sweat and Bay Rum dripping into his eyes, but all he could see were the distorted faces of two men who were being beaten by their lives. "I'm lookin' and sure, I know what you're talkin' about now. I know."

Eli pressed the razor, opening a small cut above Crutcher's Adam's apple. "You always were a liar. You get scared and you say anything to get you out of it. That's why I got my damn fingers blown off!"

Crutcher was afraid to swallow. "Bayonet?"

"You've been in that chair twenty times and you never really looked at me once, did you?"

"W-well, you're the b-barber. And The Bayonet I

knew, he was just a kid. But I always said you was a good barber."

Eli let the blade slip closer to the jugular. "Bayonet was a name I didn't even want, but it got me a place with Jess Archer's Foothill Gang. Remember now? The night I rode into camp, you laughed and called me a runt. One of the boys said I should kill you right there, but Jess put a cork in him. Anything coming back, Clyde?"

Crutcher shut his eyes and murmured, but it wasn't a prayer. A hairline of blood trickled down the side of Crutcher's neck, spotting his collar. Eli dabbed the blood with a tissue, but kept the blade pressed against the throbbing vein. "You were the gunslinger from the Canadian side who'd killed ten men. Funny, you claimed to be from up North when you really hailed from Prescott. Funnier still, I never saw you draw down on anyone. You were all mouth until The Blackhawk."

Crutcher hid his words in the back of his throat so it wouldn't move against the razor when he spoke. "I . . . didn't do nothin'."

"That's right—you didn't."

Eli angled his horse across the bend of a trail that led to a narrow gorge where Jess Archer was waiting. Archer stood up in his stirrups, his trousers and coat neatly pressed, and looked down at the drop from the rocky slope into a miniature valley that was bridged by a cross-braced trestle. The structure narrowly supported tracks for a mining train, with barely a foot of clearance on either side.

Jess tapped his bowler for attention, which was his habit. "Looks like it would collapse if you sneezed, but it's served the Blackhawk miners for ten years."

Eli peered into the gorge, "That's a hell of a fall, Mr. Archer."

"And that's good for us, son, not them."

Clyde Crutcher rode up on the side of Archer, jerking his horse to a stop. Archer checked his pocket watch.

"Sorry I'm late, Mr. Archer. Now what are we doing here?"

"I've been explaining it for two weeks, Clyde."

"I mean, what do you want me to do?"

"The other boys will be dropping a barricade that'll stop the train right here, with half the cars still on the trestle. Take care of one guard and the rest will fall into line. They'll be trapped like a pig in a well. We've all made the papers, and they're just miners working a strike. They won't want to shoot it out."

Crutcher laughed, "Not with me. What about the runt?"

Eli didn't say a word, but Archer turned to Crutcher, "You claim quite a reputation this side of the Canadian, but everybody knows about Bayonet. They'll turn over the gold. I want you boys to be ready, but nobody has to get hurt."

* * *

Crutcher's eyes were wet as Eli worked the razor against his Adam's apple, "We faced a dozen miners with Henrys and Winchesters. They were layin' for us, Crutcher."

"But you—you got away."

"Jess Archer didn't, and neither did the others. We were shot to pieces right there by the tracks. I got one in the leg and they blew my hand off. You know what they told me? The miners made a deal with the infamous Clyde Crutcher. They paid you to ride on because they were afraid of you."

Crutcher let out a half laugh and said, "They gave me more than any share I would've gotten. That's just good business. You should know about that."

Eli's hand shook as he pressed the razor against Crutcher's throat, laying open a slit of skin. "Tell me straight, how many men have you killed?"

"In a straight-up gunfight? None. I killed a fella by accident in a fight. He was kind of famous . . . and then people started to talk. I never faced nobody else for real. I swear to God."

"And by running away?"

"I-I don't know."

"I've killed six, I think. Six. For real."

"Hell. Preachers an' the penny books all say an outlaw's life'll catch up to him. If this is my time, then get it over with."

Eli said, "I should," then pulled the blade away

from Crutcher's throat and folded it into its ivory handle. "The Bayonet Kid's dead. Now I'm just a barber."

Crutcher leaped from the chair, pressing the cotton bib against his neck. Eli faced him. "Did you know I saw you on the street the day I went to the Palace for a job? If I had my right hand, you wouldn't be standing here now. But I found this place and I've done just fine over the years; better than I deserve."

Crutcher grabbed his beat-to-hell hat from the rack, his coat flaring open to reveal the holster by his arm.

Eli held out a blue towel. "You want to really use that thing?" He unfolded the towel to reveal a long metal spike, with leather wrapped around one end. "It's up to you."

Crutcher stared at the spike. "You're pretty good with your left."

"You want to find out?"

Crutcher shook his head. "I'm just a fat old man who works in a bar."

"And I'm the cripple who cuts your hair. What kind of showdown would that be?"

Crutcher put his hand on the doorknob. "None at all. And I know it."

"That's two bits for the shave and haircut."

Crutcher handed Eli a dollar. "Keep it."

Eli smiled. "A tip from The Stickman of the Year. Must be my lucky day. Yours, too."

Crutcher stepped from the barbershop and made his way down Whiskey Row. Eli watched him shake a few hands and slap some backs as he walked, not seeing the man trailing behind him. Eli wrapped the spike in the towel and dropped it in the trash as the man in the street quick-walked toward Crutcher. A patch covered one of his eyes and he was drawing something from his belt.

Eli Greene took a razor from the drawer and began to strop it back and forth against the hanging leather with an even, deliberate motion. He didn't stop as he heard the muted pop of pistol fire, but kept stropping back and forth.

Back and forth.

About the Editors

Martin H. Greenberg has edited more than 2,000 books in every genre imaginable, including many western titles, such as *Desperadoes, Texas Rangers, Guns of the West, The Best of the American West,* and The Best of the West anthology series with Bill Pronzini, as well as the Double-Action Western novel series for Tor. He was the 1995 recipient of the Ellery Queen Award from the Mystery Writers of America, the Milford Award for Lifetime Achievement in Science Fiction Publishing and Editing, and the HWA Grand Master Award, the only person in publishing history to receive all three of these honors.

Russell Davis has edited numerous novels, short stories and anthology titles, including *Lost Trails* and *Ghost Towns.* He is an avid supporter of western literature. As an author, he has written and sold numerous novels (under a variety of pseudonyms and in many genres) and short stories. He currently runs his own book packaging company, Morning Storm Books, and works with his wife on breaking and training Arabian horses for endurance riding. When he's not busy with all of that, he tries to keep up with his kids, coaches youth football, and once in a great while, gets a little shut-eye.

About the Authors

Santa Fe, New Mexico-based **Johnny D. Boggs** has won four Spur Awards from Western Writers of America and the Western Heritage Wrangler Award from the National Cowboy and Western Heritage Museum for his western fiction. A Spur Award finalist five times, he has been praised by *Booklist* as "among the best western writers at work today," and *True West* named him the Best Living Fiction Writer in its 2008 Best of the West Awards. His novels include the Spur-winning *Camp Ford, Doubtful Cañon,* and *Hard Winter,* as well as *Walk Proud, Stand Tall,* in which he first introduced Lin Garrett, the hero of "The Trouble with Dudes." Boggs's website is www.johnnydboggs.com.

Tom Carpenter is an award-winning newspaper columnist. His nonfiction has appeared in *True West* magazine and Arizona Highways. He is the Assistant Dean for Extended Programs at Northern Arizona University. He lives in Flagstaff, Arizona.

Rita Cleary is the author of six books of historical fiction for Sunstone Press of Santa Fe, New Mexico, and Five Star Western, a number of short stories for Five Star, Kensington, and La Frontera, and several magazine articles for *True West, We Proceeded On* (Lewis and Clark

Trail Heritage Foundation), *Roundup* (Western Writers of America), and Amazon Shorts. She is a past president of the WWA. She has deep roots in the West as a descendent of Private John Collins of the Lewis and Clark expedition, and she has been cited by prominent historians for her research on the expedition. Her work has been honored at the Spur Awards of Western Writers. She has served as judge for Spur Awards and for the Western Heritage Awards of the National Cowboy and Western Heritage Museum in Oklahoma City. Rita's love of horses has been lifelong, and horses figure in many of her books. She is currently working on the sequel to her Revolutionary War novel *Spies and Tories.*

Don Coldsmith (1926–2009) was the Spur Award-winning author of more than thirty-five books. After serving as a combat medic in the Pacific during World War II, Coldsmith served as a physician in Emporia, Kansas, until 1988, when he closed his office to devote himself to writing. Coldsmith and his wife, Edna, maintained a small ranching operation and raised cattle, Appaloosa horses, and five daughters, not necessarily in that order.

John Duncklee has been a cowboy, rancher, quarter horse breeder, university professor, and award-winning author of twenty-two books and myriad articles, poetry, and short stories. He is a Western Writers of America Spur Award winner and was awarded a $5,000 unrestricted fellowship for writing excellence by the Arizona Commission on the Arts. He lives in Las Cruces, New Mexico, with his wife, Penny, an accomplished watercolorist.

Former Western Writers of America president **Loren D. Estleman** has written more than sixty novels and a couple hundred short stories, including the U.S. Deputy Marshal Page Murdock series, many standalone historical westerns, and the Detroit Detective

Amos Walker mysteries. Estleman has been nominated for the American Book Award, and the Mystery Writers of America Edgar Award. He is the recipient of sixteen national writing awards, including five Spurs and two Stirrups from the WWA, three Western Heritage Awards from the National Cowboy and Western Heritage Museum, and four Shamus Awards from the Private Eye Writers of America. His latest western novel is *Roy & Lillie: A Love Story*, a historical novel about the long-distance romantic relationship between the Hanging Judge and the Jersey Lily.

Andrew J. Fenady has spent most of his adult life in the badlands of Hollywood, creating, writing, and producing motion pictures, television series, movies of the week, stage plays, and songs, including the classic "Ballad of Johnny Yuma" (theme song of *The Rebel*). Fenady has received a passel of awards, among them the prestigious Owen Wister Award from the Western Writers of America, and the Golden Boot for Westerns, the Edgar Award for *The Man With Bogart's Face*, the Christopher Award for *The Green Journey*, and three Emmys for *Confidential File*. He's worked with the toughest top stars, such as John Wayne, Robert Mitchum, Charles Bronson, and many, many more.

Born in the shadow of Pikes Peak, **Ken Hodgson** has enjoyed various and interesting careers. He has worked in a state mental hospital, been a gold and uranium miner, worked as a professional prospector, and owned an air compressor business. He has written hundreds of short stories and articles along with over a dozen published novels in various genres. Ken is an active member of Mystery Writers of America and International Thriller Writers. He lives on a small ranch in Northern New Mexico with his wife and prime editor, Rita, along with two totally spoiled cats, Sasha and Ulysses.

John Jakes is the acknowledged contemporary master of the family saga. He is the creator of the legendary eight-volume Kent Family Chronicles, the Main and Hazard families of the North and South trilogy, and the Crowns of Chicago, German-Americans whose stories interweave the history of the twentieth century in Homeland and its sequel, American Dreams. Praised as "the godfather of the historical novel," "the people's author," and "America's history teacher," Jakes mingles the lives of his fictional characters with those of historical personages and involves them in the great events of the U.S. and the world. He's a member of the Authors Guild, the Dramatists Guild, and American PEN, and serves on the board of the Authors Guild Foundation. He is married to the former Rachel Ann Payne of Danville, Illinois, whom he met at DePauw. They have four children and eleven grandchildren. They divide their time between homes in South Carolina and Florida. His latest novel is *The Gods of Newport*, his eighteenth consecutive *New York Times* bestselling novel.

William W. Johnstone is the *New York Times* and *USA Today* bestselling author of over 125 books published over the last twenty-five years, with more than 10,000,000 copies in print. **J. A. Johnstone** is the frequent collaborator of his uncle, Bill Johnstone, and is also the author of The Loner series.

Courtney C. Joyner is a screenwriter and director with over thirty films to his credit, including *The Offspring* starring Vincent Price, *Prison, Class of 1999,* and the forthcoming *Return of Captain. Nemo.* He has written extensively about movie history, and his latest book is *The Westerners: Interviews with Actors, Directors and Writers.* His story "Bloodhound" was included in the anthology *Fistful of Legends,* and he is currently finishing his first western novel, *Tracking the Devil.* Courtney lives in Los Angeles and is a member of the Western Writers of

America, the Horror Writers Association, and International Thriller Writers.

Elmer Kelton (1926–2009) of San Angelo, Texas, was the author of about fifty western and historical novels. A native of Crane, Texas, where he grew up on the McElroy Ranch, he earned a journalism degree from the University of Texas at Austin. He spent forty-two years as an agricultural journalist in tandem with his sixty-year career as a fiction writer. He earned seven Spur Awards from Western Writers of America and four Western Heritage Awards from the National Cowboy and Western Heritage Museum. His novel *The Good Old Boys* was made into a TV movie starring Tommy Lee Jones.

Deborah Morgan grew up on a ranch in Oklahoma where she learned how to shoot a rifle, saddle a horse, and gather eggs without getting snakebit. A stint as a highway patrol dispatcher gave her opportunity to pit her skills against troopers during firearm qualification. She could fire twelve rounds in under fifteen seconds (fire, reload, fire), and scored 93 out of 100 in skill and accuracy while exiting a patrol unit with rifle and using the door as a shield. Morgan was managing editor of two national treasure-hunting magazines, and later of a biweekly newspaper in southeast Kansas before moving to Michigan. Something western usually finds its way into her award-winning antique-lover's mystery novel series. She writes in both the western and mystery genres, and is currently working on a couple of western projects.

John D. Nesbitt lives in the plains country of Wyoming, where he teaches English and Spanish at Eastern Wyoming College. His articles, reviews, fiction, and poetry have appeared in numerous magazines and anthologies. He has had more than twenty books published, including short story collections, contemporary novels, and traditional westerns, as well as textbooks for his courses. John has won many awards for his work, including two awards from the Wyoming State Historical Society (for fiction), two awards from Wyoming Writers for encouragement of other writers and service to the organization, two Wyoming Arts Council literary fellowships (one for fiction, one for nonfiction), a Western Writers of America Spur finalist award for a mass-market paperback original novel (*Raven Springs*), and the Spur Award itself for his short story "At the End of the Orchard" and for his novels *Trouble at the Redstone* and *Stranger in Thunder Basin.*

Ellen Recknor, a two-time Spur winner and a native of Iowa, was weaned on TV westerns and fell in love with the genre—so much so that she moved to Arizona in 1977. After thirty years amid the cacti, she's back in Iowa and missing the cacti like crazy. As Tennessee Ernie Ford used to say, "If the Good Lord's willin' and the creek don't rise," she'll be heading southwest again very soon!

Jory Sherman began his literary career as a poet in San Francisco's famed North Beach in the late 1950s, during the heyday of the Beat Generation. His poetry and short stories were widely published in literary journals when he began writing commercial fiction. He has won numerous awards for his poetry and prose, and was nominated for a Pulitzer Prize in Letters for his novel, *Grass Kingdom.* He won a Spur Award from Western Writers of America for *The Medicine Horn.* He has also won a number of awards from the Missouri Writers Guild and other organizations. He has published more than 350 books since 1965, more than 1,000 articles, and 500 short stories. In 1995, Sherman was inducted into the National Writer's Hall of Fame. He lived in the Ozarks for over twenty years and now lives on a lake in northeast Texas. His latest book is a collection of Ozarks short stories, published by AWOC in trade paperback, *The Sadness of Autumn.*